RITUAL STRIPES

He placed a buckle-end on top of the vice and tapped it carefully with a hammer, then picked up the whole mass of straps and put it over by the wall.

'Nervous about it?' He looked full at her and Judith nodded. He went over to a wall-cabinet and took out a roll of oiled paper. It unwrapped to reveal a bunch of cream-coloured tails bound into a cord handle and he pulled her up from her seat and placed her hand on it.

'Ever had the cane?'

'Well, yes –'

'I mean proper, like. Bare bum and hard as he could lay it on.'

Or she. 'Yes. Yes, in fact, I have.'

'Well, it won't be no worse. Different, but no worse. If that's any comfort.'

RITUAL STRIPES

Tara Black

This book is a work of fiction.
In real life, make sure you practise safe sex.

First published in 2002 by
Nexus
Thames Wharf Studios
Rainville Road
London W6 9HA

www.nexus-books.co.uk

Typeset by TW Typesetting, Plymouth, Devon

Printed and bound by
Mackays of Chatham PLC

ISBN 0 352 33701 X

Contents

Prologue

Bring the punishment desk out to the centre of the room.'

The object referred to was an old-fashioned tall desk intended to give the teacher seated at it a commanding view of the classroom. This one, however, now served a different function and after placing it as ordered Judith stood watching Samantha James select a cane from the corner cupboard. Her heart sank: the chosen instrument appeared longer than usual and had a wickedly flexible look to it.

'Take down your trousers and pants and get into position. I intend what follows to be a memorable lesson.'

Beneath the composure her employer typically assumed, Judith sensed an anger that made her go cold inside. But there was no point in arguing, so she peeled the clothes down around mid-thigh and hoisted herself up over the back, torso angled down the slope of the lid. She gripped the front legs of the desk and waited, heart pumping. If only she'd kept her temper with Helen, but one impatient push had led to another and there they'd been rolling around on the office floor like a pair of teenagers when the director came in. Helen would get well leathered shortly, no doubt, but at this moment Judith was sure she was glued to the crack in the door, set to savour every stripe.

The corporal punishment of a research assistant and a secretary may have been vanishingly rare in a present-day office, but neither of them thought such treatment outlandish. Painful, certainly, but on occasion unavoidable, and by no means beyond the pale. The Nemesis Archive where they worked was, after all, an uncommon institution: one founded on the controversial exploration of female submission and domination. For the previous six months, Judith had worked hard to assess and catalogue its large collection of books and documents, and in the course of that time Helen had left Miss James's house and moved into her own flat. Now she spent more nights with Judith than she did with her former 'mistress'. The girls' cat fight amongst the furniture must have been a galling reminder of what she had lost and now the raven-haired director was frowning. Judith was about to participate in a material exposition of the Archive's central theme.

The length of rattan tapped her bared flesh and the assistant shifted uneasily. Stretched as she was over the high piece of furniture, her bottom felt acutely exposed.

'Two batches of six, one from each side. Then, Judith, we shall see if you are contrite enough to escape more.' There was an unnerving relish in the tone of voice.

'Ready?' No answer was required and Judith gritted her teeth. It wasn't true that the first stroke was the worst, but it was always more of a shock. And this time proved no exception.

Later the young women lay side by side, face down on Helen's huge bed. The pain of Judith's weals had subsided into a dull throb and she laid a gentle hand on her friend's crimson behind.

'Better?' she said into Helen's ear.

'Yeah. But that new tawse is a fucking *bitch*. And since I took off out of her bed it's a fucking spiteful bitch that's swinging it.'

2

Judith eased herself up and looked at the compact body she had first lusted after the summer before in Brittany. In contrast to her own dark crew-cut, tight curls of strawberry-blonde hair clustered round her head and the breasts that were slightly fuller than you'd expect on such a slim frame spilled out over the sheet to each side. Judith looked down her own almost flat chest past the curve of her belly to the generous hips. It was typical of the director's attention to detail that Helen's slim rear received no more than the strap, lest otherwise she might be so bruised as to rule out more punishment for weeks on end. In her own case, however, the full buttocks simply begged to be beaten with a good swishy cane and were without fail sufficiently recovered to take another dose in mere days . . .

The blonde stirred, interrupting these reflections. She planted her lips on one nipple then the other and slid her hand down to the damp thatch between her partner's thighs. Judith spread her legs, wincing at the sudden movement, then gasped as the insistent touch found her clitoris. She reciprocated by sliding down the bed to bury herself in Helen's crotch. Freshly depilated, the mons was silky-smooth in Judith's face and, pulling back a little, she pressed apart the outer labia to expose the oozing pink whorls within. Then she began to lap into the musk with her tongue.

When Helen had come home, Judith was in the bathroom dabbing rather ineffectually at her bottom with a cold sponge. The girls had fallen upon each other immediately: in the wake of whipping their need for sex was urgent, and fingers probed at once into wet cunts. Only when they fell back, gasping, from the frenzy of orgasm did the marks left by punishment receive in turn the soothing cream Helen kept for the purpose. Now, pain's residue had become pure languid sensuality, and the two supple bodies twined and twisted in their long slow ride to the top.

*   *   *

3

Later still, somnolent in the ambience of her lover's warmth and steady, gentle breathing, Judith reached down and touched the hot tenderness of her own welted cheeks. 'That is fucking *ouch*,' she muttered drowsily. It was becoming a priority to get another love interest into Miss James's life and take some of the bite out of her corrections. Got it, Judith thought, her mind suddenly sharp, what she needs is a new PA she can sweet-talk home for sex 'n' spanking (or worse). That ought to get *us* out of the firing line. There was certainly no shortage of cash for another member of staff and the lady could take charge of investigating the cult with their own name that was in the news the other day. What was the guy called? Davidson. *Professor* Davidson, and he was claiming that this sect had been around from before Homer and was still there in Victorian England. And there was this stuff about a ritual scourge that she carried at her belt, the actual whip handed down over the centuries. But he'd used the word *cat*, as in cat-o'-nine-tails, though she couldn't help thinking of the feline kind. The Nemesis Cat, he'd called it. The phrase echoed in Judith's mind and with it came a confused image of twitching whiskers that somehow grew to be thick as thongs that whistled through the air. Then her body sank into weariness and sleep came.

PART I

1

Diva

Cate shouldered her way through the swing doors to the back room of Arte's into a wall of heat and noise. The band was well under way and from just inside she could see the drummer bouncing around behind her kit, but it wasn't till she'd pushed halfway to the front that she saw the singer. Though *saw* wasn't exactly the word for it. What happened was that she was frozen to the spot by the vision of eyes black with kohl under a violet shock of hair. As she gaped, the open shirt was cast aside and breasts jutted out with nipples that were as mauve and glossy as the pouting lips of the face. The all-female audience whooped and the apparition wrenched the microphone off its stand and yelled: 'Rama lama lama'. The women shouted back 'Fa fa 'n' fa!' and the band barrelled into a manic rendering of 'Kick out the jams'. The MC5's number had become a kind of house anthem that any visitors in the know made a point of including in their set. For the next three songs Cate stood transfixed, heedless of the moshing bodies all around, her scalp set tingling again and again by that extraordinary voice. Only when the lights came up for the interval did the spell break and let her gulp down a cold beer at the bar.

To get to it she had to go out on to the street and come back in through the next door. State licensing laws wouldn't let under-21 into the gig if there was alcohol, so the bar had been closed off from the rest of the club premises and given a separate entrance. But there was still a window on to the foyer she'd just left where the minors were milling about and Cate nodded in its direction. 'Some singer,' she said to the girl serving her end of the counter.

'I guess you like them painted, huh?' The brown hair was scraped back from a freckled face without a trace of make-up. Cate coloured, suddenly gauche: she had been out of the market for a woman the whole of the past year. But latterly things had gotten pretty tense with Mark. For starters, they hadn't fucked in a month and she was restless. Not because she was stuck on being shafted but because she wasn't. That made it far worse. There were things she'd done with girls that she got juiced up just thinking about, and not a dildo in sight. No, she could do without the guy's cock, but she had the feeling that he'd gone somewhere else in his head and he wasn't telling her where. You would have to be a mind-reader to find out what that bastard wanted, Cate thought with a scowl. In the meantime here she was back among Seattle's lesbian punks on the loose for a night and already her 25 years were making her feel positively ancient. Shit, she hadn't even been asked for ID before getting a drink.

'I mean, don't get me wrong –' Ms Un-painted was looking at her earnestly '– Jynx are a good band, real tight. But the way Marissa picks up guys is the worst.' The speaker's lip stayed curled while she helped her serving-mate put out a bunch of beers further down the bar. *Marissa*. Cate tried the name out in her head and it sounded good. Her own separatist cred was shot to hell by the way she'd been living, so the singer's taste for men didn't throw her one bit – even if they were the losers the bartender had just implied.

8

She was back and Cate pushed forward the bottle she'd just drained. 'I'll get another. You been working here long?'

'Long enough to see the damage men do.' The set of her chin made her look suddenly like a rebellious kid and when she turned away to the cold cabinet the bare vulnerability of the neck gave her customer an unexpected shiver of lust.

'Name's Cate. With a C. Afraid I'm one of the guys who's been playing for both sides. Though I used to be out on the scene every fucking night.' She handed over two notes.

The girl took them and said: 'Gena.' From the till she asked over her shoulder, 'We gonna be seeing you around, or is this a one-off?' She could barely be the age required to work here yet the proprietorial tone said she was more than lowly bar staff.

'Honey,' said Cate, acting up to her shocking pink lipstick, 'if I didn't have such bad taste in women I'd be back just for you.' It was Gena's turn to go red but Cate held her eye and winked. She liked this forthright girl and was pleased when she gave an awkward smile.

'But tonight I'm kind of hooked on a painted lady –' Cate knew she was taking a chance, but what the hell '– and I reckon I need a shot of Dutch courage.' She nodded at the bottle of vodka on the bar and Gena scooped up some ice in a small tumbler and sloshed the spirit over it.

'I'd have thought by your age you'd have learned from your mistakes. You better have this on the house. And if you want to get in close when your heart-throb comes back, there's a door behind the pillar over on the right that comes out at the side of the stage.' At that moment the sound of a bass riff started up and thumped out over and over.

Cate swallowed her drinks one after the other and blew Gena a kiss. 'You deserve better than *me*, doll, but someday, who knows . . .' Leaving the words hanging in the air she took off back to the foyer. Then, edging into the hall around the outside of the jostling mass of bodies, Cate saw the pillar ahead of her and ducked quickly through the half-hidden opening.

She was in an alcove maybe three feet from the edge of the platform, right behind a speaker stack and out of sight of all but the very front of the human crush that heaved in time to the opening chords of the second set. None of the four band members so much as glanced in her direction, and Cate guessed that unless one of the spotlights picked her out she would remain inconspicuous. Weeks of abstinence plus the stimulus of being back in her old haunts was making her horny as hell and the closer view she was getting of Marissa didn't help.

Against the mostly unadorned bodies of the latter-day riot grrrls who made up the bulk of the throng the singer's daubed face and breasts were a whorish come-on, and to make matters worse she had changed her sloppy denims for a tiny pair of black satin shorts. As they banged straight into a second and then a third number without a break, Cate ached to get a hold of the near-naked body that gyrated around the fixed point of the mic stand. In a kind of trance she slid her hand inside her jeans, fingers groping into wetness caused by more than the sweat that was sticking her top to her back, and the beat throbbed right through her as in a blur song followed song.

'OK, guys. This is gonna be the last one, because we're running late.' There was a roar of disapproval and Marissa held up her arms. 'We're gonna be back next week, promise. Meantime, here's a small trophy for you.' In a trice the pants were round her ankles and tossed into the crowd. 'One, two, three, four!' she yelled and as the bass line boomed out over the scrimmage on the floor she half-turned and looked directly at the side of the stage.

Cate stood transfixed with embarrassment as Marissa's eyes flicked down to the hand between her legs. Then the singer jerked her head to the back of the stage and mouthed the word: 'Later.' Somehow Cate managed to nod. The interaction had taken barely a second and Marissa swung round, grabbed the microphone in her hand and launched into one of the twisted love songs that were Jynx's hallmark.

'Baby, do you want me?

Do you wanna want me?

Oh, baby, I'm gonna make you wanna want me.'

The strutting naked body was way beyond Cate's powers of erotic imagining. The thick pubic bush was jet black and shaved into a perfect triangle, the breasts and buttocks round and firm yet with a delicious bounce. With a supreme effort of will she pulled her fingers out of her cunt and put them in her mouth, savouring the sharp tang of her own arousal. It seemed like an omen: if the gods smiled, it would be a foretaste of the intimate pleasures that awaited her in that body she couldn't take her eyes off.

'Do you wanna want me?'

It was a high-pitched croon that grew to a crescendo and made the hairs on the back of the neck stand up.

'Oh, baby, I'm gonna *make* you wanna want me!'

The voice and guitars screamed, the song cut off dead in a single crash of percussion and the band was gone. Cate leaned weakly against the pillar, suddenly drained. 'Oh, baby, you done that – you done that *real* good,' she breathed softly as the shouts for encores began gradually to subside and the fans, grumbling, to disperse.

It was an hour later when Cate slipped out of the back door of Arte's and stood in the shadow across from the Jynx tourbus. When the club opened a decade before, the owner had fixed on the name of the exalted goddess

11

who was sister to Zeus, but Artemis somehow wouldn't stick. Just as well, since the lady had been fiercely virginal, but most of the present-day regulars probably thought the place once belonged to a guy called Artie who had a funny way of spelling his name. Cate had wanted to let the young fans get clear and was able to pass the time back in the bar catching up on gossip with two of her past acquaintances. More to the point, it gave her the chance to let a few more beers do their work on the attack of nerves that was threatening to make her chicken out of the assignation. *If* that's what it was. Maybe she had imagined the whole thing in the heat of the moment.

Then, eventually, the last few of the would-be groupies were ever so gently shooed away and Marissa stood alone on the folding steps. She was wearing what seemed to be a black shift that reached to mid-thigh. Cate screwed up her courage and crossed the road before she could think better of it.

'Hi. I'm glad you showed. Did I really turn you on that much?' She put out a hand and Cate took hold of it amid her blushes.

'You must have, yeah.' She managed a grin. 'I don't make a habit of masturbating in public.'

Marissa pulled her up into the bus and shut the door. She undid Cate's jeans and found the slippery wetness of her crotch with a sharp intake of breath. Then their lips met while Cate's hands reached down to squeeze buttocks that were temptingly bare under the loose cotton. The singer pulled away and Cate looked at her: stripped of the stage exuberance she was small, almost fragile, and the heavy make-up had become a little smudged.

She gestured at herself: 'I gotta lose the paint and the sweat. Will you wait for me?' There was a touch of anxiety in the question and Cate took the hand to her lips. It gave her a kick to taste herself on another

12

woman's fingers after all this time. Marissa seemed reassured and indicated the bunk that ran the width of the bus at the back.

'Two minutes, sweetie. Make yourself at home.' With that she disappeared into the shower cubicle and Cate cleared a space to sit and unlace her boots. She peeled off her socks, not quite believing what was happening. Here she was stripping to have sex with this sensational singer she had never met before that night. Once her feet were bare she shucked off the jeans that Marissa had unbuttoned and stood up naked from the waist down. Strictly no underwear used to be the dress code when they were teenage punks hot to get laid and it seemed to have brought her luck this time. Cate ran her hands down over her hips whose fullness felt all the more womanly in comparison to Marissa's boyish curves.

Then a movement at the edge of her vision caught her attention. There was a silver medallion the size of a saucer hanging from a strip of leather, and she leaned over the bed to take a closer look. It was at once plain that what had moved was not the thing itself but what it contained: the picture of the head and forelimbs of a cat, underneath which were the ornate initials NC. More like a panther than a domestic tabby, it appeared to snarl and ripple its muscles as Cate rocked back and fore in front of it. She had seen similar things in novelty toys but this was altogether more sophisticated and not a little menacing.

The click of the cubicle door broke her fascination and she turned to find Marissa beside her rubbing her hair with a towel. She held it out, saying: 'Please, would you?' and turned her back towards Cate to be dried. She duly set to work, taking the opportunity to fondle the damp breasts and nipples, then knelt to begin on the deliciously pert behind. Close up, she noticed for the first time a tracery of fading purple lines that criss-crossed the whole area from the top of the buttock cleft to the middle of the thighs. Shocked, but curiously

13

drawn, Cate touched them with her fingers then saw there was more. A number of faint whitish marks ran down the length of the flanks on both sides. The horizontals could be (she supposed) bruises caused by a whip, but the others were actual *scars*. Her mind recoiled from the brutality that inflicted bleeding cuts, then Marissa had turned and was bending over her.

'Oh, I'm sorry, I'm sorry, I didn't think.' She took Cate's face in her hands and lines of worry showed round her kohl-free eyes. She didn't look so much embarrassed as wearied by the impossibility of explaining to one who didn't already understand these things. 'And I don't even know your name –'

'Cate. With a C.' She spoke automatically while her brain tried to process what she'd just seen.

'Cate.' Marissa echoed the name then began hesitantly. 'Cate, you were looking at the emblem hanging over the bed. That's the Cat. Well, I mean, it's the Nemesis –'

The faltering explanation was to go no further. The outside door flew open and a tall muscular figure stood swaying slightly on the threshold. Cate recognised the skinhead drummer at once but before she could rise from her knees the woman had lurched forwards and seized her by the wrist.

'Bitch!' The force of the utterance spattered her face with saliva then she was hauled to her feet by hands that clamped her arms behind her above the elbows.

'Zadia, no! Zadia, please don't!' Marissa's cry sounded ineffectually as Cate was marched to the door and pushed out. Temper flaring, she turned, but the angry Amazon towered over her and she hesitated, fatally, and missed her footing. One leg went between the top two steps and with a sickening wrench to it she toppled sideways and landed on the tarmac on all fours. There was the short bark of a laugh and the door slammed shut. Her head was spinning from the shock of the encounter and her knees were scraped and bloody

14

but worse than either was the pain in her left ankle. Then it struck her that, save for the skimpy T-shirt, she had on not a single stitch of clothing. It was the last straw and tears welled up.

'Don't be such a fucking wimp,' Cate told herself between sobs. Then suddenly there were raised voices within and the door opened for an instant to allow jeans and boots to be ejected before it closed again. She sat on the bottom step and dressed slowly and painfully, sunk in gloom. What had happened to her? Just two short years ago, even muscles from Jynx would have got a *real* going-over from her gang of pals. They were always spoiling for a fight and to hell with the consequences. Despite her mood, Cate could not suppress a smile at the memory of the time they were all hauled off in the police truck and nearly caused a riot at the station. And look what she'd settled into instead: a job in a bookstore that was closing down and a partner who couldn't – or wouldn't – get it on with her any more.

With a sigh she got to her feet. She could walk, just, but she was in no fit state to raise some of the lowlifes she used to hang with, even supposing that she could. Anyway, what was the point? Cate felt bruised inside as well as out and turned to make her way home. There was some traffic on the main drag ahead of her but the side street behind the club was deserted. It struck her that the quarrelling voices had fallen silent in the bus and then she heard a low moaning that grew louder as she listened. A chink of light showed through one of the curtains and, gripped by a horrid compulsion, Cate stretched up to peer in. There was a clear view through to the bunk she herself had sat on, but now it was Marissa who sprawled across it on her back in naked abandon while a shaved head worried, terrier-like, at the apex of her spread thighs.

It was too much altogether and Cate set off hobbling down the road, cursing as each step made the rough denim rub her grazed knees. 'Gena was right,' she muttered bitterly under her breath. 'That'll teach you to chase painted ladies. Old enough to know better? Some fucking hope.'

2

Aftermath

It was only two blocks and a half from Arte's to her apartment but the going was mostly uphill. When Cate reached the door sandwiched between the laundrette and the coffee shop, both long closed for the night, it was locked. Perhaps Mark was already asleep; they had not parted on the best of terms and she remembered growling, 'Don't wait up,' on her way out. Or maybe he was gone somewhere himself. Either way would suit her right now: the last thing she wanted was to pick up on the mutual recriminations where they had left off. After a struggle with the ill-fitting lock Cate pushed open the battered door and stumbled into the passage. Her body ached and it took reserves of energy she didn't know she had to drag herself up the flight of stairs. The second key was mercifully easy but as she leaned on the door to click it shut she heard the mutter of a television set from the living room.

The straggle-haired and dark-stubbled figure slumped on the sofa made no move except to draw on the half-smoked cigarette between his fingers. Then when she staggered and caught on to the armchair for support the head turned and the hooded eyes snapped wide open.

'Christ, Cate.' Mark hauled his lean frame upright and looked her up and down.

17

'It's the ankle. But don't ask. Please.' If she'd been knocked down by the powerful drummer that would be one thing, but to have come to grief through her own clumsy irresolution . . . She felt ready to dissolve again and it must have shown for Mark sat her down without a word on the chest that made a bench seat and took hold of her foot. After some prodding and twisting that didn't seem to hurt as much as it ought to he declared it unlikely there was anything broken. Then he took off her boot and layered a support bandage around the joint. As a sometime medical student who had dropped out then dropped back in again he could rise to occasions such as this.

'Knees. My knees,' Cate said weakly, attention returning to her other injury. She managed to undo her jeans and assist feebly as they were pulled down. Then he disappeared into the kitchen and returned with a basin of water and some cloths. Cate closed her eyes and gritted her teeth while the raw flesh was bathed clean, patted dry and some ointment applied. Then Mark stood her up in her T-shirt and turned her round.

'What's this?' he asked, touching her bottom and she put a hand down to feel two very tender ridges.

'Must have been the steps.' She vaguely recalled scraping against the rough edge of the lowest one just before she hit the pavement.

'Steps?'

'Later. OK?'

He said no more but sat on the chest and, having pulled Cate across his lap, smoothed some cream over the sore place. Too tired to protest at the indignity of her position she lay passive under Mark's ministrations. With her head and shoulders buried in soft cushions and her wounded knees dangling free, Cate began to relax. For the first time since the incident tension was ebbing away. But, more than that, the stroking of her lower

18

behind was reawakening her sensuality and she began to move in response to it. Now the caresses grew firmer and Cate became aware there was a stiffness pressing into her belly. She felt her loins respond at once and as she wriggled on top of the swelling lump the arousal she had experienced at the gig came flooding back.

Newly energised, she got to her feet and pushed Mark back, reaching for his belt. He made no attempt to stop her as Cate stripped his jeans and underpants clear of the erection. Not since their early nights in bed together had she seen him so big: the cock stood absolutely vertical and the head that bulged out of the foreskin glistened wetly. She leaned forwards and planted her lips on it, then made to straddle the narrow bench. But he turned her round to face away from him then pulled her back in position.

What the hell, thought Cate, suddenly impatient for penetration. She stuck out her rear end at him and lowered herself, knees bending, until she felt the hardness nuzzling between her wet labia. In one movement the shaft's bulk impaled her as she subsided on to Mark's body. His hands roamed, patting and squeezing over her behind, and he moved with her to thrust and withdraw, thrust and withdraw in a lubricious squelch of engaged sexual parts. In seconds Cate was wailing in climax, but Mark had not done. He heaved her up and forwards over the sideboard, parted her buttocks and pushed the tip of his organ firmly at her anal ring. Still gasping, Cate tried to resist but he was determined and well lubricated, so she was soon penetrated where he had never been before. The ramrod hardness – he couldn't have come yet – in *that* place made her feel violated and excited all at once. Then he made a noise in the back of his throat and she felt the thing that was stuffed up to the hilt in her arse begin to pulse. Oh, God, oh, God. His cock was going to spurt its milky juice deep into her bowels. The mere idea of it set off a second wave of spasms which shook her until she slumped, shattered, across the wooden surface, held in place only by the pressure of Mark's thighs, his erection softening slowly inside.

In the morning Cate struggled out of a numbing fog to find the bed empty beside her. Mark was standing in the doorway, dressed.

'Got a class.' His voice was low and there was that troubled look in his eyes that had attracted her in the days before she understood that its direction was inward. It was about *himself* and communication with her was not on the agenda. So it was business as usual, and Cate turned over and sank back into thick confused sleep.

It was noon when she woke again in a panic, until she remembered it was her Saturday off from the bookstore. Getting out of bed was a minor ordeal with the injuries from the fall compounded by a bruised pelvis. Cate gave a twisted smile: another time, not across the sideboard. But there wasn't going to be another time by the way he kept his distance this morning. Just thinking of the manic fucking made her feel hot all over again. She put a finger to her anus: it was sore and chafed and the sphincter muscle throbbed. Christ, it's just as well he didn't want to go straight back in *there*. With an attempt at a grin Cate squared her shoulders and headed for the bathroom, resolving not to mope about what was still, on the sum of the evidence, a relationship on terminal skids.

There was no way she could hit the café downstairs for the customary espresso and bran muffin that marked a day off. The thought of having to lie to Mama Sophia about the bandaged ankle was too much. But the truth could not be told. The proprietor had known her since before Mark appeared to 'save' her from the fate of a riot grrrl, and Cate couldn't face the expression the

20

large Italian lady's face would wear when she thought Cate had gone back to her old ways. Especially when she hadn't. Well, not really. Not yet.

Cate made a pot of tea and sat at the kitchen table in her towelling robe. Much as she wanted to erase the débâcle of the night from her mind, the image of Marissa wouldn't go away. It was hardly surprising. The singer had exploded into the middle of a sex life so tame it had become nonexistent. As if infected by Mark's lack of enthusiasm, Cate hadn't masturbated for months, yet there she'd been at the gig with a hand down her pants on the point of coming. Whatever had gotten Mark going later was some kind of spin-off that she didn't understand and it was not going to be repeated in a hurry. So there was only one thing for it: to return to the scene of the crime. She just had to find out more about the extraordinary diva.

At five o'clock Cate closed the door behind her and set off past the small row of shops with her head averted. No one seemed to spot her so she straightened up and walked rather more firmly down the way than she had dragged herself up it not many hours before. She was feeling much better after a long soak in the bath and the scraped knees were already on the mend. At the corner of the street behind what was known as 'the corridor' of gay and lesbian establishments she saw that the tourbus had gone and stopped, unsure whether she was disappointed or relieved.

'Can't keep away, huh?' said a voice she recognised and Cate swivelled round. Gena's eyes flicked down to the strapped-up ankle but her tone stayed the same.

'I didn't have the lady marked down as a fighter.'

'She isn't. Unfortunately for me. The drummer showed and she put me out. Then I fell over.' The deadpan reception seemed to be making her reveal all, even the self-contempt.

21

'Guess I should have warned you. Zadia is very possessive *and* totally promiscuous. That makes for a lot of her ex-partners' partners with injuries, accidental or otherwise.'

Cate laughed. The young woman's insouciance was catching: suddenly the thing was no big deal.

'How's about a beer to dull the pain? We can go through the back.' Cate followed Gena through the rigmarole of exiting Arte's front door to get back into the alcoholic part of the same building. Once they were settled in a corner of the nearly empty bar she gave a blow-by-blow account of the events.

Gena listened in silence then said: 'Marissa's cat. Was it a wild beast sort of thing on a plaque, like so?' With her hands she indicated exactly the saucer-sized object Cate had seen hanging over the bed. She nodded and the girl raised her eyebrows.

'Well, I was dissing her for the men, but I didn't know she was into B&D.'

'B&D?' Cate felt exposed once again as older but no wiser.

'*You* know: B&D, D&S, S&M, whatever. *Sado-masochism.*' Cate thought again of the marks on Marissa's body she had left out of the story and shuddered.

'No, I *don't* know.' It seemed best to come clean.

'There's a kind of network in the city. This cat symbol says you're in and I've heard stuff about claws that would make your hair curl.'

Cate goggled. She and her pals had thought of themselves as wild, but all they'd really been was rowdy. Their main claim to rebel status was the lesbian thing, and indeed she could still remember the angst of becoming lovers with her best friend. But that was it. She hadn't even taken anything up the butt till last night. But this stuff was something else. And how was this sober and sensible young woman so clued-up about it?

Gena grinned. 'Don't look so shocked. I had a girlfriend once who was into spanking. I mean she used to go over my knee and I'd smack her arse with my hand. It would make her real horny and we'd fuck like rabbits after. But she started wanting more and I didn't fancy it at the time. And before we split up she was going on about the Cat. It didn't mean anything then but I saw her a couple of months later and, man, was she spaced out. There were scars on her face and she was mouthing off about claws and flagellation rituals. Heavy shit. Could be your fancy woman's just dabbling, though. I'm told lots do.'

Cate got up and stood at the bar to order more beers. Fancy woman? She didn't know Gena well enough to suss if that was an insult or just her flip way of talking. The girl's poker face gave little away. Back at the table she changed the subject by quizzing her about what had been going on at Arte's over her year of domesticity. But while she listened and put in the odd comment she couldn't stop thinking about those white scars on Marissa's flanks and the rake of bloody lines it would have taken to cause them. Not what you could call playing on the fringes. And what disturbed Cate more than the image itself was that the idea of the body she lusted after being treated cruelly was strangely exciting.

'I get the impression my band stories are not quite hitting the spot.' Gena's cool appraising look made Cate realise she was staring vacantly at her bottle.

'Oh, God, sorry, I'm a bit preoccupied. Put it down to the after effects of being ejected bare-arsed on to the street.'

'Or of being smitten by unrequited lust?'

Cate felt the red flush rise to her neck. Last night she had been flirting with Gena; now she couldn't even listen to what she was saying.

'Don't worry about me.' She reached out and touched Cate's hand as if reading her mind. 'I know two nice

23

femmes who'd be mine for the taking but these days I mostly settle for a good book.' Her face creased up and it was the first time Cate had heard her laugh. 'You should see your expression. I just like to play the world-weary dyke now and again.'

She was really quite delicious and Cate stared. Under the sloppy shorts and T-shirt would be a firm young body keen to do all sorts of athletic things in bed, even the spanking she'd just mentioned. The thought of Gena's hand on her butt – or, better, hers on Gena's – made her tingle and Cate crossed her legs. Goddammit, it was clear the girl needed only to be asked. What a fool she was to be hung up on the elusive diva with the yen for real cruelty.

'You know they're playing again on Friday.'

'Nah, I'm gonna give it a miss. I think it's time I got into a *real* life, don't you?' Cate wasn't sure just who she was trying to convince.

'Well, I'm off all next week. There'll be a few beers for you at the bar in case you change your mind. I'll tell them it's for the older woman with the lipstick.'

She flashed a cheeky smile and drained her bottle. 'Gotta go work, OK? See ya round.'

At 9.30 p.m. Friday the small arena of the Artemis Club was mobbed with eager fans of Jynx and crushed against the back wall by the crowd was Cate. The week had started with a firm resolve to sort out her life but the cards were stacked against her. Mark still kept his distance, pleading a heavy schedule of work for college tests she suspected were mostly invented. She tried to interest him in the scrape on her bottom – it had done the trick last time, for God's sake – but he just gave the arse she offered a quick glance and said it was fine. It *would* be fine if it had a stiff cock pumping away in it like before, she fumed inwardly. But saying it out loud would really make him run, so she didn't. Work at the

24

bookstore was getting more and more tense as the closure date loomed with still no word as to which of the staff might get taken on in another branch of the chain. As the last one in, Cate was pretty sure she would be out on her ear, but that didn't stop the two men on the staff treating her as a rival. And, to cap it all, Gena was away and she couldn't go and make eyes at her under cover of bitching about her problems.

So come the day of the gig Cate cracked. After work she took off the bandage and tested her ankle. For the first time it felt good as new and she went for some rarely used eye-shadow and face-paint. What the hell, for once she felt like it and the make-up would go with the day-glo pink lips that were to be her ticket for free beer. She pulled on a tight pair of black denims and a singlet top and consulted the mirror. Nice arse, tits *just* decent; interesting without being too conspicuous. Though, of course, she was only going to look, to see whether last week's reaction was the overreaction she had been busily telling herself it must be. Worn leather jacket on her shoulder, Cate swung down the stairs and out on to the street.

The band played a blinder, all in a single set. The vocals were as spine-tingling as before, though Marissa was clearly not well. No longer topless in satin hot pants, she wore the shapeless black shift Cate had seen in the bus, though this time the rings around the eyes were all hers. In between numbers she clutched at the mic stand, swaying as if about to fall down, and the guitarist did all the introductions. Somehow the painfully frail figure became energised once the beat started up again but each effort seemed more heroic than the last. So it was no surprise when, after thirty minutes and a cover of Blondie's '11.59' that was gruesomely appropriate, they called a halt. Marissa's indisposition was so plain that most of the disappointed audience just dispersed with little protest and Cate spilled out into the foyer with them.

What now? The interval and a few drinks were supposed to have given her a plan and she was at a loss. She just wasn't psyched up to go hit the tourbus and then maybe hit the tarmac again, face first. And anyway, did she want further in with the femme fatale and her dark doings? A hand on her arm cut through the indecision and she turned to find herself face to face with the band's drummer. Not quite face to face, since Zadia had at least four inches on her, and Cate tried not to flinch as the lady moved her hair aside and put a hand under her chin.

'My behaviour was bad – I take too much of the booze. I am sorry. Can you forgive me?' When she was speaking rather than screaming, Zadia had a marked German accent. She also looked more formidable than ever crowned with a blonde stubble so Cate was disinclined to argue with the apology.

'OK. No real harm done.'

'It will not happen again because I signed up to the rehab program. Since all week I am TT. But I shall buy you a beer while I drink a soda. Come.' She made for the door and Cate followed meekly. On previous form, Zadia was quite capable of enforcing compliance. An older woman was serving behind the bar and Cate saw her checking them out. After a minute she came over with a bottle of lager and a tall glass of lemonade which she pronounced to be on the house. The drummer beamed.

'You have friends in the right place. Good health.' They drank and she looked straight into Cate's eyes. 'Your hair is beautiful. It is so fine,' she said, reaching out to stroke it while pressing her thigh into Cate's.

Part of Cate shrank back but at the same time she felt a sharp prickle in the loins. Promiscuous she'd been warned about, but nobody had told her the lady was the

26

fastest draw in the West. Then Zadia kissed her and Cate surprised herself by kissing back. It gave her shivers all down the spine. After a short while she pulled away and gulped down some beer, too embarrassed to want to know if anyone was watching.

'You are right,' said Zadia simply. 'We are here too much in public. I have a place not far where we can go. I shall atone for causing you hurt and then we will fuck, yes?'

Cate was dazed. She was going to be taken away to have sex with the powerful skinhead. Zadia had decreed it and it would be futile to resist. Not that resistance was on her mind – on the contrary she was juiced up and raring to go. What was it with the members of this band?

But the drummer had something else to say. She leaned forward and with a flourish put an envelope in Cate's hand. 'Our Marissa writes you a letter. You will read it later, but I tell you now that she makes a date. You will see her, I think?' The long fair eyelashes fluttered, oddly coy. 'I shall cause no more trouble. I am the reformed character.'

Here's hoping, thought Cate, but what she said was: 'Marissa looked terrible. What's wrong?' As she spoke she noticed the back of the envelope was embossed with the savage cat of the medallion above Marissa's bed.

The eyelashes went again and Zadia stared down at the table. 'I don't know what to say. It is not for me to tell, I think . . .' She tailed off, then jabbed a finger at the emblem. 'What do you know about this?'

'Er, nothing much. Nothing at all, really. She was starting to explain when, when . . .' It was Cate's turn to dry up.

'You mean when I break in and interrupt you.' Her brow furrowed and she looked fierce. 'Marissa is reckless. She goes too far in *this* business –' she tapped the cat image with a pained expression '– and she is not

27

healthy. Not robust, like me.' She squared her shoulders and prominently nippled breasts were outlined through the low-cut PVC top. Cate wanted to reach out and touch but was nervous of the blonde's volatile emotions.

Zadia laughed and pressed Cate's hand to her chest. 'You show what you are thinking. I like that. But you must wait to ask Marissa about what she does. Maybe you will help her. But now we have things to do, yes?' She stood up in a way that brought Cate to her feet as well. Outside they turned down a side street and Zadia put her arms round her and kissed her, squeezing her buttocks. 'Once you repay me for being bad I make you come and come and come. OK?'

'Lead the way, lover, I'm panting for it.' Cate had surrendered control to this strong and potentially dangerous woman and she was consumed with lust. Yet, curiously, she felt neither weak nor helpless and it seemed she was expected somehow to exact retribution for the lady's rough intervention of the week before. This was heady stuff for a girl who had been leading a quiet domestic life for the past year, and she strode proudly arm-in-arm with her tall companion through the littered alley towards the pleasures of the night to come.

3

Fantasies . . .

A dozen blocks downtown from the gay 'corridor' where Cate was about to cheat on him, Mark was sitting at the bar of a back-street jazz club. In the two years spent out of school he had worked there, serving drinks and food to the tables from the small kitchen. It was a low-key establishment that he had never known to feature any big names and tonight there was a black guy at the piano playing a kind of easy-listening cross between Errol Garner and Keith Jarrett. It would do just fine: right now he wasn't looking for musical inspiration. The year he'd been with Cate the friends he had made in the place had mostly moved on to other jobs or, like him, back to college. So there was no one he knew, except the bartender by sight from his last visit six months before. But that was fine too; he didn't want to talk, just to drink glasses of beer and mull over what looked like the end of his relationship.

The day he fucked Cate in the arse for the first – and probably last – time Mark's head had been full of ideas of corporal punishment. He remembered quite clearly looking down at the anal ring stretched round his glistening shaft and seeing in his imagination the parted bottom-cheeks thick with weals from a cane that had sliced into their soft flesh. The picture had been vivid and his cock had begun to jerk inside her almost at once. He hated the fact that he dared not even mention the subject. Goddammit, she'd been turned on all right when he rubbed and stroked her arse, so fucking horny that she pushed him down to get on top. And then she came like crazy. Surely it wasn't that tremendous a jump from squeezing to a little gentle smacking to . . .

Mark shook his head in exasperation. He'd been through this line of thinking so many times and he just knew in his heart that for most girls there was going to be a world of difference between fondling their rear ends while you kissed them and putting them over your knee for a spanking. For God's sake, it was in *his* head, too: there was something shameful about this interest he had that made him keep it strictly to himself. But, try as he might to ignore it, the preoccupation was stubbornly there, and it was growing stronger. He now avoided Cate whenever possible, knowing that while he might get a hard-on it would never stay the course to bring her off. She had always demanded satisfaction, which had been no problem at the beginning. He admired a woman who was forthright about her needs and the characteristic had its benefits: he never had to go through the 'how was it for you?' routine after fucking.

But now the situation was impossible. It wasn't that Cate had changed, either. Though she didn't generally dress to turn heads, her figure was a model of classical beauty with that extra bit of sensuality in the curve of breast and buttock. But as soon as his cock stood at the sight of her he had to stop himself thinking of what disciplinary things might be done to that luscious behind. Because it was hers and they were – had been – intimate. He could picture an unknown schoolgirl he'd seen in uniform being made to bend over to have her bottom tanned, but his mind balked at the image of Cate in that position, and especially with himself doing the chastising. So the cock would wilt, and rather than confront the problem he had withdrawn from sex with her into the solitary world of the imagination. Older schoolgirls provided some of his favourite scenes; maybe because while they were sexual they were also *obedient*. At least they used to be in the classrooms of old.

'Rogers and Brooks, stand up.' Two senior pupils rise reluctantly to their feet at the back. 'You have been whispering and giggling together whenever my back was turned. I suppose you think me deaf as well as blind. Since you insist on behaving like children I shall punish you as such. Brooks, you first. Out here, *now*!'

She is a grown girl of sixteen but against the tall and broad-shouldered Miss Trent she looks positively puny. The mistress takes the solid wood upright chair from behind her desk and places it in full view of the class. She sits down and pats her tweed-covered thigh.

'Over here, girl. At once!'

Brooks obeys, going across the teacher's lap so that her hands and feet are on the floor to each side. This is clearly not a novel occurrence. Miss Trent takes hold of the pleated skirt and folds it well up into the girl's back. She raises her hand and brings it down sharply across drum-tight bottle-green knickers with a loud *smack*! The rest of the girls crane their necks eagerly to get a proper view of the proceedings; all, that is, except the one in the back row whose turn is going to come next . . .

There was masturbatory mileage too in the young secretary who must accept physical 'correction' of her errors or face the sack.

'Now I warned you, Marian, when you took the job, that I was a believer in good old-fashioned methods of discipline. Isn't that right?' From the corner cupboard he takes a standard school cane about three feet long and flexes it in his hands.

'Yes, sir.' Marian is tearful, but resigned to her fate because she is determined to keep the job. She has never been caned before but the belt was a feature of her childhood. It couldn't be much worse than that, could it?

'Very well, then. Take off your skirt.' He puts a high stool in the centre of the floor. 'I want you over this. Right over, now, and get a good grip on the legs on the other side. We want no silly jumping up until we are finished. That's good.'

In this posture her skimpy panties are pulled up into her bottom cleft, providing little protection against what is to come. At least he hasn't taken them down. Yet.

'We'll try six to start with. Ready?'

There is a *swish-crack!* and pain that takes her breath away. It burns and burns and Marian's knuckles are white. Oh, God, please. Not five more like that . . .

And then, of course, there were waitresses. Coming out of his reverie Mark saw a woman of maybe thirty or so clearing tables on the other side of the rail that enclosed the bar area. She wore black with a white top, just as he had done for the job, though there the resemblance ended. His plain shirt was replaced by a blouse that showed plenty of eye-catching cleavage, but it was the pants that really grabbed his attention. Or rather the way she filled them. The material seemed moulded to hips and thighs so that as she stretched and bent the bottom-cheeks jiggled and rolled as if with a life of their own. Not that she was fat, or even plump; just blessed with a fully-fleshed female derrière that captured Mark's gaze.

Eventually she was finished and with a loaded tray pushed through the swing doors into the back. Mark had his glass refilled from the beer tap and sank once more into his own world.

In the manager's office is an irate customer of long standing and a contrite waitress who has had the misfortune to spill some soup over the lady's skirt. The manager listens to the tirade that ends:

'I can tell you, when my mother ran a hotel dining room, if one of *her* girls had done such a thing she would have faced dismissal. Or, if not, at the very least a damned good hiding.'

The manager's eyes light up at the prospect of dealing with the situation without losing staff.

'A good hiding, you say? Well, in this day and age, that is a little irregular, to say the least.' He tries to gauge from Martha's expression whether she will wear what he wants to propose. He has had casual sex with her a couple of times, but never anything quirky. She is resolutely avoiding his eye, which he takes for a good sign: at least she has not expressed outrage at the mention of corporal punishment.

'Let me get this straight, Mrs Jameson. Am I right in thinking that if you are allowed to chastise my clumsy employee personally, you will consider the matter closed?'

The middle-aged woman inclines her head with pursed lips. 'I shall require an instrument. My mother, as I recall, used a rather heavy wooden spatula obtained from our chef.'

'Well, Martha. It's all down to you, as they say.' She meets his eyes and gives an almost imperceptible nod. He has no idea what is in her mind, but doesn't care. This is going to be *very* interesting and he can always compensate her in the next pay packet. He accompanies Mrs Jameson to the kitchen where she chooses a paddle some two feet long with a substantial business end.

'I'm afraid it has to be given bare bum, if you'll excuse my mother's plain speech. No point to the thing otherwise.' She is looking quite animated and though Martha's eyes widen at the sight of the implement she obediently rolls down her pants and underwear to her knees. The manager moves forwards, bends the waitress over and holds her under the crook of his arm. The punishment begins.

Each stroke makes a mighty *crack!* and he feels Martha's whole body jerk as the 'ah!' is forced from her lips. But she doesn't struggle in his grip and he thinks she must have been here before. It bodes well for the future, in the privacy of his bedroom, but for now he watches in growing excitement as the shapely buttocks turn from pink to red to a deep crimson. How much will the girl take before she resists? Mrs Jameson shows no sign of letting up; in fact she seems to be just getting into her stride . . .

With a jolt Mark realised the actual waitress whose bottom his imagination was in the process of mistreating had reappeared through the double doors and was headed right towards him.

'Hi,' she said brightly and from under chestnut curls her eyes gave him the once-over before she turned to the bar. Horribly caught in the collision of fantasy and reality, Mark felt as if the contents of his mind must be written on his face. In confusion he swigged a mouthful of beer then somehow forced himself to speak.

'Quiet tonight.' It was totally lame but the words helped him regain a small measure of control.

'Yeah. But I'm not bitching, though it's gonna make me short on tips.'

'Right.' He managed a smile while a part of his overheated brain registered an accent that could be Australian. There was nobody behind the bar and she leaned right forwards, straining up towards the overhead rack. His palms were damp and there was a throbbing pulse in his temples as he took in how the back seam of her pants threatened to burst its stitching. She couldn't quite reach even on tiptoe and a full second passed while Mark gaped stupidly at the haunches so prominently displayed. Then he was off his stool beside her and his extra height let him take down the glass she wanted.

'Sorry, I was in a dream.' He sat back down awkwardly, nostrils full of her scent. What the fuck had he said that for?

'Thanks.' She took the tumbler from him with a half-smile. 'Don't fret about it, I'm like that half the time. And especially after a long day.' The bartender stuck his head round the door at the far end and she gestured at him.

'Will you let me get you that?' Mark emptied his beer and put his glass alongside hers.

'Sure. Rodney knows my poison. Just give me five out back and I'm through for the night.'

Mark paid for the drinks and made a serious attempt to get a grip. He took the beer and the vodka martini to a small table in the corner with two chairs and sat down. In an effort to empty his mind of unmentionable images he thought about her. She was an Aussie all right and close up he had to put her age at thirty-five minimum, which gave her a good ten years on him. So what? In fact that could be a good thing. The affairs he'd had with girls his age or younger hadn't worked out. Now a woman who had been around a bit, maybe she'd, she'd . . . She'd what? Cure him of his fantasy life? He was back at the same sticking point: it wasn't age that was the problem, the problem was in his head. He was drinking deep in his frustration when she appeared again with a shoulder bag.

'Great.' She slid into the seat opposite him and raised her glass. 'Cheers. You're Mark and you used to work here, right?' She laughed at his expression and went on. 'I have my spies in the kitchen. Well, Janey's the name and I guess I started here soon after you left.'

'I met a girl and went back to school. Well, I *did*, but it's over now, or almost. I mean, I'm still in college but the girl, the relationship . . .' Mark gave up, tongue-tied, but Janey came to the rescue.

'Hey, handsome, I figured out Mr Happily Married wouldn't be here on his tod, but I'm not asking to see the separation agreement. I could use the company for a couple of drinks and if you could too . . .'

'Yeah, er, sure. I mean, that would be great.' Why couldn't he string two words together?

'As long as I'm not intruding. You seemed pretty deep in thought a while back.' She was looking at him with an eyebrow raised and again Mark had the feeling that she could read him. Especially the things he didn't want read. To hide his blushes he stood up.

'Let me get you another. Then if you like we could go somewhere else?'

At three in the morning in a less than reputable part of town the medical student and the waitress were locked in an embrace. For an hour they had stayed in the club, talking first about its characters then as the alcohol took hold both ventured a few disclosures about their current lack of sexual partners. For Mark's part he was careful to avoid mentioning the main cause of his relationship problems and he assumed Janey to be doing the same, though what she might be censoring he couldn't guess at. Then at her instigation they took a cab to her own neighbourhood where for the past two hours in a hot smoky room with more black faces than white, they had drunk lots and danced even more. Jiving and jumping had given way to moving close and slow, though she turned away from the lips that tried to find her own. Now, outside in a deserted back alley, she let him nuzzle into her neck while his hands were exploring the rear end that had so aroused his lust.

'Feels good, yeah?' Wriggling her butt provocatively, Janey nibbled his shoulder and whispered close into his ear. 'How would you like to give it a spanking?'

'What . . . what . . .?' Mark could not – dared not – believe his ears, but his already stiff cock went rock hard at once and he felt her hand on it.

'This guy here heard me just fine. *He's* telling me I'm going over your knee for a good, sound spanking. I thought it by the look in your eyes, fella.' Janey gave a delighted chuckle and unzipped his pants, adroitly avoiding his attempts to kiss her on the mouth. She squatted down and in the dim lighting he could just make out her upturned face.

'So we got a date, Mark, am I correct?'

'Yes. Oh, God, yes.'

'OK. We'll go to my place. But first I reckon this big boy's in need of a little milking.'

Her lips closed over his engorged organ, working back and forth, and his hands were in her hair.

'Oh, God, I'm going to . . . aahh . . . I'm going to . . .' He felt her grasp tighten on his hips as the spasms started to pump out his pent-up fluid.

4

Amazon

Hours before her straying partner ejaculated in another woman's mouth, Cate was following muscled thighs up an outside stairway just a stone's throw from Arte's, savouring an eye-level view of miniskirted arse-cheeks that rolled at every step in their PVC sheath. At the top she held open the screen while Zadia found a keyhole in the peeling wood of the door and let them in to her apartment.

'It is not smart,' she declared in the hallway, 'but I am alone here. I do what I like.' Crossing the worn linoleum of the kitchen she took a beer from the fridge and held it out. 'For the visitor. I have a cola later. Please sit and drink while I prepare.'

Cate sank down thankfully at the table and put the bottle to her lips. They had walked for only five minutes yet the high sexual excitement in which they'd left the club had all but dissipated and she was feeling apprehensive about what was required of her. After a second swallow she looked round the room. While shabby, it was clean and tidy and the whole place had the air of being little used. Maybe Zadia spent her spare time in the tourbus giving head to Marissa – just like she'd last seen her doing. Cate pursed her lips with the irritation she still felt at having been usurped in Marissa's bed that night.

Then Zadia reappeared in the doorway with a solemn expression on her face. She held out her palms across both of which lay a piece of black leather the length of her forearm. Stopping in front of Cate, she inclined her head in a brief bow.

'Please take the instrument. It is named a tawse.'

Surprisingly heavy, it had a greasy feel and Cate handled it gingerly. At least a quarter-inch thick, it was wide enough to be cut into two substantial tails at one end while the other was shaped into a handle. Tawse, the lady said. There was a Scottish uncle vaguely in her memory talking about getting it at school, though he called it 'getting belted'. And surely that was on the hand? Cate turned the thing over, perplexed. Did Zadia want her to . . .?

'You will use it, yes? Just come with me.' She led the way into a fair-sized room with a double divan bed in the middle of one wall. Two pillows had been placed on the edge of the mattress and there was a low footstool on the floor below.

'Take off my skirt, please, then we begin.'

Feeling more than a little out of her depth, Cate dropped to her haunches and found a hook at the front of the garment on top of a zipper that held the whole thing together. When she pulled it down the shiny material sprang apart and fell to the floor, revealing Zadia's unshaved blonde bush. Almost in a reflex Cate put her mouth to the hairs that were damp with the drummer's excitement, but she drew back with a sharp hiss.

'*Ach, nein*! After I atone.' She turned and knelt on the stool then lay right forward, the pillows under her belly. Cate stood hesitating with the strap dangling from her hand. In the position Zadia had taken up, the buttocks were raised and parted, and she longed to dip her fingers into the secret furrow and taste fully what the pubis had merely hinted at. But she was expected to chastise the Amazonian lady, not caress her. At least, not *yet*.

Cate looked again at the tawse and swung it through the air experimentally. Then, taking a deep breath, she raised it and tried to bring it down square across the proffered behind, but at the last moment she pulled the stroke and the tongues licked feebly against a naked flank. The woman waiting for punishment turned her head then eased herself up. She frowned a little, but there was no impatience in her eyes.

'I go too fast. I did not understand. This is the first time for you, yes?'

Cate nodded, profoundly embarrassed. Here she was, the tough ex-punk who couldn't bring herself to hand out a spanking with a bit of leather used on schoolkids. What a fucking joke!

Zadia took her arm and steered her to an upright chair by the bed. 'Sit,' she commanded gently. 'First we will remove the jeans and make you more at ease.' Lifting one of Cate's legs, she uncovered the sixteen-hole Doc Martens and beamed. When the denims were off she put the boots back on and laced them up tight over the ankles. 'Very good. Now stand.'

When Cate was on her feet the black nylon singlet came just to the crotch and Zadia turned her round, making approving noises. Cate felt hands slip into the wide armholes and cup her breasts, squeezing the nipples; then they withdrew and reached under the hem to pat her bottom. There was an immediate stab in her loins and she gave a little shiver of pleasure. Zadia picked up a cushion and placed it where Cate had been sitting, then picked up the tawse.

'Now for this. You hold it so –' she gripped it a little down from the end then lifted it above her head '– and bring it down so!' With a dull thud the cushion gave up a puff of dust. 'Now you try.' Cate had no difficulty imitating her teacher (though with the left hand) and once again the dust flew.

'Good. So you show me what is the difficulty? You punish the naughty cushion, no problem, but you do not want to punish me, yes?' Zadia took her by the shoulders and looked hard into Cate's eyes. 'You forget what I did. Now think. Think!' She tightened her grip and Cate shrank back at the drummer's strength. 'I burst in when you want to make love, yes? And I take hold of you and shout, yes?' Her voice was getting louder and the gestures made Cate flinch. 'And then I put you out in the road, so!' She lunged at Cate who stumbled to her knees, knees that were still sore from the earlier occasion.

She cried out and was transported back to that night when on the tarmac she wept bitter tears of self-pity and impotent rage. Then something shifted inside her and the remembered fury was reignited. This woman had wrecked her hot night of sex, then she'd abused her, and now she was pushing her around all over again. Cate got to her feet and looked down at the wisp of clinging material that topped the full-on dyke boots. Keyed up by an adrenaline rush, she felt strong, sexy and *mean*.

'OK. Get back in position. Now.' She enunciated carefully, trying to keep her voice level, and without a word Zadia obeyed. Cate moved to one side of the bared hindquarters and measured the distance with her eye. Then she raised the strap and brought it down three times in succession with as much strength as she could muster.

The aim was perfect and the pure white skin coloured immediately into three pink bands that overlapped across the crown of the buttocks. Cate's mouth was dry and her heart thudded as she laid on six more strokes: the leather felt alive in her hand and the way it thwacked into the meaty curves thrust up at her was

41

indescribably thrilling. So far the recipient had not made a sound so her chastiser continued at a measured pace. As she worked, the hot anger that had fuelled the first blows became transmuted into a cold flame of revenge, and Cate's fierce pleasure mounted as the fiery red of the buttocks became streaked with darker purple. Each stroke was now met with a gasp of pain and when she held off to wipe the sweat from her palm Zadia made to get up.

'Enough. Please, enough.' But she did not turn her head and, as if from a distance, Cate heard her own voice speaking.

'*I* say when we are finished, not you. Get down.'

Zadia obeyed at once and six more bruising strokes made her cry out loud.

Then Cate threw aside the instrument and said quietly: 'Now it is enough.' Suddenly she was drained.

The chastened Amazon got up on to her knees and rocked, holding her behind for several seconds while Cate watched. Then Cate took Zadia's tear-stained face in her hands and stooped to kiss it but she was rebuffed.

'Now you come. First you hurt me, then I make you come. It is the way.' So saying, Zadia wrapped her arms around Cate's waist and pushed her mouth into the soaking crotch. There was no resisting her: the new-found enthusiasm for the tawse had brought Cate already to the brink and the long skilful tongue took her to a shuddering climax where they stood clutched together. And only when the process had been repeated more slowly on the bed did Zadia allow her new lover to soothe the hot and swollen parts she had zealously thrashed and do some mouth-work of her own.

Cate woke and peered at the digital clock: it read 7:02. Another hour before she need think about getting ready for work. But there was something wrong. These figures were green, not red like the ones on her alarm, and when she tried to move there was a tangle of sheet and another body that stirred and groaned. Memory flooded in and Cate sank back, dizzy, on to the pillow. She hadn't just fucked a woman for the first time in a year, oh no. Nothing as simple as that. She'd beaten her. Walloped her butt with a thick leather strap. And it had been the most exciting thing she'd ever done.

The figure beside her rolled on to her side and the cover slipped down from her haunches allowing Cate to make a nervous examination of the punished area. With relief she saw that the spectacular colouring of the night before had mostly gone, except for a line of purple marks down the left flank where the tails of the instrument had dug in. She fingered these cautiously and Zadia stretched then pushed her behind right out.

'Mmm.' The voice was thick with sleep. 'You kiss it better, *ja*? Mmm.'

There seemed nothing for it but to comply. One thing led to another until in the afterglow of orgasm Cate found her eye once more on the illuminated dial. Only this time it read 8:25.

'Oh, shit. Oh, *shit*.' She leaped out of bed and began to cast about for her clothes before it occurred to her that a semi-transparent top and bone-tight jeans would not pass muster at the bookstore. And while she could just make it for nine from Zadia's, no way was there time to go home first. 'Fuck!' Cate was staring crossly at the black singlet when it was taken out of her hand.

'You need to be respectable for work, yes? I help. Come.' The tall naked figure swept out of the bedroom and Cate followed her to a cupboard in the hall where she flung open the door. 'My sister keeps things here. She has the size of you, I think.'

Cate stood bemused in front of the rack filled with clothes and Zadia pushed past her. 'Here,' she said, handing over an expensive grey suit and a white silk blouse. Back in the bedroom she opened a drawer and

43

drew out something small and scarlet. 'You wear *my* panties, yes?' She gave a deep throaty laugh that made Cate want to pull her back into the rumpled sheets but the drummer pushed her in the direction of the bathroom. 'Now be *fast!*'

The morning passed in a kind of dream. Cate worked at shelving new stock that had come in the day before while the other staff served customers. The gear fitted her as if made to measure and the hateful Anthony who normally kept up a string of jibes at her 'studenty' dress was reduced to a pop-eyed silence. She resolved to improve her wardrobe, then remembered that the end of the month would likely see her unemployed. What the hell. Landing some other job could only be easier if she looked like she did at that moment. Come lunchtime she browsed the shelves on sexuality in the back room and took down a volume called *Erotic Pain* whose subtitle promised to explain the essentials of 'Dominance and Submission'. Gena had said D&S: that was what it stood for. Cate slipped the paperback into her jacket pocket and headed out down the street.

In the corner of a quiet coffee shop she learned that there was an extensive and varied subculture devoted to what she had stumbled on the night before. For some people it was their whole life, for some an irregular pastime, while others remained, through choice or lack of option, located in a world of fantasy. She read with a sense of recognition that an assertive woman could quite easily take to being a 'top' without prior indication and was reassured to be told that it was only natural to find the sights and sounds of someone getting a powerful butt-warming to be a real turn-on. Then with a jolt she realised it was two o' clock and hared back to the store, her mind fizzing with new words and new ideas.

When she went to return the book to its place a woman in motorcycle leathers was examining a neighbouring volume. On her third finger was a signet ring with a large silver disc that carried the image of the cat Cate had first seen in the bus, then stamped on the back of that envelope. Oh, God, the envelope. Though she patted her pockets automatically, Cate knew where it was: lying on the kitchen table in Zadia's apartment. Shit. A letter for her from Marissa and she hadn't even brought it along to read.

'Hey, sister.' A pair of intense blue eyes were fixed on her: she must have been staring at the ring. 'You want to take a closer look?' She held out her hand with the emblem uppermost. 'I thought at first you were one of us.' The voice was kind of weather-beaten to match the complexion and seemed to invite an explanation.

'I saw it before, twice. Well, that's twice from the same woman. But I don't know what it means except it has something to do with all this –' She gestured at the small row of books about sadism and masochism.

'And you want to find out more?' The woman finished the sentence and Cate nodded. 'Any experience?' The gaze pierced her and it seemed pointless to dissemble.

'Last night was the first. I –' she hesitated for a second then plunged on '– I used a strap – a tawse – on a woman. Not the one with the cat like yours. And I never felt so alive.' Oh, God, why was she telling this to a total stranger? Cate fingered the throat of her blouse, feeling naked and exposed, but the woman wasn't looking. She had taken out a pad and was writing. Then she tore off the top sheet, folded it in two and held it out.

'My first time turned me from a housewife into a leather dyke. Overnight – though it took twenty years more to get the details right. You need to talk, here's a time and a place. This will get you in.' Cate took the paper and pocketed it while the woman put her book back. She picked up her helmet then turned before she left. 'Don't do too much reading, now, sister. Just get out there and do the business.'

* * *

45

It was well after six when she climbed the stair and opened the door into Zadia's place, calling out her name. In a waft of cooking smells the lady herself appeared wearing a halter top and scarlet pants.

'Cate.' She reached out a hand and drew her into the kitchen where the table had been set and there was a clutter of pots and pans on the side counters. Pouring out two glasses of wine she said, 'I have one with you, yes? We celebrate. I do not hit you any more; *you* hit me. But in a special way.' She gave a pantomime wink and a giggle and the formidable figure with the shaved head was for the moment a gleeful little girl, one who, Cate became aware, was holding something behind her back. Then with a flourish, she produced it and swished it through the air. Cate saw it was a yard-long cane with a crooked handle and she saw also the seriousness behind her lover's delight.

'Tonight you get the second lesson. But first we eat. Give me your jacket, but you keep the rest, yes? You will look like the part you play.'

She took away the things and they sat down to dinner. There was a bubbling casserole, crusty fresh bread and a salad and the two women ate hungrily in silence. Then Zadia made coffee and handed over the missive from Marissa. 'You read, yes?'

Cate opened the envelope to find an A4 sheet copiously inscribed in a small neat hand. The whole of the first side and most of the second was taken up with what the writer would like to do with the reader's delectable body and its parts: it was, well, more of a *sex* letter than a love letter and Cate skimmed it uneasily in Zadia's presence. But at the end was written: *125 E Simpson, May 19 evening. Show the envelope at the door. Till then. xxxx M.* One twenty-five East Simpson Street. She'd seen that address before, and very recently. Cate got up and went to the jacket hanging on the back of the door. There it was on the folded piece of paper: same number, same street, same day.

46

Zadia had cleared the table and she pulled up her chair while Cate told her about the woman in leather and showed her how the dates and locations were identical. The drummer wrinkled her nose.

'Maybe it is – what do you call it? – opening day.'

'Open day.' The idea of the D&S practitioners and their gear on display for the public made Cate smile.

'OK. OK.' Zadia frowned, picking at a loose thread on her sleeve. 'Look, Cate, I know not much about this Cat. Only what Marissa says sometimes and she knows I don't like, so she says little. I don't do what she does. I mean, I don't do until the night, the night . . .' The German woman's English was deteriorating in her agitation and Cate took hold of her arm.

'Oh, Zadia. Are you saying you'd never had the strap before last night? Or anything else? Then we were both virgins, right?'

'*Ja, ja*, I understand. Both virgins. It is good.' Eyes brimming, she flashed a watery smile that brought a lump to Cate's throat as they looked at each other across the table. Then Zadia got abruptly to her feet. 'Come. Nobody beat me but I beat others before. Marissa one time. So I teach you, yes?' She led the way into the bedroom where a tall stool had been placed in the middle of the floor and handed the cane over to Cate.

'Take this and feel it. Once it moves in the hand I do not need to make you angry, I think.'

It was not far off eleven on the clock when she surfaced and stretched. The chaotic bedclothes were becoming familiar and there was no longer that unpleasant lurch of waking in an unknown bed. Her lover was sleeping on her face and the second morning's inspection revealed buttocks marked with a score or more of dark lines that fed into a solid mass of bluish-black down the left flank. Cate bit her lip, remembering the fierce

47

pleasure of making the tip of the bendy rattan whip in to force a cry from her lover. Lover. Oh, God, *victim* was more like it. Victim-lover. She sighed and nosed into Zadia's neck then nibbled her ear until she stirred.

'It's gonna take a lot to kiss this better,' she announced as much to herself as to her sleepy companion, and moved down the bed to put her mouth to the discoloured flesh.

By two o'clock they were eating a belated and hasty breakfast of waffles and strong coffee. Zadia had nearly finished packing a bag for the tourbus which was leaving from the back of Arte's in a half hour. She had resisted any special treatment and sat on the usual wooden chair at table, but Cate noticed with a twinge of remorse how each shift of weight made her wince in discomfort. The band was gigging Monday through Thursday, then again, after a long weekend, until the end of the month, so they would not be meeting for more than two weeks.

'Your bottom needs a rest,' said Cate lightly, trying to ignore her feelings of guilt, but Zadia shook her head.

'You hurt me, and now I am sore. So be sorry, if you want. It is part of it all, yes? But remember: you do not force me. Later, maybe you will. Or maybe you move on. Or maybe I do.' She shrugged as if to say that they should leave such things to when they came. 'We did what we did. Now I go to play the drums, it is settled. But what do you do now?' She got up without waiting for an answer and began to stuff another pair of jeans into the holdall in the corner.

Cate was caught unawares. For nearly two days she had lived in the present, as if closing off thought about the next day would help her assimilate the momentous step she had taken. But Zadia's was a good question. In less than an hour she would be back in her flat and very likely Mark would be there. The prospect filled her with

48

dismay. Fresh from sex with her new woman and with so much stuff to ponder and absorb, the last thing she needed was to deal with the stale remnants of her failed year with a man. It was simply and plainly intolerable.

Zadia straightened up with her shoulder bag in place. It was time to go and Cate picked up the jacket she had brought with her. As her lover locked up outside, she suddenly knew what she was going to do. It had to be a clean break with the past. No messing. 'I got the first bit, lover. It's my apartment and I want it back. So he's gone. *Finito*. Not next month, not next week, but right fucking now!' The idea of ordering this man out of her life in a peremptory fashion gave Cate a wild exhilaration that made her hoot with laughter. For a moment her companion stared, nonplussed, then she caught the mood and the two women bounded down the stair and, giggling hysterically, ran helter-skelter through the startled pedestrians of the Sunday afternoon street.

5

. . . and Realities

When Mark surfaced the pain in his head made him wish he hadn't. But there was no going back, for the pressure on his bladder that had roused him was demanding release. Unsticking his eyes, he lurched to unsteady feet and saw a door to the left of him ajar. In the bathroom he directed the flow into the bowl with considerable relief then drank a glass of water and splashed some on his face.

Lying down again, he tried to get his brain to process what facts he could marshal. Here he was in a strange single bed, alone and hung-over. Badly hung-over. He could remember quite clearly the drinking, then the dancing and drinking, though that was a tad more hazy. But afterwards, in the alley, the words in his ear that were straight from one of his fantasies and the feel of her mouth working his cock were both clear as crystal. So where was Janey? Had he spanked her? Had they even fucked? Mark turned on to his side and groaned with the effort of recall that made it feel like his skull was bursting.

Then the door opened and she marched in with a tray. 'Now don't you say a word, not one word. Just get this down you first.' Janey held out a fizzing glass but Mark drew back. A picture had come to mind of her pushing a glass at him last night with the same words and bit by bit memory returned. When they'd come in she'd opened a bottle of Scotch. That explained why he was so wrecked: after the earlier boozing they'd sat and guzzled whisky. Or, rather, *he* had. Realisation dawned that she'd got him smashed quite deliberately so that he couldn't do anything to her. And then he recalled how all evening she had kept his mouth well away from her own. She'd sucked him off but she wouldn't let him kiss her, as if that was somehow too intimate. So what now? He took and drained the concoction with a grimace at its bitterness and it was several moments before he trusted himself to speak.

'So we didn't –'

Janey held up a hand to stop him. 'If *sir* would like to use the facilities –' she nodded in the direction of the bathroom he'd already stumbled on '– then he'll find me waiting for him in the next room.' He noticed that with a starched apron she wore a black roll-neck and thick black stockings, but her face gave nothing away. Bemused, he watched her take the tray and when she turned to leave he was startled to see that at the back of the pinafore there was neither skirt nor underwear. From the waist to the stocking tops behind Janey was quite naked. By the time she had made a leisurely exit in a display of undulating flesh he had an erection and his head was beginning to clear. Whatever game the lady was playing, he wanted in.

The flow of hot water and use of a razor completed his recovery and he put on the silk dressing gown that was hanging beside his towel. Next door he found Janey sitting demurely on the end of a chaise longue and at his appearance she jumped up and gestured that he should take her place. Then, without a word, she lowered herself over his lap so that while her feet were on the floor the upper part of her body rested on the upholstered seat. Relieved that she did not seem to want dialogue improvised

51

around the theme of her naughtiness, Mark lifted his hand and brought it down. Diffident at first, he soon realised from the way she pushed up her bottom that he should smack harder. And harder. In fact, he should slap her with as much force as he could muster. As he worked, the anxiety his extraordinary situation provoked at first began to leave him and he watched the pure white swell of the buttocks turn pink and deepen into red. His lust was now rampant and when Janey's belly began to press harder on to his erection he knew suddenly he could not last.

'Oh, Christ, I'm sorry – I can't stop it –'

In a trice she was on the floor, his robe was spread and her mouth closed on the first spurt of his semen. She sucked until the pulsing stopped and he was flaccid, then she stood up. 'If *sir* would now finish his excellent work . . .'

There was the hint of a smile as she lowered herself once more into position for the spanking to continue.

And continue it did, though it was not long in reaching a conclusion. To the quivering of the globes was added a rhythmic gyration of the hips, and Mark aimed his smacks low into the base of the cleft. All at once the cries were squeals and then the squeals were shrieks and it was all over. The spanked woman subsided into shivers and moans while he held her waist and stroked the back of her neck. Then she got up and went to the head of the couch, pulling him with her. She bent over it and said in a thick voice: 'Between the cheeks. Not inside, understand. Between. OK?'

He was hard again and grew poker stiff at the sight of the nether lips that glistened in damp brown curls of hair between the split hemispheres. He longed to plunge his oozing cock into their warm wetness, but the message was clear: no penetration. For the second time his need was pressing so without argument he took the option offered and, moving up behind her, lay his organ along the furrow. He dug his nails into scarlet buttock-flesh, making her gasp at his roughness, but she clenched the rear cheeks on him and in seconds he came deliriously, spattering up over the small of her back. Afterwards when they showered she held him very tight, and knowing this time not to attempt a kiss he contented himself with returning the firm embrace.

Later she put on jeans to match his and an old sweater and they went out to a diner in the next block. This time they both drank beer and when the food came they wolfed it down. She talked about how she liked the run-down neighbourhood where she'd lived for the past ten years which bordered on black and Latino enclaves, and he explained that while moving out of Cate's apartment was essential he was unsure whether he wanted to be somewhere too near the medical school. Back at Janey's place she made coffee while he took in for the first time the details of the room where they had played the morning scene. Aside from the centrally placed chaise longue there were two upright armchairs by an old heavy writing desk and a bookcase. On the wall there was a striking medallion the size of a small plate showing a fierce cat that seemed to move with any movement of the viewer and Mark took it down to have a closer look.

When Janey came in with cups and a steaming jug, he got to his feet. 'I'm sorry, I didn't mean to pry,' he began, embarrassed to be found examining her possessions, but she waved him back to his seat.

'Carry on, Mark. Make yourself at home.' The way she said his name it came out 'Meck' and he liked it. Perhaps Meck could be an improvement on the unhappy impotent fantasiser Mark had become. She handed him his coffee and sat down with hers.

'What you're looking at is more important than you probably realise. It's in this room for a reason, because nobody gets in here unless they're doing the kind of things we did earlier.' She took a mouthful of coffee and paused for a moment, as if considering. 'You've been really good, Meck. You didn't just catch on to my peculiar ways, you respected them, and that's more than a lot of men would have done. So I guess you deserve to know a bit more about me, even if it puts you right off. Though if being knocked out with a whisky bottle didn't drive you away, maybe nothing will.' Her tentative smile showed him it wasn't easy for her to talk like this.

'I couldn't leave without a hangover cure, and once I'd seen what the waitress was – or *wasn't* – wearing then you couldn't have *made* me leave. So you've got yourself a captive audience.' He grinned at her in what he hoped was a reassuring way, his curiosity whetted by her diffidence.

'Relax, fella. You're not getting my life history. The age *I* am that would take us till the end of next week.' She reached over for the medallion he'd been studying. 'No, it's this guy here you need to know about. The Nemesis Cat is his proper name – you see the initials right here underneath the picture – but he gets called just The Cat. If you've got one of these on your wall it means you're into s/m – sado-masochism, yeah? – and you do stuff in the network.'

Mark nodded to the query, though the porno magazines he'd used now and again didn't use the term, preferring the neutral-sounding 'CP' (for corporal punishment) or the mild-sounding 'spanking' and he'd avoided the psychology books because they made it all sound really pathological. But what was 'stuff in the network'?

'I'm not supposed to tell anyone about the network because how it runs is dead secret. But I couldn't even if I wanted to because I just don't know. What happens is that every so often I get to meet up with other Cat people for a session. The idea is you get together with someone to do something elaborate or extreme, the kind of thing you need a stranger for, yeah? The clever bit is getting a match so that first of all it works and, more important, that you're safe.'

'Sounds fine. A more sophisticated version of the contact ads in magazines.' Mark meant to be positive, but he had the feeling there was a twist coming.

'Well, not quite. Thing is, being a masochist I get paid. Not invariably, but nine times out of ten. I get paid by sadists who do things to me they can't do to a wife or girlfriend. By arrangement only, of course, but on occasion I've needed a whole month to get over what I agreed to. Crazy, yeah? What you've got to realise is that as often as I can stand it and not often enough to make a good living I'm a professional submissive. That's the nice phrase. To put it bluntly, Meck, I'm a *whore*.'

She stopped and looked down at the emblem she had been holding on her lap. After the drama of the declaration Mark didn't know what he felt. Whores were whores, he didn't think much about them, and he certainly didn't have a knee-jerk revulsion to women who worked in the sex industry. It made sense, of course, of the aversion to kissing that yet permitted a blow-job, though he wondered if the ban on penetrative fucking applied to her 'sessions'. None of these things really bothered him, however. What did was the idea of Janey being tied down then flogged with a whip or thrashed with a cane to the limits of her endurance, and maybe beyond. Not because of the way it made him feel sick, but because at one and the same time it had given him a hard-on that was straining uncomfortably against his jeans.

Aware that he must say something, Mark blurted: 'It's just a word. I've never paid for sex but that doesn't mean I think it's wrong. If I'd had more guts I would have tried some of the contact ads in magazines, not that I'm loaded with spare cash.' While true, he feared it was too feeble to hide from her the uneasiness he was not voicing.

'Thanks, but I shouldn't have laid all that on you. Forget it, OK?' She got up briskly and gathered the empty cups. Then at the door she put down the tray and turned. 'Tell you what. I know a thing or two about you closet spankers, and I'm willing to bet that you go for the naughty schoolgirl scene, complete with regulation underwear. Come on now, admit it.' She gave an infectious giggle and despite his blushes Mark had to smile. 'Well, you just have a look at this.'

Out of the top drawer of a cabinet she took a paddle made of polished wood and handed it to him. 'I had this made specially as a copy of one I saw used on a girl back home. For my sins I was at a private school in Melbourne, very "English" and proper. Three of us were called in to the headmistress's office to see a fourth girl get it on her knickers. Such a thing was completely unheard of, right? But she'd done the real no-no of getting caught in a nightclub in town, so as well as punishing her it was supposed to warn off girls like us who might be tempted by the idea. Well, she howled the place down and jumped up after four, so my two mates had to hold her down for a full dozen from scratch while I just stood there and watched. I was dying to know what her bottom looked like after, and even more what it *felt* like. I never found out the first, it was never talked about and that was our last term. And then it was two years before I arranged to be on the receiving end.'

Mark stared at her, his erection back with a vengeance. 'So do you want to do it, fella? I've got all the gear we need and if you give me ten minutes you'll have the minx of the senior common room on your hands. And if you reckon I was dead cheeky to bring up your fantasies, then you've got an obvious come-back.' She went out then stuck her head around the still open door. 'A couple of things, Meck. I'm keeping my pants – panties – on because it stings like the very devil. And when I say I'm sorry, it means I'm done. Well, kind of. Give or take. Get me?'

On her return Janey came in without a word and walked slowly over to the raised end of the chaise longue. It was quite a transformation and Mark was wide-eyed. He'd expected that even though she was twenty years out of school her basically petite if curvy figure could carry a uniform without it seeming ridiculous. Yet he was unprepared for the submissive demeanour – so at odds with her normal assertiveness – that carried all else in its wake. With the longer curls tied back to leave a fringe that hung down over the bowed head, what filled out the blouse and skirt was turned from womanly flesh into pure puppy fat. And when she bent over the couch and rested her hands on its seat he lost no time in hoisting up the skirt to get a better look at some of it.

It was in an authentic brown serge material that took several stages to pull up over the hips, eventually to reveal fully cut knickers of a matching colour in thin cotton. Having folded the skirt with care so that it would stay in place, Mark stepped back to take a proper look at the full snugly clad bottom and the white thighs that tapered into brown woollen knee socks and sensible brogues. Fantasy was no match for this actuality that was making his pulse race as he went over to the desk for the paddle. Once in position he patted each arse-cheek experimentally a few times, then raised the instrument and delivered the first stroke. Then the second, the third and the fourth. The sharp *crack!* and the bounce of the impacted buttock went straight to his head and he laid on with a will until a sharp cry from the recipient brought him back to earth. How many had he given? He would guess a dozen, a dozen and a half max: surely plenty of scope to continue. Mark counted out twelve more strokes each one of which made the body twitch and gasp though the hands remained in place.

Then at thirteen there was another yelp and a muttered 'sorry' so he applied two more with force.

'Ah! Ah! Oh, I'm sorry, sir.' Still she stayed down and he did the same again.

'Oh-oh-oh-oh! Please, sir, oh, please . . .'

The blood throbbed in his brain and he fought to control himself. Four more, just four more. She could take it – would take it.

And she did. He dropped the paddle and was beside her; an arm round the waist to keep her bent and a hand pressing hard into the gusset between her legs. At his touch she came, jerking in his grasp with harsh cries.

'Stay,' he ordered and released his grip. Behind her he peeled down the underpants to just below the crown of the cheeks and unzipped to release his bursting cock. He could feel the heat from the flaming imprints of the paddle as he pressed the slick head of the organ against the rim of her anus. She stiffened with a sharp intake of breath, seeming to sense that he was poised on the brink of buggery, but he mastered himself and after a frozen moment she pushed back. It was a small movement but he began ejaculating at once with a painful intensity and he clutched at her hips, watching the fluid well up in the cleft and run down into the bunched cotton below.

When it was finished, he rolled the garment back and delivered a smack to the prominent wet patch that made her yelp again. As they went to clean up he held her close and she laughed when he said: 'I wonder how many paddled schoolgirls have had to wash a guy's sperm out of their panties after.'

On the Sunday morning she came naked to him in his single bed and offered her bottom for inspection. It was declared well on the mend so she went over his lap there and then. Afterwards she squatted over his face with a hand on his organ while he tongued her to climax, then she leaned forwards and took him so that when he discharged in her mouth he was unforgettably engulfed in the tastes and smells between the hot spanked globes of her buttocks.

Over a late breakfast, she said: 'You know the terms by now, Meck. You're looking for a room, you said; so take that one you've been using.'

Mark looked across the table at Janey with her rich brown curls spilling over the collar of a robe open to the swelling breasts and felt a renewed stiffening in his groin. He said: 'When we've eaten I'd like to book you for an hour on the chaise longue. Then I'll go and start moving my things.'

Back in Cate's apartment he packed two suitcases full of clothes and made piles of books and CDs that he didn't think she would want to claim. The dozen or so magazines hidden at the bottom of the wardrobe he put in a bin bag of rubbish. Their sketches of CP scenes had been a useful masturbation aid in the past months but now he had the real thing. OK, he hadn't fucked Janey in the standard manner – maybe never would – but the only hand that was likely to be on his cock was hers and it would do the job without the need of pictures.

Then he heard a key in the lock and after a moment the click it typically made as Cate leaned back to close the door behind her. When she came in to the living room he saw spots of high colour on her cheeks and her mouth set in a line.

'Mark, there's something I need to say. I've made a decision –' She stopped, looking bemusedly at the operations she had interrupted. He straightened up and took the chance to get his piece off his chest.

'Cate, I've made a decision too. Made it this morning. I'm going to move out. Er, now. Right now.'

6

Examinations

Cate stood speechless. There was Mark in the middle of
packing his things. She had come to throw him out of
her flat and out of her life, and he had beaten her to it.
The bastard was leaving *her*! In the kitchen she made
coffee, telling herself for fuck's sake get a grip. She
wanted him out and he was going; that had to be a
successful conclusion to the matter. But there was an
anger inside her that she had lost control of the
situation, and it persisted despite her attempts at
rationalisation. She took Mark a cup and was glad to
see he had almost finished.

'I'll come back for those tomorrow when I've emptied
the cases.' He pointed at a small heap in the corner and
Cate nodded.

'You got an OK place? Can I get the address? You
know, mail might come and stuff.' Awkward herself, she
noticed that he too was embarrassed by the request.

'I, er, I can't tell you the address. I don't mean I *can't*
tell you, I mean it's in a friend's place and I don't know
the number. I'll leave it tomorrow.'

With relief she saw him to the door with his belong-
ings and with an effort managed a peck on his cheek.
'I'll see you around, eh?'

At seven in the evening Cate sat in front of her dressing
table, freshly bathed, staring moodily at her reflection

while she brushed her hair. The fact there was no Mark to be avoided made the place seem suddenly empty. And on top of that, the euphoric decision of the afternoon to eject him had blown up in her face and the whole sense of a new departure seemed tarnished. What was it Zadia had meant? That maybe they just did what they did and they'd both move on? As if it was all just a series of unconnected happenings without any implications or any direction. Well, perhaps it was.

She decided against make-up. Untouched the face was harder and if she looked tough maybe she'd start to feel tough. Making a resolution to leave out underwear of any kind she reached for a black sweatshirt and jeans that were ripped at the butt. Boots laced, she stood up, stuffed some notes into her pocket and went out the door. Fingers crossed, Gena would be back on tonight; and if she wasn't a beer or six would make the world feel a better place.

When she reached Arte's the lady was there all right – in close conference with a pretty little blonde in red lipstick and tight pants who looked more like fifteen than the twenty-one she had to be to get past door security. They were at the far corner of the bar so Cate bought a drink and sipped it. When she turned round it was to find them beside her.

'Hi. Melanie's just going.' Gena gave the girl's prominent rear a slap saying, 'Later,' and she tripped out in a fit of giggles. 'The kids today, what can you do? Want to grab a seat?'

Cate was getting used to the deadpan remarks of this young woman who was little older than the girl she would plainly be bedding when it came to 'later'. But the hair fastened back from the paintless freckled face and the serious demeanour added years to the impression Gena created. It all made sense once she knew the history of quitting school and parents at thirteen and being taken in by her aunt to help run the club.

'Well, are you going to keep me in suspense? I heard the gig was short and sweet, but what about the femme fatale?'

'When I get to her, I'm sure she'll be very sweet. As it was, she looked real sick and I chickened. But then you'll never guess who arrived and swept me off my feet.' Cate sat back and emptied her glass with a flourish. Gena got up without a word and in two minutes came back with more drinks and set them down slowly on the table.

'I give up, I give up. Now, if you don't tell all immediately, I'm gonna get the bouncer over and have you put out for – oh, I don't know – being aggravating. Patty's one-hundred-sixty pounds of pure muscle and she never lost an argument yet.'

Cate held up her hands. 'OK, you win. It was Zadia.' Savouring the surprised chuckle the name produced, she launched into the story of the drummer's insistence she made restitution for the tourbus episode and the results of that over the weekend. She tried not to get too carried away, but when she finished it was clear her new-found enthusiasm had communicated itself.

'Wow. So the Amazon likes a tanning. Who'd have thought it.'

'Don't know about *likes*. But she was turned on by it after. Though maybe that was a one-off, or should I say two-off.'

'But the lady I'm speaking to sure likes to hand it out. No doubt about that, huh?'

'Well, er, yeah. I think she does.' There was no point in lying about it; indeed it was a relief to be able to acknowledge the fact to a third party.

'Guess I'd better level with you then, if we're doing honesty. I told you there was a girl I used to spank; what I didn't say was that since then I got to like some of that treatment myself. Not all the time, but, you know.' She was looking a bit sheepish. 'Truth is, it's embarrassing. At my age being a dyke who likes femmes isn't exactly right on in the first place, but being one that likes her butt warmed really confuses the picture.'

They both laughed and drank. Cate's confidence was coming back and she giggled her way through three more beers and tales of Patty Pecs, as she was fondly known, and her numerous adoring lovers. Then out of a companionable and slightly tipsy lull Gena took the proceedings into a different gear.

'I can't stop thinking about the D&S stuff earlier. You know, you getting off on the D and me admitting to a bit of the S.' Cate looked sharply at her friend, but she was staring at the table. 'There's an office upstairs we could use if you wanted us to be alone. Shit, I don't know what I'm saying. I mean, I'm not asking you to, to . . .' Uncharacteristically agitated, Gena downed her drink in one and stood up. 'Forget it. Must be the booze talking.'

But Cate was on her feet first. Something told her she had to take charge here though at that moment she had no more idea of what would happen than Gena seemed to have. 'Show me the way, doll, and don't fret. If it's all a big mistake then the booze can take the blame for it.'

It was not a prepossessing room with its desk, filing cabinet and a few wooden chairs all harshly lit by an overhead strip, but Cate had the bit between her teeth. Once they were in she clicked the latch on the door lock and made Gena stand on the open patch of tiled floor in the middle. From behind her she unbuttoned the girl's loose cotton shorts, pulled down the zip and let them fall round her ankles. She bunched the long T-shirt up at the back and took a spring-clip from the desk to hold it in place, then hunkered down to study what she had uncovered.

The hips were quite slender and it was a heavily dimpled boy's behind that stood out above the sturdy thighs and calves. The golden skin was covered with a fine down and Cate, enchanted, thought of the figure of a young god as she stroked and petted its contours. Gena stood quite still and upright during these attentions, then she said: 'In the desk, the big drawer.' Under a handful of files Cate found a thick piece of rubber the size and shape of a boot-sole.

'Lean forwards and put your hands on your knees, OK?' Cate swung the implement with a resounding smack to the left and right and, dropping to her knees, waited to see its exact shape appear in red on the two buttocks. Well tucked in at their base were genital lips just visible through a frizz of brown hair. Close up, Cate caught the sharp scent of them and it made her realise how her own cunt was lubricating. On her feet again she gave six full whacks to each side then sank back down and pressed her cheek into the bottom-cheeks to feel on her face the mounting heat she had created. Throughout the girl had remained motionless and now long moments passed while Cate held on to her legs. At last she released her grip and got up to return the rubber sole to its hiding place.

'I reckon your date will be waiting for you. Do you think?'

'Reckon so.' Gena pulled up her shorts and Cate unclipped the T-shirt and smoothed it down. Her palms were wet and she could see small beads of sweat on Gena's upper lip. The air was heavy with sex yet there seemed a mutual understanding there would be no physical consummation. It was as if their desire for each other was to be saved for something more than fucking. Cate cleared her throat.

'Friday night. Can you get Friday night off?'

'What's on?'

'The Cat people. I'm going to investigate and I have an extra pass into the place. I'd really like it if you came too.'

'Yeah.' Suddenly Gena's face broke into a broad grin and she took Cate's arm as they made for the stairs. 'Yeah, sure. Cool.'

East Simpson Street ran half across the city and neither of them knew where one twenty-five was. Then Gena dug a piece out of *Dyke Digest* on Jingles Bar whose address was just four doors away, so they had arranged to meet up there on the night around seven. However, in the afternoon notice to quit the bookstore had arrived for Cate and Sally, while the hated Anthony was offered a post at another branch. In total outrage they demanded to speak to the manager's office, and when, after much prevarication they got through, Cate raised the spectre of a sexual discrimination suit. The threat worked in the sense that an extra job was found in the space of an hour, but it was then offered to the more docile Sally who had not given the boss's deputy an ear-bashing.

So it was almost eight when the cab deposited a still indignant Cate at the bar door and she hurried inside to scan the spread of early-evening drinkers. Seeing no sign of Gena she ordered a beer, puzzled. The girl couldn't have given up on her already, could she? Further along the counter there was a guy in a suit talking with a flashy little number in stilettos and seamed stockings. Straights slumming, she thought, before she realised with the frisson it always gave that the 'guy' was in fact a woman. Then there was a second, bigger shock. The figure turned and Cate saw that this was not *a* dyke, but *the* dyke she had come here to meet, astoundingly cropped and tailored.

'Hi. I wondered if you were having second thoughts.' Gena straightened up, pocketing a piece of paper and said to her companion: 'Gotta go, hon. I'll call tomorrow, promise.'

Cate gawped: the brown hair that was always worn up had been cut mannishly short at the back and sides with the top slicked down to the head. And the clothes were as much of a transformation: knee-length culottes hugged the hips and there was a matching jacket over a glossy tank top. But the freckled smile was the same.

'Well, girlfriend, how do you rate the costume?'

'Wow. Another shock like that'll kill me. You can buy me a vodka to settle my nerves. And, yes, you look terrific.'

Gena took hold of Cate's shoulders and looked her up and down in turn. 'You too. I just love the boots with that skirt.' Cate sat down while the drinks were bought. Angry and flustered after the debacle at work she had cast about for gear to shift her mood. The Doc Martens laced up to the calves made her feel assertive, while the little black dress that flared out around the upper thighs was certainly daring. In fact, in public without underpants it was positively foolhardy, but what the hell.

'Here's two shots to brace us up for the Cat, OK?' Gena sat down and gestured at her outfit. 'It's not for keeps. Thought tonight might call for something special.'

'Well, it seemed to work on your latest femme, or is it just the force of personality that slays them?' The comment produced a faint blush and Cate grinned.

'Don't let it get to you, doll. I'm envious as fuck. But I'd better tell you my bad news and get it out the way. In two weeks I'm unemployed.' She recounted the shenanigans of the afternoon and it felt better to get it off her chest.

Gena sat back, considering. Then she said: 'Only one thing for it, girlfriend. You're gonna have to make a career change from bookseller to *domina*. The lady with the whip. Who gets paid for her expert services.' She drained her vodka and stood up. 'So if you're ready we better go along the street and see if we can get you started.'

* * *

Their destination turned out to be a slightly run-down establishment with the sign HOTEL BOND. It occupied the corner of a block and employed a doorman who gravely directed them round to a side entrance. That was emblazoned at head height with the emblem of the wild beast, though this time in an intricate painted carving. Cate pressed the bell three times without response, then noticed they were being inspected through one of the cat's eyes. The door opened a fraction on a heavy chain and a voice said: 'I cannot admit two at once. It is most irregular. Those we invite are usually selected so that they are not acquainted in outside society.'

'We met earlier in the bar. I didn't know she was coming here until this moment.' Cate thought it would not be politic to say Gena's invitation was second-hand.

'One of you, then. Let me see your note of admission. The other must wait outside until we are ready for her.'

Cate hesitated, unhappy that they were to be split up. 'You go ahead,' said Gena and pushed her forwards to hand the letter through the gap. In an undertone she added, 'Your need is greater than mine. Catch you later down the road.'

After a pause the door opened to admit Cate and she watched the slight, greying woman close it with a thud. She wasn't the obvious choice for the job of repelling intruders, but maybe they didn't get past the chain in the first place. Taking back the letter, Cate remembered Marissa's explicit prose with a twinge of embarrassment but the lady gave no sign that she'd read anything untoward.

'Follow me.' She led the way into a small room on the right that was empty save for a sideboard against one wall and an upright wooden chair in the centre of the floor. Out of a drawer she took a silk band that was elasticated at the back. 'Please sit. I hope you understand it is necessary that one under examination should wear this.'

Cate sat down with a shrug, affecting nonchalance, and allowed the blindfold to be put in place. Then she heard the door open and a murmured exchange before it closed again. Her skin prickled and there was a touch to the side of her neck.

'Allow me to take your jacket. The air in here is rather warm.' The new voice was low and husky and there was a trace of scent in the air. Marissa? But the accent sounded sort of Ivy League and the formal tone was difficult to square with what she knew of that lady. Cate allowed the leather to be removed while she struggled to recall what the diva had actually sounded like in their brief encounter but with little success. The drastic end of it seemed to have erased such details so she made an effort to put the question of the speaker's identity out of her head.

'As I believe you are aware, the Cat is the symbol of a network. We are all people with an interest in the discipline of the flesh, and I understand you may share in that. Shortly, we shall give you an opportunity to demonstrate your aptitude, but before that I should like you to give an account of a recent important experience. If this is all new to you it may well be your first such encounter and in my opinion you would do best to focus on your feelings and endeavour to make them clear to yourself. Do not concern yourself with justifying anything to me.'

The speech was elaborate, even theatrical, and Cate tried her best to focus. She was there first of all because Marissa had invited her and she still wanted to continue the bed-scene that had been so rudely interrupted. But things had changed and maybe this organisation could do things for her. Hesitantly at first then with gathering momentum she began on a description of the weekend with Zadia and how it had been a revelation. At the end of it was the ambivalent reaction in the cold light of morning to the bruises she had caused, after which she lapsed into silence, uncertain how to round off what she had told.

'You said your friend wanted to make restitution for manhandling you. Am I right? So would you say that the punishment was, in effect, carrying out her orders?'

'Not exactly.' The joy she had felt in handling the cane was vivid in her mind and she made an effort to put it into words. Then she added: 'I hurt her a lot. More than she expected and I'm sure more than she wanted. But then later I think she was glad of it.'

'Good. That is admirably clear. Now I am going to ask you to stand up as you are, move round to the back of the chair and bend over it. This will be difficult – perhaps especially for you – but it must be done if we are to go on.'

It occurred to Cate that there was nothing to stop her walking out of the room and out of the building for good. But then it piqued her to think she was the sort of person who couldn't face something 'difficult', so she got up and did as she was told. The folly of wearing a very short dress with nothing underneath was apparent in a way she hadn't expected. But what was going to happen? Was *she* going to be punished? Well, they could stick that. Or –

The questions were answered by the pressure of a cool finger against her exposed labia, and since they were moist with the reliving of Zadia under the cane, it slipped easily inside and began to make stroking movements. Cate gritted her teeth: it was bad enough being deprived of sight and made to offer her genitals for examination. But this woman was going to make her come and, aroused as she was, there was no way to stop it. Well, not short of leaving and her pride wouldn't allow that. Besides, the finger had been joined by a second and they were engaged in doing things to her clitoris with only one possible outcome. And that was going to be very, very soon.

Afterwards Cate hoped she had not made too much noise: at least she had managed to hang on to the chair. The fingers were withdrawn and there was from behind her the unmistakable noise of a stifled giggle followed by a just audible exclamation that sounded very like 'Shit!' After a silence the voice resumed but now the posh speech sounded as fake as a bad piece of amateur dramatics and it brought Cate uncomfortably close to the giggles herself.

'That was excellent. Such a strong sexual response can be, if properly channelled, a real asset in our work and I look forward to testing it again a little later.' Bet you do, thought Cate while she strove to suppress a smile. Whether or no it was Melissa acting the part it was cheering that the lady had been turned on by her own act of masturbation.

'Now I shall take you into the next room where a client has been prepared for you to deal with as you see fit. That is all I shall say. When I leave you there remove your blindfold and begin; later, you may put it back to give a sign that you have finished. Is that understood?'

Once the door clicked shut Cate peeled off the silk band to see a wooden A-frame about her own height with a naked figure secured to the side of it that faced her. Naked, that was, save for a leather mask that was stretched tight over eyes and mouth and the leather straps that circled the waist and ankles. Moving round the structure she saw the wrists were tied halfway down the front of it opposite a long though flaccid penis that protruded through the slats. Otherwise the space was empty apart from a table where instruments of punishment had been set out, though part of the wall to her left was a large rectangle of reflective glass from behind which she was certainly being watched.

OK. This was a test and she had to rise to the occasion. It was necessary to act the cool and self-possessed character she was far from being inside. But

70

she could be literally cool. In two deft movements Cate hoisted her skimpy dress over her head and deposited it on the floor. She stood for a moment, naked in her heavy lace-ups, a little shocked by her own audacity, then approached the table to inspect its contents.

The shiny black whip coiled on the left she had little idea how to handle, so that was out; and a tawse on the right was rejected as being too lightweight. The cane was a different matter: it was a straight length in a leather binding embossed with the cat-head and the way it quivered in her grip made her tingle all over. Reluctantly, however, she laid it down again on the rudimentary grounds that the figure was fastened flat to the frame and people were supposed to bend over to be caned. That left another whip, but one with multiple thongs each of which had a stiffened end. It occurred to her that it could be called a 'cat' too, even though she was vaguely aware that the naval article would have been made of rope. Whatever, it still seemed like an omen. She had of course never used such a thing and could easily make a fool of herself, but it sat well in her grasp and did not seem difficult to control.

She realised that the headpiece on the immobilised young man made it unlikely he could know what she was doing, or even that she was there. So Cate stroked the tails of the whip over his back and flanks to indicate the instrument she had chosen and the body went at once rigid with a muffled cry of surprise. Once the muscular tension had subsided she placed a warning hand on the nape of his neck then stepped back and struck four times, hard. There were noises from under the gag but the body seemed braced to receive the vivid red stripes that sprang up across the white flesh and Cate saw with a frisson that in their wake the male organ stood proud.

She took it as a seal of approval and gave her impulses free rein. Pacing from side to side she lashed the instrument down again and again, scoring darker and darker lines into the abused flesh; yet the penis seemed only to grow more and more rampant. She had to stop, but not yet. Please, not *quite* yet.

Cate plied the thongs to the right until it glowed red there too then forced her trembling hands to desist. Still the cock stood miraculously erect and she knew suddenly what to do. Moving to the right of the frame, she swung the whip up under the swollen organ so that it coiled over and the tails lapped at the scrotum. There was a strangled bellow and the thing reared up. It was like some monstrous animal whose purple head emerged half out of its sheath to spit a gob of white fluid into the air. And when she flicked the leather tails some more it did it again and again. Eventually the ejaculation was done, leaving the floor spattered with the viscous milk for a yard ahead.

Cate drew back and took a couple of deep breaths. If that wasn't an ending she didn't know one. There was just the discarded dress to pick up and the blindfold to restore. And when she had done those things she stood still until she heard the door behind her open.

When she arrived at Jingles bar, Gena took her straight to the ladies where she bared an arse that was a rich ruby red and impressively hot, explaining to Cate that there had been a spanking session with two other girls. 'They came real easy, you know, and I reckon I could too with practice. So they're gonna help me out.' At the table she sat down with an exaggerated 'Ow!' and put a hand to her butt. 'It's sore, all right, but it's kind of nice sore, yeah? So that's me, girlfriend, now what about you? Gonna spill the beans?'

In her enthusiasm for a new way of getting into sex with pretty femmes, Gena looked for once young and vulnerable and it put Cate in a quandary. After the whipping she had climaxed at a single touch, to the examiner's great delight. Then she learned that an assignment was to be offered to her on the spot, with more to follow when she'd been trained in the use of other instruments. But the need for secrecy had been emphasised in the strongest terms and it was that that was giving her pause. How could she keep her friend in the dark when she was expecting to share confidences? Then, as she sat searching for the right words, Gena forestalled her.

'Hey, Cate, me and the girlies, we were just playing games. But you weren't, were you? What you did was serious stuff and you're not supposed to tell. Am I right or am I right?'

'Both of them. You put me to shame, girl. But maybe I can redeem myself. I just had a brainwave, so listen up.' She leaned forwards conspiratorially and Gena did the same. 'I got a top-secret session booked next week, but it's out of town at this big house and the lady said that if I was feeling uptight, first time and all that, she'd send someone along to keep me company. But, if you could see *yourself* doing such a thing –'

'– you mean being a girl Friday who carries the gear, the whips, whatever –'

'– *and* holds the nervous hand of the aspiring, er, aspiring –'

'– domina. I told you earlier that's the word. And you are on, girlfriend. The trainee domina has her hand-maid, as of tonight.' She sat back and they both grinned at each other.

'Well, in that case, I daresay the job description entitles her to hear as many of the sordid details as she can stomach. How about this, for starters? I know you're not a fan of men but the one tonight did have a talent. I swear to you, doll, after my special treatment this guy would squirt you right in the eye at five paces. No bother.'

'Squirt? You don't mean –'

73

'Oh, yes, I do, I most certainly do.'

'Oh, fuck.' The face was screwed up in distaste as the image registered then Cate caught her friend's eye, and heads turned from the surrounding tables as the two women exploded into raucous laughter.

7

Cat Work

In the month since Mark learned that Janey took clients through The Cat his desire to be present at a session had grown and grown. Following the move to her spare room, in which he always slept alone, she had led the way into a pattern of spanking and mutual masturbation which, in itself, satisfied him fine. He never asked why penetration was outlawed and never pushed her to take him in her mouth. When she did he regarded it as a bonus. After all, his orgasms were intense and frequent and the real s/m action was an immeasurable advance on the scenes he used to play in his head. While they had died out, this one thing had emerged from them: where he once imagined a woman being beaten he now wanted actually to watch. When he spanked or, rarely, paddled Janey he could of course see the results of it, but he wasn't really an observer. He was in charge and he had to regulate the chastisement, to keep an eye out for signs that he was going too far. So now Mark's dream was to become a *voyeur*. Another person's idea of what was sufficient punishment could be quite different to his own. Janey had said as much herself; she had experienced it. And he longed to be there, hidden, absolved of all responsibility, to witness the work of an individual whose zeal might require the whipping to go on, and go on, until . . .

The door to the apartment banged shut and he started up guiltily. Janey was back from her waitressing at the jazz club to surprise him in a fantasy of her mistreatment, just as had happened the time they first met. She put a bottle of vodka down on the table and drew up a chair.

'I've had some news that deserves a little celebration. But there's something I want to ask you as well, OK?' Mark hadn't touched any spirits since that first encounter she had just brought back to his mind. But clearly something was in the air, so he found some tonic water, cracked open a tray of ice and produced two glasses. Presumably she was not aiming to get him paralytic and out of action for a second time.

'I've just been offered a special gig for Friday night, and I get the tip-off that if I do well it could be regular. I don't know all the details yet, but it'll be staged for a small mixed party – loadsamoney – and it will net me more than I ever earned before. So, cause for a small celebration, eh, boy?' Mark poured two generous shots over ice, added tonic and they clinked glasses.

'Sounds good. Though I get the impression there's more to it, yeah?'

'Right. But nothing's perfect. It's a new lady who'll be dishing out the pain and I'm told she's hard. And when Sophie says that, it means she's fucking severe, so I'm gonna get taken a good way down masochist's row before she lets me off. What the fuck –' Janey shrugged but Mark could see the nonchalance was mostly an act '– I've been there a couple of times and it ain't pretty, but with pay as good as that . . .' She emptied her glass and then, as if she had been reading his mind all these past weeks, dropped in a casual bombshell. 'Should be some show. If you fancied a ringside seat, Meck, I think it might be arranged.'

At 8 p.m. on the dot Mark hesitated outside HOTEL BOND until the doorman emerged and forced him to take

76

the plunge. Handing over the embossed card, he was directed to the second door on the left with no hint of disapproval at his informal sweatshirt and jogging pants. 'You won't want to be wearing tight jeans,' Janey had said with a giggle the night they'd emptied the bottle, so he had taken her advice.

When he knocked a woman came out with heavy eye make-up and red lips. 'You must be Mark, right?' When he nodded she took him down a corridor where two couples in evening dress were being ushered through double doors. They continued past into a small room lit only by a dim overhead bulb. She indicated an armchair placed before the viewing window and handed him a paper. 'It's all pretty basic but you'll be on your own here. The guys you saw are paying for this so they get the posh suite with the drinks cabinet.' Then, on the way out, she turned. 'It was Janey got you in tonight, but aren't you the guy who used to live with Cate a while back?'

Mark looked at her, bemused. 'Yeah, that's right. But what . . .'

'Oh. So you're not really in touch with her any more?'

'No. I've hardly seen her since I moved out.'

'You don't know, do you? Oh, my. Well, have a good time.' She gave a chuckle and closed the door behind her. Trying to shrug off his irritation with this puzzle, Mark looked around. The glass in front of him gave on to the long axis of a rectangular room with the walls ahead and to the left lined from floor to high ceiling with books. The right side contained a long mirrored surface that must be the other observation suite the woman had referred to.

In his hand was a printed leaflet headed *NC Productions Inc.* which he squinted at in the low illumination. It began with a paragraph in italic script:

We do not consider amateur dramatics to have a place in our demonstrations since the corporal punishment is real, and not in any way simulated. But we do offer a peg on which to hang what you will see, and that may allow for a surprise or two. Enjoy!

Underneath that he read:

The setting is the library of a remote boarding school run by the headmistress with an iron hand. In the evening rounds of the buildings she has discovered the new gym teacher in a compromising position with a pupil. Both have agreed to accept summary discipline on the understanding that the errant mistress is the more culpable and therefore will bear the brunt of it. The scene opens as they await their fate.

The lights went down just as he finished, and when they came up again after several seconds two figures were standing on his left, their backs to the rows of books. His pulse quickened at the sight of Janey, shapely in white lycra with her curly hair tied up into a topknot, and next to her he saw a boy in full school uniform with jacket, tie, short pants and knee socks. On the desk in front of them lay a long straight cane and an elongated paddle made of a single piece of thick leather. The pair stood quite still, heads a little bowed, and stared into the middle distance. Then from somewhere beside his viewing post a door opened and a woman in a dark suit swept up to the desk chair and sat in it. Leaning over she opened a far drawer and took out a tome ostentatiously labelled PUNISHMENT BOOK. When she straightened to face the waiting couple Mark saw her profile for the first time.

It was Cate.

The shock sent his mind reeling. This woman he had lived with for a year, too scared to confess his interest in spanking, *she* was the new 'hard' lady who was going to give Janey a severe caning. Cate? *Cate*? Mark shook

78

himself and wrenched his attention back to the scene. It was too much to assimilate there and then and he was missing the action. The 'headmistress' had clapped the book shut and was speaking.

'. . . and a further dozen for leading your pupil astray. As for you, boy, a thorough spanking with the paddle should suffice. Come here!'

So how many was the 'gym teacher' going to get? *Two* dozen anyway and with that wicked-looking length on the desk. Mark's scalp prickled: he couldn't quite believe it, but he was going to see Janey get soundly thrashed. And by a Cate who had never looked more beautiful in a brilliant white blouse with a brooch at her throat, her eyes shining as if anticipating the delights to come.

The boy's jacket was removed and he bent over, hands on knees. Cate held an arm crooked round his waist, and the very short grey pants clung enticingly to him while she lambasted their seat with the substantial leather oval. Then they came off and he went over her knee for some resounding slaps with her bare hand, followed by a fusillade of blistering paddle strokes. There were yells and cries and tears before he was let up to nurse a behind that had become an impressively deep cherry red. Then he turned to face the viewers and it all went topsy-turvy once again. Between the front tails of the shirt there was a brown pubic bush that had been shaved into a perfect heart and beneath, quite hairless, were labia that pouted pink and wet. In the words of the song: 'he was a she', and Mark's hard-on went a distinct notch harder.

Now it was the turn of the second and principal culprit to take her punishment. She was directed to bend and hold her ankles, then the 'head' took up the cane and laid six measured strokes across the prominent posterior, each one of which made the body jerk and Mark flinch in sympathy. The second skin of lycra now bore the impression of six perfectly parallel lines. Five more were delivered in similar fashion but the sixth sliced into the upper thighs and the 'teacher' leaped to her feet, clutching at the injured part.

'I shall repeat that stroke. You know the penalty for a further lapse.'

She stayed down for that and the next five, with Mark willing her to hold on, but number eighteen was her undoing. 'Ah! ah! ah!' she cried, prancing and her chastiser stepped back.

'Boy, fetch the steps.' Under cropped hair, the spanked boy-girl was snub-nosed with freckles and with red bottom-cheeks on display made an arousing sight. When the short stepladder had been positioned, the unfortunate 'mistress' was bent over its top step and tied hand and foot to its legs with four lengths of rope. Then the implacable agent of discipline took a broad strip of leather and fastened it tight over the victim's mouth.

'We shall have no further interruptions. You were warned, and now we begin again from the beginning.' With a long paper-knife from the desk she sliced neatly through the waistband of the white leggings and, taking hold of the two ends, ripped open the back seam to uncover startlingly wealed buttocks and thighs. Then she picked up the cane and raised it in the air, saying: 'Boy, you will count out the full measure.'

Mark was in turmoil. Two dozen more? On top of, what was it, eighteen? Oh, God, she couldn't take punishment like that, could she? He ought to intervene, ought to stop this barbarity. But of course he didn't. Horrified yet prodigiously excited he watched, riveted, as stroke after remorseless stroke took the tally to its eventual destination.

Then the room was empty save for the ladder and the figure still bound to it. Mark shook himself out of his daze and, stumbling out of his cubicle, found his way in. When he removed the gag Janey stirred and moaned.

He would release her in a minute, but first he couldn't help it, he just had to … The jogging pants fell round his ankles and he held his swollen, dribbling cock to the ferociously welted flesh. Janey arched her back and the well-thrashed hindquarters pushed out towards him. Then the organ's head was inside the anal ring and just as he tried to control himself and withdraw she pushed again and he thrust right inside. He began to ejaculate at once as the body he had penetrated went into spasms that matched his own.

Then he became aware that they were no longer alone in the room. Behind him stood Cate, flushed and radiant, and Mark froze. Whether he was covering Janey or just shy of pulling out of her in front of his past lover, he stayed put, and screwing round his head he saw the 'headmistress' still held her instrument of pain.

'Why didn't you *tell* me? All that time and you didn't tell me.' Mark tensed as the cane was tapped against his bare behind but he felt his cock stiffen again.

'You are a *naughty* boy –' the tone was best schoolma'am and, coming from the blonde beauty, it jacked him into a ramrod, distending the tight hole '– and you know what we do with naughty boys, don't you? We teach them a lesson.'

His mind was frozen in disbelief – this could not be happening to him – and he cried out in shock as the cane bit. He heard Janey cry out too, but she was coming for a second time, and then, unbelievably, and in a rhythm with the stinging cuts across his buttocks, so was he.

'Your ex has come up in the world, eh? I bet you never thought she'd be giving you six of the best on your rear end. And they are beauts!'

'Ow! Careful, Janey, take it easy.' She was applying ointment to the stripes in question and they were incredibly tender to the touch, but as soon as he spoke

81

Mark felt ashamed. He got up and manoeuvred Janey into his place over the end of her chaise longue, saying: 'You're the one who needs attention, not me.' In the two hours since her ordeal she had returned to her usual jaunty self, but he was sure the experience would stay in her mind. He spread the soothing cream as gently as he could, relieved to see that the swellings had gone down somewhat.

Janey oohed and aahed her way through his ministrations. 'That'll teach me. I could have stayed down, you know, but I was pretty sure the lady wanted to give me more.'

'You mean you jumped up so she'd have an excuse to tie you up and start again? It wasn't in the script.' Mark was incredulous.

'Script? Oh, boy, you've got a lot to learn. The point is to put on a show so you've got to take risks. Mind you, those guys sure got value for money tonight with the extra buggering scene thrown in.' It took several moments for Mark to grasp what she was saying. He'd given no thought to the other guests, in the thick of the event or since. They, of course, would have been watching his entry into the room and all that followed.

'Oh, shit. Shit!'

'Don't worry about it, Meck. You'll be a porn star yet.'

He shook his head at the unwitting exhibition he had made, though the remark made him aware of his state. At first stricken with remorse that he could be so excited by Janey's pain, his tending of her had brought it back. Anointing the weals that covered her bottom and thighs had given him an erection that was growing firmer as the slashing action of the cane replayed in his mind.

'That feels easier, thanks. But it's going to be a while before you get to lay a spanking hand on these cheeks.' Unerring in her appraisal of his state, she reached back and found the hard organ before he could sidestep her hand. 'I thought so. Look, fella, I'll be stiff as a fucking board in the morning, so I reckon it's now or never, at least for the next week. So, speaking of buggery as we were, how about it? I'm not sure I want to make a habit of this, but strike while the iron's hot and all that, eh?' She stuck out her haunches and Mark needed no further invitation to line himself up between the empurpled glistening globes and sink his throbbing cock once again deep into her behind.

8

Emissary

The director of the Nemesis Archive in England pressed
the bell beside the emblem of the wild cat long and hard.
Her attendance at the conference in Seattle had been
accomplished without a hitch, but the attempt to recruit
a new assistant was proving more troublesome. Eventually the door opened a crack.

'I have no instructions to admit a caller. Give your
name.'

'Samantha James. Let me in, please. I am already late
for my appointment.' The door closed firmly and
remained closed for a further five minutes during which
the appellant's ill-humour grew. Then she heard the
chain rattle and the door was flung wide.

'Miss James, do come in. I'm so sorry, there has been
a misunderstanding. You should have been received at
the main entrance. And of course brought to it first.'
The grey-haired doorkeeper ushered her through into a
wood-panelled office with traditional furnishings. But
the young woman who rose to her feet was anything but
old-fashioned.

'I'm Marissa Scholes.' She held out a hand but it met
with no response. While the visitor did not exactly
repudiate the gesture, neither did she accept it, being for
once in her life deprived of self-possession. The author
of the sober letters that had been exchanged was in the

flesh a mauve-haired figure in transparent top, clinging hot pants and stiletto heels. The chief mover of 'The Cat' whose experience and expertise she had come a long way to learn from looked like nothing so much as a common whore. Albeit a rather fetching one.

'When I'm not oiling the wheels of our network, I'm the singer in a band.' The remark was made as if it explained the choice of such an outfit for office wear. 'But I'm sorry the wheels did not turn smoothly today. I'm afraid I only just discovered that the car I sent for you arrived at the wrong meeting, so you must have had to make your own way here.'

'That is so, and with difficulty. I hope you do not suppose I make a habit of being late.' She made the words as icy as she could and saw an answering moment of decision in the young woman's heavily mascara'd eyes.

'OK. Right. I don't make a habit of shirking respon-sibility either. So I'm giving you my apology and a chance to deal with the lapse. To "correct" it, yeah? Isn't that the word used in England?'

For the second time the visitor was wrong-footed, but there was no mistaking Marissa's meaning when she continued: 'I got all sorts of straps and whips and stuff, but I guess it'll be a cane you want, huh?' The lilac-glossed lips were a sexual invitation all of their own.

'Yes, indeed. For summary "correction" – you are quite right about the term – I find it without rival. In my view a smart dose of the cane is the real "short, sharp shock" after which one moves on. And I have my own with me.' Samantha unzipped the long black bag and removed a rod that was a mere two feet long but bent easily into the shape of a C between her hands. She watched Marissa clear a space beside the monitor on her desk, then lower the brief shorts and lean forwards on her elbows. The trim buttocks were unmarked, though whitish scars ran in vertical lines down both flanks. They seemed old, but just visible between the parted legs were fresh lacerations that curled right up into the genital fig. The thought of bearing *their* infliction was enough to make even a seasoned chastiser wince.

Samantha James sighed and lined her weapon up to the curves that were as yet unscathed. This young lady plainly did not spare herself and there was thus no reason to hold back. Six strokes followed, each applied at full stretch and each taken in exemplary silence. Once the velvet pants had been gingerly restored, the dispenser of discipline watched with satisfaction how the recipient eased herself down gently into her chair, a flush now tinting the pallor of her cheeks.

'Sweet Jesus. That instrument of yours has the bite of something twice its size.'

'Top-grade Malay rattan. A present from my assistant when she joined the Archive on a permanent basis. She has had occasion to make much the same comment.'

'I'm sure she has.' The rueful smile made the director long to subject her host to some of the more exacting forms of discipline to which the girl was clearly no stranger, but she made an effort to rein in her imagination.

'Your apology is accepted, Marissa. Please forgive me for ignoring your hand earlier.'

'Of course, Miss James.' They shook firmly and the older woman tried not to notice the way the small breasts moved under their transparent cover. They and the buttocks she had just striped were kindling a lust that threatened to cloud her judgement.

'Samantha, please. Call me Samantha.' She was implacably opposed to the use of her first name by staff and her secretary Helen had not used it even when she had been a regular occupant of her employer's bed. But Miss Scholes – that was how she had thought of her during their correspondence, hating the Ms form for daring to suggest that any woman she dealt with could ever *marry* – was a different matter. Despite the calculatedly disreputable image, Marissa had to be treated as an equal. Having erred, she took it upon herself to make reparation through corporal punishment, unlike an underling who did so only under threat of dismissal. The logic was impeccable, but she felt uneasy in her demand and sensed that the young lady did too. However there was business to do so she put the matter to one side and leaned forward with a smile. 'Now, my dear, what can you tell me about this namesake Cat of yours . . .?'

'Let me see if I have understood you correctly, Marissa. Your organisation runs without a hierarchy which means that your principal function is simply to put people in touch with each other.'

'That's it. Once you have a small nexus of enthusiasts that can be contacted electronically – though that isn't essential, merely faster – then you're away. So new people only get in through one of our core members, though we may give them a little examination, usually in a practical situation involving the dominance/submission axis. Also if there are any special ideas I quite often put my own body up for use. As you may have noticed, this can make for interesting results.' There was an ironic detachment to the young woman's embrace of pain and the shadows under her eyes seemed the darker for it. Beneath the sexual provocativeness could be glimpsed a sense of limits regularly tried, and it was deeply affecting. The director shifted in her chair and continued in what she hoped was a matter-of-fact tone.

'From the examples you give it works well, and I do appreciate how much safer it is to have no central register.'

'Yeah. I could assemble one in a day or two, but the way things are if we were raided nothing would be

87

found except our rooms and some gear. I'd maybe go down for running a brothel and that would be that. Not that I really want to investigate the gay scene in a women's jail at first hand.'

'Oh, my dear, you would soon be under the protection of the toughest dyke on the block, take my word for it. Though you could expect to be well spanked when you didn't toe her line, but no doubt also when you did.' She stopped, a little embarrassed at her flight of fancy, but Marissa was grinning, so she cleared her throat and went on. 'I am sure it isn't going to come to that. To return to the subject of the Cat, I have to say it's all rather anarchic for me. I'm afraid that I am too fond of handing out instructions and then correcting deviations from them.'

'I know that last bit.' Marissa put a hand to her bottom with a look that went straight to the director's loins. 'But of course you don't plan to set such a system up yourself?'

'Indeed, no. As you are aware the main reason for my actual presence here is to take a closer look at the young lady you have recommended to me as ideal for the task. A Miss Carpenter, I believe?'

'Cate, yeah. I'm asking you to take a lot on trust here. When you meet her later you will of course make your own assessment, but you have no way of evaluating how she would be – hopefully *will* be – in the field. And objectively she doesn't cut it, being a beginner of a mere five weeks' standing. Perhaps you'll let me fill you in on her recent history and try to explain.'

Samantha James nodded assent, already intrigued by the unlikely candidate on offer. In matters of deviant sexuality she had come to believe that the risky option often took one to places that were not reached by playing safe. So the director settled back in her chair to hear a story of how a chance episode in the band's tourbus had occasioned the drummer's penance and

Cate's subsequent induction into the network. Or rather, how Marissa had intervened to bring about the sequence of events.

'Well, I glimpsed something in her eyes when she saw the marks –' she ran her hands over the material that now covered the curious scars '– so I made the most of the opportunity and sent Zadia to her. It was a long shot, but I hoped I could bring out what I thought I had seen there. And I was right. Then I lured Cate here on the expectation of meeting me on – well, on a tryst, I guess. But instead she underwent a test I'd planned, and passed with flying colours. And since then the novice has gone from strength to strength. By the way, she was blindfolded at the time and still isn't sure I was the examiner, and I'd like to keep it that way.'

'You can rely on my discretion, Marissa. Would I be right in thinking that the two of you have become – how shall I put it – rather close?' When the young woman looked a trifle taken aback, she went on. 'Oh, I don't mean to suggest there is anything reprehensible in advancing the cause of one's lover, if that is what you have done. But perhaps you think that an English woman who has passed forty will disapprove of sexual relations among colleagues. Let me put your mind at rest by confessing that I used habitually to bed my secretary once I had reddened her bottom with a good piece of leather. Unfortunately, her affections are now occupied elsewhere, so while I still enjoy applying the strap, matters go no further. But this is more than you are interested to know. I fear I become garrulous with age.'

'Not at all.' Marissa's smile was seductive as she stood up. 'It's a pleasure to speak with you. Can I take you to your suite, where we could continue over some lunch?' The director followed the young woman up a flight of stairs, captivated by the long limbs that preceded her. Once inside, Marissa clicked the catch on the door and set down the bag she had been carrying. She looked diffident, but somehow determined.

'I want to say something. Well, it's two things really. First, I'll be much happier if I can call you Miss James. I guess you noticed I couldn't get the first name out once, yeah? But I don't want a misunderstanding here, because the second thing is I want to ... to ... oh, I can't say.' She turned her head aside and the director felt as if a hand gripped her vitals.

'Go on, my dear. Please go on.'

'I want to do something real intimate. But I want to do it with *Miss James*. Does that sound stupid?'

The 'Miss James' addressed didn't trust herself to speak. She simply bowed her head while the young woman dropped to her knees and unbuttoned the expensively tailored breeches to draw them down. Underwear followed and she parted her legs to keep the garments at mid-thigh while allowing Marissa the intimate access she desired. Then there were fingers that spread the lips and Samantha heard the half-gasp of surprise with a smile. It had been thirty years since a tutor had lengthened her clitoris by an excruciating and extended process involving needles and miniature clamps. But she had never regretted the ordeal. Beyond a general enhancement of sensitivity to the touch of a sexual partner, there was a quite specific benefit. During any prolonged punishment – and a strapping was ideal for the purpose – the engorged thing's friction against a silk gusset would bring her to peak most satisfactorily just at the height of her victim's pain.

But now the stiff protuberance was between Marissa's nibbling teeth and coherent reflection was at an end. There was only the point of honour, never yet betrayed, that she should maintain control during the first orgasm from a new lover. Perhaps later she would have the chance to unbend between the sheets, but for the present, as the climactic waves began to roll and break,

90

it was going to take every ounce of iron will Samantha James possessed to hold upright to her position . . .

'Honey, I'm telling you, the fucking thing was the size of your pinkie.' Marissa looked up from her position between Cate's thighs. 'I mean, don't get me wrong. I just love hunting for your sweet little bud. But this piece of anatomy was something else. Shee-it. And you've seen what she did to my butt. I mean, OK, a good whipping is my bag and I'm just not used to the cane, but even so –' The speaker's flow was interrupted as Cate pushed the head back down into her crotch.

'Keep your mind on the job, boss. Or I'm gonna be late at the beauty salon before my all-important interview.'

'I'm not your boss and you know it. But she will be.' Below the eyes fixing hers were lips wet with Cate's secretions. 'Can you cope with that?'

'The job sounds great, but I'm gonna have to put her right on one thing before I take it. There's no fucking way she gets me bending over with a bare arse for the treatment you got. Though I suppose –' still speaking she opened her legs wide and drew up her knees '– I might want to get a peep at that monster of a clit. Oh. Oh!'

Thus talk was suspended as her own hard morsel of flesh came under investigation. For the second time in the space of an hour Marissa had the bit between her teeth – that crucial bit of erectile tissue – and Cate was for several long minutes quite beyond words.

The tall raven-haired Miss James was an impressive sight in her dark suit and brilliant white shirt. As they were introduced her penetrating glance made Cate thankful she had devoted some time to her own appearance. Then, once they were seated in the office and had begun to discuss how a network might be established around the existing institution in England, Cate started to relax. With her newly styled blonde bob and wearing pencil skirt, stockings and sensible heels, she felt she looked the part she was hoping to get to play for real: that of the thoroughly professional associate to the director of the Nemesis Archive. And as for the missing underpants, well, who was going to notice?

'Very good. Now I should like to turn to the other aspect of the appointee's duties. Miss Scholes does not know why the organisation's full name is the Nemesis Cat but she has undertaken to question some of its long-standing contacts. Perhaps you have some thoughts on the matter.'

'May I ask why you use the name? Isn't Nemesis to do with vengeance?'

'Yes and no. There is reason to think that her status as agent of divine retribution is a later accretion to an older persona of nymph-goddess who was associated with acts of ritual flagellation. She was typically portrayed with a scourge hanging from her belt, in the manner of the Furies to whom she is indeed related. So an appropriate figurehead for a private collection of women's sado-masochistic writings, while not being too plain an advertisement of their nature to all and sundry. Now, the name of the Archive has no history beyond being my choice. But I am hopeful that there will prove to be some past link between your network here and the research of Professor Davidson on the shadowy cult with its postulated whip for which he uses the identical name. It is all very curious, since he appears to have had no knowledge of your existence, being satisfied to trace things through to the nineteenth century. However, my assistant Judith is engaged in a search for documents to bring the study on from that period and if we can acquire someone to work from the present backwards, so to speak, fortune may smile on us, and, who knows . . .'

She broke off abruptly with a wry face. 'I must apologise: my tongue runs away with me too often these days. You are, of course, familiar with much of this from reading Judith's preliminary report. I should instead use my time here to learn more of your own activities. Indeed, I understood there may be the chance of a little exhibition later?' The piercing eyes seemed to light up at the prospect.

'My young friend Gena has been assisting me, but unfortunately she has the lesbian club Artemis to run now that her aunt has become ill. When I started off she appointed herself as "handmaid" to the new "domina" –' Cate blushed a little at the terms but saw Miss James nod amused approval '– and accompanied me to all my appointments. Now she's had a haircut and taken to dressing as a boy; in fact, rather a caricature of an English schoolboy of half a century ago whose behaviour often requires his tight grey shorts to come down for a good spanking. Nothing more severe than that, but we think it makes an appealing display and would be pleased to demonstrate. Then there is Zadia, the German lady who initiated me. She is made of sterner stuff and would, I'm sure, consent to the use of your preferred instrument.'

'Capital! I have a rule of thumb that six strokes should leave a girl able to sit, albeit with some care, whereas twelve or more should make her keen to avoid that action at least for the rest of the day. Earlier, I was mindful of Miss Scholes's need to work at her desk, but the Fräulein will have the whole night to recover, will she not? This is becoming a visit I shall remember.' The director's enthusiasm led Cate to decide it was now or never for the statement she was determined to make.

'But there is one thing I ought to make clear, Miss James, and I'm not sure how you'll react to it. I don't – ever – submit to corporal punishment myself.' She steeled herself to continue under the probing gaze. 'If

that disbars me from working with you, then so be it.'
There was a pause while Cate stared at the floor
conscious of the beating of her heart. Then the director
broke the silence and it sounded as though she was
weighing every word.

'I place a high value on the ability to say difficult
things. That is my first response. Next I should tell you
something. Before she joined us full-time, the Judith I
have mentioned resigned rather than accept discipline
with the tawse. Then, after becoming reconciled to her
own inclinations, she returned to present me with the
cane I now carry everywhere, and present herself for its
first application. And thereby, of course, take back her
position. But you see, Miss Carpenter, Judith is by
nature submissive in these matters. In other respects she
is an assertive young woman, but at root it thrills her to
be beaten and despite, or perhaps because of the pain
(these are deep matters), she craves it.' A further pause
gave Cate the nerve to look the speaker in the eye before
she resumed.

'From what I have learned today I do not think that
would be true in your case and therefore the question of
coercion that would serve your ultimate interests does
not arise. In other words, my dear young lady, rest
assured I shall never attempt to chastise you against
your wishes if you come to work for me. And I shall be
delighted if you will accept my invitation to do exactly
that.'

The phrase 'against your wishes' left something rather
too much like a loophole for complete comfort – what,
after all, had been this Judith's real wishes? – but Cate
was in a mood to shrug off any doubts. Miss James was
regarding her with a questioning look so she said
simply: 'Thank you, I'd like to. I'd like to very much.'

PART II

9

Memoirs

The chair in the Rare Books reading room had an irritating creak that seemed to worsen the more she tried to sit still. Scanning the autobiographical jottings of Edwardian libertines and rakehells for a Cat – with a capital C – had in any case become a thankless task and Judith decided it was time for a break. At the outset she had been excited about the search. Miss James had leaned on the Vice-Chancellor of the University with the aid of some photographs from her days as madam of a flagellation brothel, and he in turn had applied pressure to the keeper of the Private Case who depended on him for a lucrative trade in illictly photocopied extracts. Thus was a pass procured for the director's assistant to peruse the recently bequeathed and as yet mostly uncatalogued additions to the British Library's collection of restricted documents.

On her first visit Judith took particular pleasure in the barely concealed outrage of the two men at the front desk that a young woman should have access to such things. And she had compounded the offence by arriving in shiny black trousers so tight they turned heads on the street, topped with a lemon blouse and her customary dark crew-cut. It was hardly the dress of a scholar, but the rarely issued permit could not be gainsaid, and it took her through the general study areas with their automated book request points to a staffed counter at the rear of the building. After a pursed-lips consultation, it was decided to give her access to a list of titles on which she could mark down what was required for the day. These would then be retrieved from the annexe opposite, where they were housed apart from the massive complex of the new library, and delivered to her table. That, too, was set apart from the rest, though whether the arrangement was to protect the room's other inhabitants from her or her reading material Judith wasn't entirely clear.

In the tea room she sat alone with a mug of coffee, turning over in her mind the changes afoot at the Archive. Miss James had arrived back from Seattle in unusually high spirits over a fortnight ago, bringing with her pointers to the writings Judith was presently studying. Less welcome was the news of the assistant hired on a two-year contract that she insisted on calling 'Miss Carpenter', though she could be little more than Judith's age. She and Helen had schemed to get a new submissive into the director's bed to serve as a focus for her disciplinary urges and take the heat off the two of them. Now it seemed the incoming lady was a top and nothing but a top, apparently calling herself a 'domina'. That was a new one on Judith, but it was obvious what it meant. She would be baring *her* arse for nobody and, worse, it didn't sound like she'd be getting her head down between the boss's legs. So they were no further *forwards*.

Meanwhile they were all in a tizzy over this affair of the Cat. As far as she understood it, the eccentric prof had convinced himself – if not the academic world at large – of the existence of a Victorian secret society whose lineage could be traced back to pre-classical Greece. Basically a loose grouping of whipping clubs, its members were united by their use of a kind of cat o' nine tails and the emblem of the other kind of cat

98

behind which they hid their real identity from the wider society. One crucial text asserted the instrument was a replica of the scourge of Nemesis; not, of course, actually *hers* – in pre-Hellenic myth she was the Moon-goddess turned nymph who chases the sacred king round the seasons – but the one employed in the flagellation cults dedicated to her name that Davidson argued were rife in the ancient world.

That was all fine and good: it could take its place alongside all the other unverifiable speculations about pre-history and no one would get too excited. But then he'd gone on to claim that the conjunction of whip, feline symbol, and, if less commonly, the name of the goddess recurred at key points in European history, notably at the time of the first millennium, alongside witchcraft beliefs of the seventeenth century and most recently in the England of the 1880s. In so doing, he became a classicist who had ventured into periods beyond his competence to earn the sneering dismissal of the relevant specialists.

There it might all have rested but for the invitation Miss James received to a North American conference on dominant women in history. Enclosed in the letter from a past colleague of hers was a sheet headed with the image of a panther-like cat and an email address that led to the circle of s/m practitioners in Seattle. Quite how they originated nobody seemed to know, but the reputedly severe Miss Carpenter had been detailed to make enquiries before she joined them in England. Then the director got wind of some hot memoirs from the early decades of the last century so after the necessary strings had been pulled Judith had been installed in a small hotel in London while she searched them for traces of the double cat.

But so far they had eluded her and after just a couple of days the 'confessions' of entirely male and mostly unimaginative sexual exploits began to pall. Now, at the

99

start of the second week, and not yet halfway through the material, Judith was heartily sick of the whole thing. However, the last MS had dropped hints that the subject of flagellation was treated in a certain privately published volume absent from her list though surely present in the actual BL collection. From the window beside her she had been watching the boy with the courier's satchel who brought her requests over from the end-terrace house across the road. Unlike the supercilious pair who manned the counter he looked approachable, as did the older guy with a beard she had seen going in and out who was presumably his boss. If she could get to the books themselves, there might be all manner of discoveries to make. There was only one way to find out so, having drained her coffee, Judith headed down through the exit and out on to the street.

At the bottom of a short flight of steps, the handle turned to give access to a short corridor with a door at the end that was simply marked PRIVATE. Judith tapped on it but there was no response so she slipped quietly in. Shelves ran from floor to ceiling on each wall of the room and she glanced round, at a loss. Then she spotted two of her files on a single high shelf amidst some unfamiliar spines: that looked like a place to start. So she moved the steps over and was halfway up them with a book in her hand when she heard the door open right beside her. Aware that her pose was already provocative, she mischievously made it more so by bending over and reaching for another title.

'If I had a daughter who came home in trousers like that –'

'– you'd take them down and put her across your knee.' The words were out before she could stop herself and, twisting round, she saw a man in his forties unashamedly studying her behind.

'How *did* you guess?' He laughed and so did she, then he went on. 'Now, I know I'm risking a slapped face to tell a young woman the way she dresses is just asking for a smacked bottom –'

'– but then, if that's exactly what she *is* doing –'

'– and when we add that she's flouting regulations by being unsupervised amongst the naughty books –'

'– then there's really only one thing for it.' The conclusion had a logic all of its own – what more was there to say? – and she accepted the offer of a hand off the rickety step-ladder. He was a bear of a man but there was a softness about him too, and his eyes were a warm brown. It seemed he was quite *easy* with the subject of their dialogue while for her part a year at the Archive had served to dissipate much of Judith's initial embarrassment about these tastes.

'If we go into my office in Cataloguing, we shan't be disturbed. That is, if I'm not completely misreading the situation . . .' He left the sentence hanging and there was a window of doubt in which Judith stood on the brink of walking away. What was she doing? This guy was a stranger she'd seen a couple of times in the distance and that was it. But her assertive spirit came to the rescue.

'Lead on, stern patriarch, and do your duty. Just don't say how it will hurt you more than it hurts me, OK?'

Inside his room he put the book he was carrying down on the table. 'That's for you, but I'll explain after we've attended to business.' No more was said and Judith peeled down the offending garment while the man placed two upright chairs side by side. He sat on one and she went over his lap with her upper half resting on the other. It was a solid, reassuring lap and she was content to feel his hand explore the buttocks left quite uncovered by her string briefs. Then he began to smack, at first gently, then with increasing force. The audacity of their encounter – on both sides – had made Judith wet before he even started and now she pushed herself up to meet the slaps as they landed, knowing, as never before, that if he'd only keep up the same kind of pace she was going to come. And he did, even reading the signs of her excitement to smack into the base of her bum at exactly the right time.

After that, there was only one possible course of action, whatever the lesbian sisterhood might have to say about it. She unzipped him and he let her pull out and hold his satisfyingly distended organ with blue veins that pulsed up its sides. Then, pants down over the table, she felt him enter and move in a way that rubbed directly on her clit. God, he was good at this too! The last prick in her cunt had belonged to a cold and ultimately violent guy and it had put her off men for the whole year since. But here she was, about to climax for the second time in ten minutes, and she just might have to rethink her separatist position.

Back at the desk that was piled with manuscripts Judith sat savouring the delicious sensations that ran through the parts of her body pressed against the seat of the wooden chair. Nicely spanked and well fucked on a Monday morning: things were looking up. Of course, it was odds on her lover Helen wouldn't be very impressed, but then why should she find out? Judith took up the book that had been given her by Harry (for that was his name) and smiled at the way introductions had been made only after 'business' was concluded by making a date to do it again on Wednesday. The hand-bound volume had markers inserted in several places he had thought relevant, so she settled down to examine it. The first two were disappointing, however, since the references to 'the cat' seemed linked only to naval punishments. There the action of its thongs on bare flesh was described in loving detail and made Judith wonder squeamishly if the bear-like cataloguer might fancy doing something like that to her. Then she struck gold with a passage dated September 7 that began:

* * *

I woke this morning with a throbbing head and the feeling that something important had happened. Then I remembered the paper I had been given by S— bearing an address and a date. At the top was an embossed seal of a fierce beast which he said was the symbol of the Cat, a secret organisation devoted to rituals that claim descent from ancient myths and legends, rather in the manner of what we know of Freemasonry. It is set apart, however, by its devotion to what the psychologists call sadism and masochism. I am aware of my leanings to the latter yet, being only recently of age, and raised in a household that eschewed bodily correction, I have lacked the opportunity to investigate further. Now it is time to repair the omission and I mean to present myself on the 17th of this month as directed.

That was better: a proper feline appearance and even the prospect of Nemesis herself materialising out of 'ancient myths'. The writing, too, had a directness sadly lacking from the earlier pages, even though the title credited only one author. But then she found the preface which explained that a collection of 'recollections and reflections from maturity' had been followed by diary entries written more than three decades before in the year of the author's 'first dalliance with the thonged mistress'. Judith was not impressed by the style of the man's 'maturity' that managed to be pompous and gruesome at the same time. No matter. What she wanted was going to be in the young man's record of fresh experiences and she turned eagerly back to the final section of the book. What she wanted was the entry for the day after his visit, the 18th, and there it was.

On arrival I was told at once, by a senior gentleman, that an earnest of my good faith was required before

I could proceed and that an agreement to receive thirty lashes would suffice. As a complete novice in these matters I was far from tranquil at the prospect but it seemed a *sine qua non* of my admittance and I gave my consent. Thus I was led into a chamber that contained a slanting wooden frame to which I was fastened at wrist and ankle. My breeches were drawn down to my knees while my shirt was folded up. Two masked ladies entered in white robes, each bearing a whip with many thongs of a strange cream-coloured leather.

They took up positions to either side of me and began without delay, applying their strokes in alternation. I do not doubt that the assigned number were delivered, but I kept no count. The procedure can have lasted no more than five minutes by the clock, but they were minutes during which my consciousness was filled with pain to the exclusion of all else. When my bonds were released I clutched at the upper thighs, where the hurt was most extreme, certain that I should find blood. But the skin was uncut, though laced with raised welts exquisitely tender to the touch. A gentleman offered me his arm to step back from the frame and as I reached down to resume the lowered breeches I found that my member was standing. Giddy with the after-effects of my first whipping, I was less embarrassed than surprised at this consequence: nothing had been further from my mind.

There was a row of dots and the next paragraph took up the story from much later. Damn. These were extracts from the original account, presumably selected to focus directly on the initial flagellatory experiences. But Judith wanted more of the engaging young man's thoughts, quite apart from the details of the Cat she was there to research. But for now this would have to do and she read on.

At the end of the night I was returned to the first chamber to take my place with the three other newcomers. A senior acolyte to the goddess named Io was brought in and stripped of her robe and mask. She stood before us in a chemise that concealed little of her matronly figure while J— explained that she had sullied the sacred whip with her supplicant's blood. That he had consented was no excuse and now the instrument must be ritually stained with the offender's own before it could be cleansed for further use. To that end Io was tied to the frame whose acquaintance I had made earlier, as indeed had the other young men beside me. Her undergarment was raised and pinned below the shoulder blades and we were instructed to administer ten lashes each in rotation, continuing until the desired outcome had been produced. Attention was drawn to the privilege of our situation: it was, we learned, only in the exceptional circumstances of such a breach that the thongs could be wielded by anyone other than the acolyte herself.

Chosen to begin, I acquitted myself of my quota although my degree of nervous tension prevented a proper appreciation of what I was doing. But as I watched the operation proceed in other hands my excitement grew, so that when I took up the whip again I savoured to the full how the heavy hindquarters, already well streaked, juddered with each blow. I enjoyed in this way a third turn which made the lady cry mercy, and after it three more lashes were enough to redden the pale leather in the manner required.

But the ritual was not quite done. Startled, I heard J— command that we move in close to the moaning figure on the frame, take out our members and anoint the errant acolyte with our seed. Weird and fantastical to my daylight pen, the act seemed in the heat of the moment to be fitting, if unexpected. It was evident

105

the others were as aroused as I, for it took but little manipulation for all to comply fully with the order. While the copious discharges bespattered the whipped globes, I was moved to reflect that one day this lady would whip me and it would be all the harder for what that night I had done to her. And as I put away my spent tool, I shivered in a compound of fear and delight at the prospect.

Phew! This was hot stuff for a reader recently reconnected with the male organ. Judith could see all too vividly in her mind's eye the spurting cocks and wondered if Harry's could be persuaded to do just that ahead of schedule. He was off the next day, which was why they'd fixed on Wednesday, but how about the present afternoon? Well, it was really still lunchtime and there were matters arising from the material – other than her sex life – which needed to be addressed. Most obviously there was the white leather whip; now that was exciting. What could be more appropriate for a Nymph-goddess of the Moon? It was the first mention of a special instrument and maybe that was what her boss was really looking for. After all, surely s/m clubs were ten a penny these days, but to turn up the authentic Scourge of Nemesis, that would be something else. Judith shook her head impatiently. She was wool-gathering: no actually ancient piece of leather could have survived in usable form. In any case she remembered reading in a flagellation manual that the thongs wore out with use unless they were pickled so hard they ripped the skin at once – ugh! – and that was obviously not the case with the implement described.

Judith picked up the book and skimmed through the remainder of the extracts with a sinking heart. There seemed to be no more about the society of the Cat, only accounts of other 'firsts', notably his birching at the hands of a retired but vigorous governess. They would make a good, arousing read, but took her no further in the quest. Now, it was a fair bet that the original diary spelt out the nature of the organisation and very likely its origins and connections. The boy's descriptions were nothing if not thorough. She stood up decisively. It was Harry who had conjured up this volume; maybe he could get hold of what she wanted. And the best way to find out was to go and see him in person.

Her confident knock on the door marked CATALOGUE DEPARTMENT was met with a booming 'Enter!' but once inside Judith was suddenly tongue-tied. The man in charge, however, rose from his chair with a grin.

'I was wondering if you could last out, since I don't think I can.'

'I've actually got something to ask you about this book.' She waved it at him then dropped it on the table. 'That is, after, er –'

'– business?'

'Yeah, business.' Judith grinned too and turned to latch the door shut behind her.

'There's just one thing. All joking aside, my hand's sore.' From a drawer of the desk he produced an oval piece of stitched brown leather with a wooden grip and held it out for her inspection.

Uh, oh. A paddle. It would be the whip, next stop. But the thought was oddly unperturbing and Judith nodded assent, reaching for the fastening on her trousers.

10

Bitter End

While the research in London was busy getting to the
bottom of things – in one way or another – Cate's
efforts in Seattle had met with little luck and her time
was running out. To start with it had all looked so
promising. Marissa turned up the name of a woman
who was active in the early days of the network some
twenty years before who would be happy to be inter-
viewed by a young enthusiast and talk about the glory
days. Which she duly did, and although there were
entertaining stories aplenty, it became clear that she
knew no more about the antecedents of the present
organisation than her younger questioner. However, the
visit was saved by the production at the end of the
afternoon of an old index file with the cautionary words:
'I think you can be trusted with this, but don't get too
excited. It's at least ten years since I heard from anyone
in here and it's more than likely they have all moved.
But it may be a start. When you return it I'd like to
know how you got on.'

Cate 'got on' with difficulty. Of the thirty names
listed, twenty-three were unknown to the present occu-
pants of the addresses in the box. Six had left forward-
ing information behind, but then the trail went cold at
the next stage. It was beginning to look like folk with a
penchant for unconventional sex moved a lot, or maybe

they just *got* moved by a combination of outraged neighbours and hostile landlords. But then, at the end of the alphabet – and a long week's work – the last door was answered by Henrietta Zander herself. A spry little bird of a woman (66, according to her card) she took Cate in as soon as she heard mention of the Cat.

'It's been a long time since anyone used *that* name to me,' she said, 'far too long. I'm not up to much myself these days, you understand – not anything demanding, that is – but it would be nice to be kept in touch.' After they were settled with a pot of tea Cate explained how she had come by the address and gave the lady a brief history of her own involvement in the network. Then she broached the issue of where the name had come from.

'Well, my dear, I *can* as it happens tell you that, but I'm not sure it will really answer any of your questions. But first, let's be comfortable with a nice cold glass of wine.' As she got up and went out Cate suppressed her irritation. It was already five in the afternoon and she was due at Arte's for the Jynx gig by mid-evening. In two days' time she'd be heading across the Atlantic to the Archive so it was positively the final performance. But with a sigh she accepted the drink offered and settled back: this was *work*, part of her new job, and it had to be done.

'Now, the name. Well, it actually came from *me* though I'll need to explain that. You see, there were half a dozen of us back in the early 80s who wanted to do something for kids getting switched on to s/m. It was of course taboo – as you know it still is in lots of ways – but there was a flurry of interest. So we thought that some old hands like us could provide a set of contacts to help the novices along and I thought straightaway of the experience that started *me* off, where I first heard of Nemesis and saw the emblem and the flail. It was that of course that was the real cat, though it was actually a cat of more than nine tails.' She refilled their glasses and Cate drank, trying to resign herself to a late appearance downtown.

'The story starts way back in the early 50s when I was sixteen. I lived with my aunt, in this very house as a matter of fact, and my cousin Hector was staying for the holidays – a distant cousin, I should say; you'll see why in a minute. That particular summer my aunt began to make mysterious evening trips from which she would not return until after we were asleep and then not emerge from her room until lunchtime the following day. And she was normally such an early riser. Naturally we were very curious but all our attempts to draw her out were turned aside so in the end we decided to take our own steps to investigate by hiding under the rug she kept in the back of the old station wagon.

'It was an anxious wait until the ignition fired, but then we had soon driven beyond the city lights and after about a quarter of an hour the car was crunching up a gravel drive. Once the driver's door banged shut we peered out and saw we were parked among a row of vehicles to the side of a largeish country house. The moon was bright and we snuck round the back and found an open door. Now it sounds crazy that we were so bold – I suppose we must have egged each other on – but we went in and crept along a deserted corridor with rooms opening to both sides. Then there were voices ahead and we dived through the nearest door, only to find ourselves behind a corner screen at the front of a small audience. And I tell you, dear, what they were looking at just took my breath away.' The wine bottle was emptied and another procured from the fridge. The lady had a fine sense of the dramatic pause and Cate's urge to get away early was tempered by a desire to hear the rest of the story.

'There was a raised platform that went back in a semi-circle between two Greek columns with carved

110

cat's heads, and in the middle of it all was a rough wooden block half-covered by a sheet. And over that was the naked body of a woman with her legs tied apart. I had never seen or imagined such a thing; she was spread so wide it was like a mutilation of flesh split open and turned inside-out. The shock of it fixed the whole sight in my mind, so I can still see every splinter of wood, every fold of that obscene pink gash that looked as though it should be bleeding.' Henrietta stopped, flushed, and took a drink. Cate gulped at hers, unsure how to react to these overwrought memories. But no response was needed as the story continued.

'As you can imagine, Hector was pop-eyed. Thing was, though, it affected *me* in the way you'd expect of a young male and after that summer I went for women mostly. Then the ladies in white came in with their whips – their "white cats" – and started on her. Somehow they didn't hit her *there* – on the thing I couldn't tear my eyes from – but the red streaks were all around it and I thought I was going to pass out watching. Hector must have been feeling the same because he suddenly pulled me out by the hand and we hurtled across the passage into an empty room and when he pushed me down on the bed it seemed like the only thing to do. We'd played games as younger kids and we'd fooled around a bit in the last year but I'd never seen him hard and standing out. Enjoyment wasn't the word for it – though, don't get me wrong, he didn't force me. I must have been ready for him too because he got in easy and it didn't hurt, and I guess I had an orgasm because I certainly shrieked, but the first time and all that, it was scary more than anything else.

'Well, that was it, really, because before we could pull apart the door opened and we were caught. I'd never seen my aunt so angry and we were whisked straight home a lot earlier than she normally came back. Once there she barked at us to change into our pajamas while

111

Mrs Jones was fetched from next door – an old battleaxe who was only too pleased to hold us down in turn while we got the hiding of our lives. I assure you, dear, in spite of what I've done – and enjoyed doing – since then, there was absolutely nothing sexy about that hickory switch. We both howled the place down with no thought to our teenage dignity. The strange thing was she didn't seem annoyed about the fact we'd done what the local kids used to call the dirty deed. She was bothered far more by what we'd *seen*, and in the morning after our punishment she kind of apologised for overreacting (which we accepted, glad to be back on good terms), swore us to secrecy and gave us some packets of rubbers on the grounds it was better to be safe than sorry.'

'Quite a lady', said Cate, wondering when they were going to get back to the point.

'Yes, and she was right too. The marks she'd left on us were an exciting reminder of the whole adventure and as soon as she was out of the way we stripped off for a detailed examination. Thus we spent the whole afternoon fucking, as we now brazenly called it, savouring the word. We had three days like that then Hector went back home and it was as if I'd finished with the male organ. There was an older girl just down the street started making eyes at me almost at once – it was as if she could sense I'd seen something I couldn't get out of my mind – and before long I was studying her cunt close up. She made me call it that and it was a thrill for the sheltered teenager I had been to use such bad language. But, my dear, I'm rambling.'

'No, no. Please carry on.' Cate made an attempt to deny her impatience, but it had plainly been visible and Henrietta looked hurt.

'I'm so sorry, you must be wanting to get away and I'm boring you with an old woman's reminiscences. The only other thing you need to know is a week after that there was a fire. I recognised the house in the local paper and my aunt went about really grim for a while, though true to our agreement I never mentioned it and nor did she. The owners died in the blaze and the press made veiled remarks about there being the remains of "outlandish apparatuses". Then a later report said that a collection of documents and books had been utterly destroyed and my aunt became visibly more cheerful. It seemed her disreputable participation in the flagellant society was not going to come to light.'

'So is that it?' Cate at once regretted her choice of words. 'I mean –'

'No, you're quite right, dear. It's not much to come all this way for, is it? But that's all I can tell you, I'm afraid. We took the name and the idea of a cat emblem from that one visit. For my aunt the subject was closed and by the time we were setting up the network that you're in now, she had died. There is just one more thing, though I don't suppose it's any use. There was a name that came up a few times after the fire: Inglewhite.'

'*Inglewhite*? Who's Inglewhite?'

'Well, I haven't a clue. First I thought it must be the owners but their name was in the papers and it was Johnson or some such. Now that I think of it I remember the exact words I overheard my aunt once use on the phone. She said: "It's not lost, then. Inglewhite will have a copy." But as to what it means, well, your guess is as good as mine.'

All the way back downtown Cate sat in an ill-tempered silence in the back of the cab. Damn it, it wasn't her fault. If Henrietta Zander had kept in touch with her old crowd from the Cat she wouldn't need to rabbit on to a stranger. But she was well aware that it would have cost little to be more civil and disliked herself for letting her feelings show. Now she was going to miss the gig

113

anyway, and her behaviour had managed to achieve the worst of both worlds.

Rather than stop to eat she went straight to Arte's where, as she feared, the band had long since finished and the audience dispersed. Gena was not in the bar and the woman serving just shrugged when asked if she knew her whereabouts. Her mood worsening by the minute, Cate stomped out the back and headed to the tourbus, but at the steps something made her hesitate. There was a noise coming from inside – a smack-smack, smack-smack, smack-smack – that sounded all too familiar. It stopped and Cate put her eye to a gap in the curtain with the nightmarish suspicion that the past was about to repeat itself. And indeed, in full view over the back of a small couch were arrayed the hindquarters she had come to know and love, now with a long tongue busy in the cleft. As she watched, the figure with the shaved head stood back and the black paddle slapped the crimson buttocks in the repeated rhythm she had heard: forehand and backhand, smack-smack, smack-smack, smack-smack.

Cate pulled away from the window and walked quietly down the street, tears of mortification pricking her eyes. One week. A single fucking week. That's all it took. She'd been one week out of touch with Marissa on the wild goose chase of the address book and already her lover was spreading for Zadia. They couldn't even wait until the day after next when she'd be out of the country. Cate sat down on the kerb and pummelled her fists on her knees in impotent rage. And there she stayed frozen in place and devoid of feeling until a drunk's unsteady progress along the pavement made her get up and head for home.

The following afternoon she forced herself to return to the club where she was booked to do a video shoot in an upstairs room. By repute the camerawoman – who called herself simply Jag – was a whizz at a 'total voyeur

114

thing' which avoided stilted scripts and hammy acting to home in on 'whipped bums and wet vulvas'. Into these lingering close-ups would be cut facial expressions: a sternly set jaw here and eyes entreating mercy there. Cate had liked the sound of this applied to their naughty schoolboy routine so as she dressed in the rarely worn stockings and suspenders with knee-length skirt her spirits lifted a little. But then Gena arrived subdued and it was a relief when Jag bustled in with a mouse of a girl in a baseball cap and began arranging lights.

They had planned the scene to be in three parts. First the mistress would have the boy lean forwards while she lifted the back of each trouser leg in turn and smacked the sensitive area right at the top of the thigh. (Gena had read that this was done in some English schools of half a century ago.) Next he would bend over the back of a chair with his trousers tucked up in front to pull them snug to his bottom for six of the best. In the final part he would go to the bathroom, strip to reveal 'his' true gender, and the mistress would rub cream into the welts she had raised while the camera zoomed in.

The chastisement went well, though without really meaning to Cate found herself slapping and caning harder than she had done before, producing yelps of pain that were, she guessed, far from feigned. So it was a red-faced 'miscreant', breathing rather fast, who went to undress. Then, on a whim Cate threw off her blouse, stepped out of the skirt and marched into the bathroom in her garter belt and heels. Jag made no complaint and followed closely while the massaging of stripes took place, but then a second departure from plan brought the scene to a rapid end. What possessed her she did not know, but Cate plunged her greased fingers between the slick labia and worked them vigorously. At once Gena gave a strangled cry and shot upright, eyes blazing.

'I can get a dozen girls to do *that*.' She spat flecks of saliva in her outrage and tears spouted. 'How *could* you,

Cate, how could you ruin it all . . .?' Grabbing at her clothes she lurched out of the room and the door banged shut behind her.

'Wow. I guess that was what you call an exit.' Jag shook her pony tail and put the camera down on the table. Cate stared at where Gena had been, tight fingers of misery clutching at her insides.

'I petted her once or twice, like *there*, but – oh fuck. What have I done? Fuck, fuck, *fuck*.'

After a silence Jag picked up the cane and gave it a couple of experimental swishes. 'Y'know, I got a small fanbase for pics of *my* butt getting worked over and you looked pretty goddamn nifty with this weapon. How's about it? I can take more than young madam who flounced out.' Without waiting for an answer she went to her bag and extracted a sizeable dildo with an attached belt. 'And this should help take your mind off your troubles. It's my own design, and if you'll just open your legs I'll demonstrate.'

Sick and now bemused, Cate gave herself up to the lady's attentions. Anything to do with sex could only make her feel better. First fingers explored her genitals and located the clitoris, then adjustments were made to one end of the plastic shaft. When the harness was fitted round her waist and thighs there was a thick leather plate over the vulva with a spring mechanism into which Jag inserted the dildo. Then she pressed back on the shaft and the intensity of the sensation made Cate's knees buckle.

'Jesus fucking Christ,' she said weakly, clutching at the edge of the table.

'Sorry. A tad too much projection. I'll sort it.' The next time it was deliciously right and Cate took a few paces around the room, familiarising herself with the novel weight and pressure of the phallic appendage.

'OK?' Cate nodded and Jag gave her camera to Mouse who had been watching with interest. 'Do your own thing, kid, but not too fancy, yeah? Make sure you get the basics.' She dropped her baggy jeans and stepped out of them to reveal black shorts stretched across surprisingly plump cheeks and without any preamble took up position over the chair back.

It took six strokes to establish that the camerawoman meant business and she took another six without a sound. For six more Cate rose on to her toes to gain a little more swing and was rewarded by audible grunts of pain. Then she peeled down the thin silky covering, leaving the damp crotch between Jag's thighs, and laid on six more. The fair skin was angrily barred in reds and purples and Cate tingled all over. Subduing a fierce desire to draw blood and break this woman's self-control, she delivered six measured strokes that avoided the worst of the marks while Mouse kid ducked about shooting up from underneath the cane-slashed buttocks.

When she penetrated Jag's vagina they both came at once but Cate wrapped her arms tight round the slim waist and carried on. The spur that dug into her clit with each hard thrust of the black shaft caused pain as much as it gave pleasure but that was what she needed. And from the noises Jag was making, it suited her fine that Cate was going to fuck them both brutally into temporary oblivion.

11

Installations

'And this, Miss Carpenter, is our newly constructed video and observation suite.' Samantha James opened the door and followed the young woman in. With her blonde hair, blue eyes and pale pink lips, the new personal assistant had the looks of a Nordic ice-maiden, and one who had insisted the job description exclude both corporal discipline and sexual services. But there was a certain air of voluptuousness that sustained her employer's hope the stipulation could be withdrawn. First she would have to get the girl showing more flesh: even if the costume was nicely moulded to the curves of the figure its length was too conservative. Miss Scholes in Seattle had hinted of a wayward past and as Samantha watched her employee bend this way and that to inspect the cameras and recording equipment she could detect no signs of underclothing beneath the conventional exterior. Good. That was a start.

The two women were in the basement of the Nemesis Archive after completing a tour of the several floors of books and documents above. The whole was contained in the converted stacks of the old University Library, left vacant with the completion of a new building on the out-of-town campus. The purchase had been financed by the US-based Oceanus Corporation to house works relating to the topic of female sado-masochism and the price offered had been high enough to silence most critics of the scheme. Ranging from the scholarly and the clinical to the most blatantly pornographic, the materials of the original collection had been expanded under Miss James's direction to include a whole floor of unpublished documents, and Judith Wilson had been duly hired to assess and catalogue them. Now the paymasters in Chicago had given their backing to the setting-up of a network and the facilities (in which they were now standing) to record the activities of some of its participants. That was Cate Carpenter's principal task and she was to begin recruiting at once; in respect of her secondary investigations into the origins of the Cat the director had been less candid, giving for instance no sign when she learned it of how important the name Inglewhite actually was. Neither of her assistants had been told of her main interest, something that had fascinated her for years: the shadowy Rite of Nemesis, with its attendant robes and whips. The professor's recent work had thrown up some useful things but he plainly failed to appreciate the significance of what he had discovered. For him it was all history, dead and gone; for her it held out the promise of power . . .

Samantha James pulled herself back to the present where her disconcertingly pretty new worker had finished examining the equipment. 'Well now, do you think it will suffice?'

'It looks to me first rate, though of course I'm no expert. I'd better crack on to provide subjects to match the set up.'

'Excellent. Now, if you'll come with me I'll show you to your office. It adjoins mine and has recently been completely refurbished.' On the way up in the lift she said: 'I hope you won't take this amiss, my dear, but I do not expect my research staff to dress as if in a formal office. Whatever *you* would be comfortable wearing . . .'

She left the sentence hanging, uncharacteristically awkward under the attention of those clear blue eyes. Their owner simply nodded in acknowledgement leaving it impossible to tell what she might be thinking.

Upstairs she proposed a toast to their future collaboration with a glass of single-malt whisky. After she had poured a second dram the young blonde cleared her throat. 'I don't know if I should raise this so soon, Miss James, but maybe a fresh eye can see things the boss doesn't. It's about your secretary, Helen. That's her name, yeah?'

'That is correct. Go on, please.'

'Well, now that we're going to be dealing with a lot of sensitive matters, do you really think she's up to the job? I have to say she was quite confused when I arrived, and while I was waiting for you I heard her being real snappy with a client on the phone.'

The director was taken aback. This American girl had hardly got a foot in the door and she was criticising the Archive staff. Yet she admired her boldness and it was true that Helen had been looking strained and distinctly scruffy. No doubt Judith's continued absence was responsible, but such patent pining in one who had been her own, once devoted, bedmate was, to say the least, irksome.

'You see, Miss James, it's like this. I have a core contact at the business college here in the town, and I know they would be keen to provide you with an integrated package of technical and secretarial services. But as things stand . . .' The shrug was eloquent.

'Well, I'm glad you have brought this up. It seems that the interests of the Archive may lie in the direction you suggest. I tell you this in confidence, of course, but Helen has no contract and no proper qualifications, having started work here in the days when she was my, ah, sexual partner. And she does occupy a rather attractive company flat around the corner that might be

120

just the thing for you. Leave it with me, Miss Carpenter, I shall make a decision without delay.'

Before the week was out Cate was well ensconced in her plush office and the first-floor furnished apartment that backed on to the area behind the old library. OK, she ought to feel bad about Helen, but she hadn't actually *made* her homeless. Once sacked, the silly girl had upped and fled the town to stay with her sister. And plainly there was more to it than being out of work: from the wastebasket full of torn-up letters it seemed there had been love betrayed. As the tear-stained scripts revealed – and Cate *had* blushed a little at the invasion of Helen's privacy – her paramour Judith had a history of straying, but this time she had really done it. She had dallied – was presumably still dallying – with a *man*.

Cate had taken a chance in causing Helen to be ousted, but it had paid off. The replacement Grace was a demure nineteen-year-old that Miss James had taken to at once, with the result that through the dividing door could be heard almost daily the smack of leather on flesh. From the way Grace would emerge, flushed, to perch herself on a cushion it was clear there was a pair of cheeks under the skirt as red as those on her face. It made Cate wonder whether the girl's duties included the oral servicing of that monster of a clitoris she had heard about but had yet to see. While she wanted to keep the boss at arm's length until she had consolidated her own position, one day she just had to find a way of taking a look . . .

With a sigh the new occupant of 3A Warden's Close got up and stood in the sunlit window of her living room. Outside the immaculate green quadrangle was bounded by old grey stone and the slated roof to the right was topped with a clock that struck the hours. There had been a few changes in little more than a year: from lesbian riot grrrl through bookseller with boyfriend to domina. The word made her think of Gena and she felt a pang of emptiness. Here she was in an ancient university town in the middle of England having split from what the kids back home would call her 'bestest friend' – and in the worst of circumstances. Would she ever see her again?

Cate took off her jacket and slung it over the back of a chair. OK, she'd come a long way from the disorderly punk days, but now she had played with this new gear for a while it was getting to be a burden. The boss had said less formal, so that was exactly what she was going to get. At the bottom of the extra case that had come – expensively – by special air freight were the pair of sixteen-hole Doc Martens. They would do for starters. As for the rest, it was time to go shopping.

Two days later the first candidate for a key position in the new Network (it had been decided to avoid the word 'Cat') had arrived for examination in the basement suite. These early recruits had to be more than mere enthusiasts for the 's' or the 'm' or even the whole 's/m' hog, since they would have responsibility for introducing others. So the fact that Marjory was a handsome woman in her late thirties and the deputy principal of the college was a recommendation of its own. After introductions had been made Cate escorted the immaculately clothed and perfumed visitor into the observation room where unseen cameras were making their silent record. The removal of her skirt revealed the substantial buttocks of a mature woman, framed by suspender belt and sheer black stockings and covered in a wisp of silk. Cate too was in black, but the clinging leotard and ankle boots could hardly have been in greater contrast.

'May I say I *do* like your outfit. *Very* hard.'

If that means I look as if I'm gonna flog the fat arse off you, lady, then you're dead fucking right. The brattish response evoked by the plummy voice stayed

122

put in her head; all that came out was an awkward 'Thanks.' But something had made Marjory look newly apprehensive as she eyed the stool in the centre of the floor that was no higher than the seat of an upright chair and Cate maliciously decided to raise the anxiety quotient a touch more by giving an explanation.

'The point is to give you like a focus for your position without providing any bodily support. So you're on your own for this one, and if the knees give way . . .'

'I see. Rather clever, really, I suppose.' The older woman sounded less than keen but she placed her feet as required to each side of the thing. When she bent to grasp its front legs halfway down the muscular tension was palpable. Cate picked up the three feet six of springy rattan in her customary left hand and stroked its tip down a succulently bare thigh.

'You understand, Marjory, that we're going to play this entirely by ear. Ideally we end kind of mutually, but you only have to straighten up to call a halt, OK?' Deliberately Cate had omitted to mention the possibility of the college woman being left wanting *more*. She had come to know that once she gripped the cane it gripped her and there was no danger of leniency.

As it happened, however, the occasion was carried through with honour on both sides. The gossamer panties were soon in shreds: it was a nice touch, clearly intended and Cate warmed to the posh examinee. She was, in any case, a stalwart character whose only response to the chastiser's best efforts was a small jerk of the body and a grunt. But she guessed that when the sound began to increase in pitch the limit was near, and she contrived to end on a round six times six. At that, the deep-hued rump was wedged in a solid bruise to the left which Marjory explored with her fingers, breathing hard.

'I say, Miss Carpenter –'

'Please, Cate.'

'Cate, I haven't been so neatly thrashed this whole year. I have to confess the riding crop is my usual choice, but I could come to change my mind. The way you make the cane whip in you can do so much with just three dozen. It was three dozen, wasn't it? I'm afraid I rather lost count there towards the end.' There was a silence as she stepped out of the tatters of silk and inched the skirt back into place over swollen hindquarters.

'Well, I do hope we can do business. As you no doubt appreciate, it will be a couple of weeks before I could attempt anything similar, but after that . . .'

'Yeah, sure, Marjory. I'll need to consult with Miss James but –'

'You have of course been filming our little encounter?' The eyes regarding her were sharp and Cate had the grace to blush. In addition to her prowess in taking punishment this lady was no fool.

'There is one thing. In the intervals between sessions, I do like to divert myself with a little spanking. Just with the hand of course, but having a really *bad* girl over one's lap can be *quite* stimulating, I find.' Cate looked at the broad, heavy palms and saw in her mind's eye bottom-cheeks bouncing under heavy slaps. The image was vivid, all too vivid: she was going to have to get a 'bad girl' of her own, and soon.

'I don't suppose you have any interest in obliging, do you, dear?' Cate had bent to pick up the stool and she realised the woman's gaze was directed at the fabric stretched over her butt. Her jaw dropped and she backed away in a kind of reflex.

'Oh, I'm sorry. How silly of me. Please forget I asked. It's just that *some* dominant ladies do like to switch now and then, and I thought . . .'

Cate felt a trifle ashamed of the strength of her reaction. Here was this woman who taken what by any reckoning was a severe caning with scarcely a murmur,

124

and she was running at the mere mention of getting her arse smacked.

'No, no, Marjory, don't apologise. I just, er, never do.' As they left the room she made an effort to recover her poise. 'I'm flattered you rate me "bad" enough to qualify for your knee, Marjory, but I wouldn't have thought one with your looks would be short of volunteers.' Now it was the older woman's turn to blush at the compliment and they both laughed.

'I'll call you later tomorrow to talk about where we go from here.'

'I look forward to it, Cate. Very much.'

'Cool gear.' Grace was looking up at her with a tentative grin, so Cate grinned back and sat on the edge of her desk, showing off the gleaming white lycra that swathed her upper thighs.

'Thanks.'

'I couldn't get away with those, worse luck, my bum's too big. Besides, Miss James wouldn't like it. It's all right for you but a lowly secretary is supposed to wear the uniform.'

'Yeah, I guess. You wouldn't want to give her another excuse to reach for the strap.'

'Oh, she's not bad, really. Last job I worked for a man and got a real swishing every Friday. The old bat from Accounts used to egg him on to strip me first and I ended up stiff and sore all weekend. But what *she* does here just leaves you hot and tingly, really.'

Grace had a killer of a shy smile and the talk was making Cate hot and tingly in another place. But it was not going to help her advancement to poach on the director's territory.

'I think Mrs Rowleigh was quite pleased with yesterday.'

'Marjory? You know her, then?'

'Well, actually, I'm booked to go round on Saturday afternoon. But don't tell Miss James, will you.' She looked suddenly worried and Cate chuckled. Anything less like a bad girl was difficult to imagine.

'Your secret's safe with me. Just don't turn up on Monday with a lot of new bruises.'

'Oh, no. She doesn't spank hard, and it's not long before she wants to move it to the bed –' Grace put a hand to her mouth and stopped in blushing confusion. The girl was a bubbling fountain of cute indiscretion and Cate longed to lift her skirt and make a close inspection of the parts deemed too big for clinging shorts. But before she could let temptation get the better of her the door was flung open and Miss James swept in.

'Good morning, ladies.' While they replied she deposited a long flat package in front of Grace. 'A fine new Lochgelly complete with three tails. You know where I keep the bottle: give it a good oiling and report to me in an hour. And, Miss Carpenter, could I have a word in your office, please?'

As Cate sat down she was aware of the director's scrutiny of her white two-piece and chunky trainers to match. 'Some young women might have taken my remark about formality as a cue to wear perhaps an occasional pair of trousers or even jeans. Your reaction, on the other hand, is nothing if not decisive and I have to say I am glad to see it.' While the eyes were amused there was also a kind of hunger in them that made Cate faintly uneasy. Then it passed and the lady cleared her throat, picking up the three videotapes she had brought in with her.

'Turning to more serious matters, Miss Carpenter, I am quite impressed with your performance. It is clear why you were so well thought of in Seattle. I am sure Mrs Rowleigh had a most intense experience; yet not I think in any way excessive. Finely judged, I should say, and no easy task given the lady's reserve under the cane. Now it's your decision, but since you seemed to have hit it off by the end, I suggest that you enlist her services forthwith.'

'That's what I'd thought, Miss James. I'll call her today.'

'Excellent.' She put down the tapes and handed over a typescript. 'This report came in yesterday from Judith – Miss Wilson – who is still in London. I should like you to read it and see if it connects in any way with your own information.' Cate took the stapled pages and flicked through them.

'Yeah, sure. But wasn't she meant to get back more than a week ago?'

'Indeed she was, and while I am happy to have received what you are holding – I find it interesting and well put together – she should have consulted with me earlier.'

'That does sound rather lax . . .' Cate paused, praying she had read the signs right.

'I think impulsive more than lax, but it is a fault and must be corrected when she returns next week.' Miss James made to leave then stopped at the door with a smile. 'Perhaps, Miss Carpenter, you would care to assist me in the administration of discipline.'

12

Misses

It was Monday lunchtime before Judith got off the train and shouldered the travelling bag to walk to her flat. Though she had meant to leave at the crack of dawn Harry had held her down until she promised to keep in touch, then had smacked her bum just in case she didn't keep her word. 'Because if I don't, I may not get another chance,' he'd said and she had to admit it made a twisted kind of sense. So by the time he had fucked her fore and aft, with some sharp slaps to the thighs in between, it was well after ten o' clock when she strode, all aglow, into the concourse of the station.

But the extra – unauthorised – fortnight had been more than one long spankfest. Harry had helped unearth other records of the cult of the goddess with its fetish of a white whip. One of them, which called it the Cat of Nemesis without any prevarication, was the personal diary of an acolyte 'priestess' based in an English country house during the years 1930 to 1933. In that year, in the midst of scandalous disclosures in the press, the secret society dispersed and at least one of its members left for North America. And Judith was carrying with her – quite against regulations – an even more recent find which she wanted to keep to herself for the present. Becoming certain that Miss James was not telling her the whole story, whatever she might be telling

128

the new assistant, Judith had decided to probe as far as she could on her own.

Other things, though, occupied her mind as she turned into the park that bordered on her home street. She ought to have known it was a bad idea to phone Helen after several beers because she had (of course) mentioned there was this guy helping her get stuff and then (of course) promptly denied there was anything between them. She squirmed afresh at the memory: Helen had drawn the correct conclusion – who wouldn't, it was all so crass – and rang off, sounding really hurt. Then just a few days after there was no answer from her phone. Judith hadn't wanted to get her at work in case she might have to explain to Miss James why she was still in London. She hoped that the report sent in would have squared the boss by now, but things with her lover were hanging unresolved and she was not looking forward to facing her in the office after lunch.

There was a pile of mail in her box in the hallway and she climbed the stairs leafing through it. Judith was inside before she found the handwritten envelope among the junk circulars, and she sat down at the kitchen table, feeling weak. It was from Helen and the fact that she'd sent a letter could only mean the worst. She took out the single sheet covered in a neat script which began 'J' – since they had first become lovers in France Helen had called her by the initial alone – and with a lump in her throat Judith read the message.

Well, that's it. The call was a shock, but I've got over it now. I know you're not the faithful type, J, but I didn't expect you to pick up a *man* the first week in the big city. But I suppose it gives me the chance to make a clean break. That and getting sacked the next day.

I'm at my sister's working for her company – they make sex toys, ha ha! – but I'm not telling you where that is. Don't try and find out, I think it's best you just keep away. Miss James was looking for an excuse to get shot of me once I moved out of her bed, but that new Cate Carpenter gave it to her all right. She's a bitch and a half. Watch out, J, you'll be next!

I might look you up after a while, who knows.

Helen x.

Tears had come after the second line and now Judith sat and blubbed uncontrollably, overcome by a mixture of shame and grief. Then she raged in her head at the Carpenter woman and the boss who could let personal considerations dictate the dismissal of a good secretary. And after that, she cried again at the realisation she had no chance to try to make things up with her lover. Ex-lover. Slowly she pulled herself together. For fuck's sake, she had a lover – and he was in London. If Helen had been there she'd have tried to talk her way back into her bed and ended up deceiving two people if she could get away with it. Women complained about guys thinking with their dicks; it seemed what brain she had was firmly located somewhere between arse and cunt. Well, that had to change. Judith washed her face in a mood of resolution and went out to sit on the grass in the park. After a while she felt calm enough to make her way to the Archive in order to check in before the end of the afternoon.

Prepared as she was, it was still unnerving to see the brown-haired figure at the keyboard where Helen used to sit. But she made herself go over and stick out a hand.

'Hi, I'm Judith. You settling in OK?'

'Grace. I'm sorry your friend isn't here any more.' She coloured and blurted in a rush: 'There was gossip at the college, I mean, I know you were, er . . . and I just want to say it's all wrong 'cos you can tell from what she left behind here that she was doing a good job.' Judith looked at the flustered youngster, touched.

'Don't worry about it. I'm still a bit shocked because I just found out two hours ago. And we've split up, too.'

'Oh, no! That's an awful thing to come back to. I wish I didn't have to be here like this, but my Principal got me in, so . . .' She made a gesture of helplessness. 'I heard it was the new broom that got her chucked, but I don't think she's too bad really. She's been nice to me, but it's the way they carry on with their "Miss James, this" and "Oh, Miss Carpenter, that" you'd think they were a couple of old biddies.' In spite of herself, Judith gave a giggle; this girl was a real charmer in a bashful kind of way. Then, as if to illustrate her point, the door opened and the director herself stood there in her customary black breeches and high boots. From behind, in an astonishing combination of lemon-yellow leotard and bovver boots, came the new recruit.

'Miss James,' she said, 'I advise we go straight down. The first applicant should be ready and waiting.' Then she saw Judith and stopped.

'You're quite right, Miss Carpenter. But first, meet our cataloguer, Judith Wilson. Judith, this is Cate Carpenter from Seattle.' She forced herself to smile and nod; whatever her feelings it would help no one to show them at this stage. The striking blonde took her hand and squeezed it without a word.

'Thank you for your informative essay, Judith. I have left some comments and questions upstairs for your attention. However, you have still to account for the fact that you extended your work at the British Library by a fortnight without consulting me. I shall expect you at ten o' clock in the morning to answer to me on the subject. Now, Miss Carpenter, after you. We are due in the examination suite.'

They headed out for the lift and Judith opened the door on to the stacks. She caught Grace's eye and said: 'I'd better go to it while I can still sit down on the job.' The girl made a rueful face back and pointed to the cushion under her. Clearly it had become a tradition of the Archive that the secretary was *ex officio* prime recipient of the director's strap. Judith climbed the iron stairs to her cubby hole amongst the books somewhat cheered that there was a fellow sufferer in the building. It was just a shame Helen couldn't be there too.

At the appointed time Judith stood in front of Miss James's desk far from happy. While she was not actually marked, a fortnight's regular paddling had left her bottom distinctly sensitive. To make matters worse, the Carpenter woman was in attendance and there seemed every likelihood she was going to watch. Then Judith spotted the cane she was holding behind her back and mutiny welled up inside her. Accepting a justified beating from the director was part of the deal: it could hurt intensely yet deep down she thrilled to the idea of an authority exercised over her through corporal punishment. But no way was she going to take it from this upstart who was the same age as herself.

'Judith, do you agree that you were at fault and deserve punishment?'

Well, of course she did. She should have got approval for the extra stay in London. Now it was pay-back time and she had to submit to Miss James's will, whoever was to be its agent, otherwise she would be following Helen down the road.

'Yes, I do.'

'Very well, it shall be a dozen shared between us. Fetch the desk and take up position.'

Judith willed herself through the mechanical stages of placing the high desk in the middle of the room then rising on to the balls of her feet to stretch over and get hold of the legs on the other side. String briefs under trousers had become the order of the day for routine chastisements which the boss seemed as a rule content to deliver across one thin layer of cloth.

'A little tighter please, Judith.' She duly strained down another inch with her hands and gripped again. Lying as she was down the slope of the lid, her behind was pushed out and sheathed as closely as if she wore the blonde's lycra shorts.

'Now, Miss Carpenter, I'm sure you observe the fine jut of these buttocks and the slight bulge at the crease. With this posture I find you can inscribe a long line right across the swell of them with every cut.' She used her instrument as a pointer to illustrate the remarks and Judith clenched her teeth. For the duration she wasn't a person, merely a pair of arse-cheeks to be appraised and then whipped with a standard length of rattan. The boss delivered her six first. They were hard but Judith had experienced worse at her hands and was bracing herself for the remainder when the new assistant spoke.

'Miss James, it's really not my place to say this, but do you always leave her pants on for a caning?'

Pants? Oh, God, she means trousers. She wants them down.

'No, of course not, Miss Carpenter. But I had thought the offence this time not too grave in view of the good work done during the time away.' The voice was almost wheedling, quite unlike the usual directorial manner, and Judith's heart sank. Her Miss James was under the thumb of this 'Miss' Carpenter. It had to be unrequited love or something and because of it she was going to have to bare her bum.

'If you would rather strike uncovered flesh, I'm sure our culprit will oblige.' Mortified, Judith lowered the trousers around her spread thighs and went back over the desk. What else could she do? At least the band of her thong stopped the bossy American getting a prime genital display.

'Just six now, Miss Carpenter. But if you catch her right in the overhang you should get a reaction.' The limber rod lashed down and its tip bit excruciatingly into the left flank, unused to such treatment. Judith clung on, desperate in the pain's white heat, and a second followed almost at once. She fought to subdue a wave of panic: these strokes *must* be borne. To let the blonde sadist force her up before the end was unthinkable.

Three and four passed and she was still in place, panting. There was a taste of blood where she had bitten her lip. After five seared her there was a pause and every muscle shrieked for release from the intolerable tension of her posture. For several seconds the tick of the clock was the only sound then a boot thumped the floor and an effortful grunt brought the final jolt of agony. At the very edge of her endurance Judith found from some-where the means to stay in place until she had been told to get up. Through the haze she had the impression her cruel chastiser was disappointed and the thought gave her strength to draw up the trousers without a wince and return the desk to its corner. Then she fled to the bathroom.

She was still leaning weakly against the washbasin when there was a gentle knock at the door and a low voice said: 'It's me, Grace. Can I help?' Judith let her in and was in no state to resist when the once-shy secretary took surprising charge of the situation. In no time she was stripped from the waist down and stood in the bath while the bruises were swabbed with copious amounts of cold water. Then a fluffy towel was used to pat her dry while she made an effort not to cry out at its touch. Finally Grace uncorked an amber bottle and bent her patient over an upright chair.

'Witch hazel,' she said, and started to smooth some, little by little, into the ravaged flesh. 'Oh, these marks here are brutes. That new "Miss", she must be a left-hander.'

'A fucking vicious one.' Judith said it with feeling. 'But how come you're such an expert?'

'Ah, I spent two years in an institution abroad until I got rescued by Mrs Rowleigh. Don't ask any more because I would much rather forget about the whole thing. But the point is there was always one of us getting whacked – it was pretty random – so we all got plenty of practice. It didn't have to mean like making a pass, but then there were times, you know ...' Her hand slipped down low between the cheeks and she giggled. 'Ooh, Jude, do you always go really wet like this, even when it's been sheer bloody hell?'

Judith gasped as fingers found the centre of the throbbing mass of sensations in her nether regions.

'That's great, you're built just the same as me: a hot line straight from arse to cunt.' Grace put an arm round her waist and Judith seized hold of the chair until the climax passed. She stood up and pressed against the girl's body and they held together in some long drawn out kisses. Then a door banging outside made them spring apart and after a minute Grace stuck her head cautiously out of the bathroom. 'It's OK, I think the Misses have just gone downstairs. But we'd better be careful, eh? I mean, I'm up for more of the, er, aftercare –' she giggled again and Judith longed to find out how wet *she* was inside her knickers '– but you don't want to go the way of your friend.' Mention of Helen reminded her of the resolution to stick to one lover at a time and Judith felt ashamed of herself.

'Fuck, you're right, girl. We should be out of here. But thanks a bunch, I feel tons better, and if I can ever return the compliment ...'

'I could well take you up on that. For all we lesser mortals know, the Yank's got her eye on *my* bum for the next go at waving her magic wand in-house.' Judith left her still grinning in front of the monitor screen and made her own way up to the eyrie on the top floor that looked across the quad and out over the surrounding rooftops. That lotion was fabulous stuff: with the help of the down pillow kept for the purpose she might just be able to sit and get to grips with the latest instalment of tales from the sisterhood of the white whip . . .

13

Sex 'n' Sympathy

Cate was not best pleased with herself. When she woke it had been to memories of the previous afternoon in the observation suite, where Marjory Rowleigh had introduced two women of thirty or so who had recently abandoned their roles as suburban housewives to embrace a world of deviant sex. While a mild dose of the strap was at present their limit in the submissive mode, they offered themselves for it with such enthusiastic lewdness that it seemed clear there was a place for them in the growing network. That was well and good, but later over breakfast coffee Cate's thoughts turned back to the morning in the director's office. She had really not intended to hit Judith so hard: the idea had been to humiliate her by the mere fact of taking part in her punishment and then to emphasise her lowly place in the pecking order by having her strip.

But with the cane in her hand the aim changed to one of breaking her. If Miss James hadn't been there, she would have thrashed Judith until she screamed for mercy; as it was six strokes had not been enough, even though she had scored them into the lady's bare arse in a way she was going to feel for days to come. Cate stared out of her window at the buildings gathered in their old tranquillity around the sunlit lawn while she was shut into a world of warring impulses. A small voice

inside her insisted it was simply not right that Judith
had been severely treated for an action that the director
on her own would likely have let pass, or at most
rewarded with a routine six to the seat of the trousers.
Self-interest told her too that it had been a tactical error
whose main consequence was to create even more of an
enemy than her role in Helen's dismissal had done.

On top of these, though, was the feeling of a
discarded opportunity. The girl was tough and plucky
and in another situation could have been a friend. Or
more. The thought of that dark-stubbled head between
her thighs like Marissa's used to be made her cunt
prickle. And Judith had a real peach of a butt. In fact,
two ripe peaches that demanded to be flogged then
spread for a suitable instrument to plug the tight hole
between them. Cate got up and paced the room. The
image of the girl thrusting out her well-thrashed arse to
be violated made her shiver with lust and she felt sick.
The reality of her situation was that intimate connections from the past had been severed and, to make
matters worse, she was without the current option of
even a one-off fuck.

And then there was a further worry that seemed set
to grow with time, a worry about Miss James herself.
When Cate had stuck her neck out in the interview to
declare she never took punishment herself and then,
after a drink or two later in the evening, that she never
gave head it had felt like she'd won a real concession.
(The second bit wasn't completely accurate: she *had*
been known to stick her face in among a girl's freshly
whipped parts, though since she was never going to
whip her boss it was effectively the truth.) But it was
beginning to seem a hollow victory. More and more she
could sense the piercing gaze stripping her arse bare
whenever she was turned away and those long bony
fingers itching to set to work with a cane. It was all
getting very tense and it looked like something was

going to give. And that wasn't going to be her. Suddenly she had a thought that halted her pacing and put a smile on her face: maybe, just maybe, she could deal with two of these problems in one go. It was something that Marjory had said at their last network session, something about a college girls' club . . .

'Cate, this is Cassandra and this is Charlotte. Girls, this is Cate Carpenter from the Nemesis Archive.'
    'Cassie, please –'
    '– and Charlie. Good to meet you, Cate.'
    Marjory had explained to her earlier that the young women were not at her college but were students from the university who financed their studies by a little prostitution on the side. The practice had become common enough that they had formed a society for the purposes of mutual advice and protection. The two members present were anything but provocative in their scruffy denims, though Charlie's impish smile lit up features otherwise grave in a way that made Cate tingle. The business of the meeting was to arrange for the girls to 'service' the Archive's director in a planned series of sessions that would satiate her lust sufficiently to take her mind off Cate. Terms were soon agreed and the party headed to the pub just across the road to seal the arrangement with a drink. After one round, Marjory cried off, pleading work in the form of a report to digest before the morning; and after the next Cassie left for a rather different kind of work appointment.
    By this time Cate was in the mood for more and Charlie proposed taking her to a couple of low dives that only whores and students frequented. The fact that Cate was got up in sober skirt and modest heels to match was brushed aside as being an obvious disguise. Anybody could see she was a tough cookie underneath.

'The thing is, you fit in to The Cobbler's whether your loins are girded with a tarty wisp of black or a pair of motheaten old bloomers. Or even, of course, nothing at all.' She paused and raised her eyebrows in a frank query that had Cate blushing. Denial of her pantiless state was impossible.

'Ha! I was right. Now that wins hands down. A *real* hard case.' Laughing, she grabbed Cate's arm and hauled her down the narrow alley that ended in the faded pub sign of a boot on a last.

The next hour and a half passed in a whirl of booze and ribald stories from Charlie and some mates about the pitfalls of dabbling in sex for money while Cate responded with tales of sessions in the Seattle Cat. Come closing time, they were ambling back the way they had come in an inebriated silence when Charlie suddenly asked: 'Why won't you have sex with your boss? She's quite a looker, regardless of age, and *I'm* not going to mind getting to grips one little bit.' She stopped and once again the curious eyes were fixed on Cate. 'I mean, it's not as if you've got someone else here or anything, is it?'

Sober, she might have bristled at the questioning, but as it was Cate simply started to explain that she'd left behind – *lost* – a friend and a lover, but before she finished the first sentence the tears were running down her face. Charlie pulled her into a dark doorway and they sat on the step while the whole story poured out of how she'd found her lover back with the drummer after she'd been gone just a week and then how she groped her best friend and drove her away. And now she was here and while she thought she'd got it all under control she was afraid it was all starting to go wrong . . .

Eventually she ran out of steam and Charlie offered a handkerchief with which she dabbed at her eyes and blew her nose loudly. But before she could start to feel ashamed of letting it all hang out – God, when had she last done *that*? – her companion stood up.

'Come on, Cate, I'll walk you home. And if you feel like it you could ask me in for a nightcap. It'd be ace to see some of your gear.'

When the bottle of Polish vodka had been cracked and a hefty shot consumed by each, Cate produced what she called her 'box of tricks'. Declaring herself to be fainthearted about s/m, Charlie picked her way through a variety of whips and tawses to seize on a martinet fashioned from thin flat strips of leather.

'I think this is about my limit for an arse-warmer.' Then she took out the thick black dildo with the metal plate that had been a present from camerawoman Jag in Seattle on her last day. Cate produced the straps for it and Charlie's mouth fell open as she fingered the hooked end. 'You mean this goes into *you* while the other end is in *her* –'

'– and you can both hit the roof together. That's it, kid.' She poured them another tot of the potent white spirit and watched while Charlie examined the device, looking tipsily thoughtful.

'Y'know, Cate, I've got a special thing – I don't think I said, yet – that guys come to me for. It turns me on getting it, er, up the bum.' She was colouring, eyes down. 'I've been like that since way back. I can remember my mates starting to play about between their legs and I pretended, like, to be the same; but what I was doing was sticking things up my arse and worse, doing toilet games.' She looked up as if dismayed by her own words. 'Oh, God. Do you think that's really sick?'

Cate put a hand on Charlie's shoulder. 'Honey, lots of women like a good butt-fuck. It kinda goes with the territory if you get off on spanking and such. Now if you're asking me to stick that ugly great weapon right up between your cute bottom-cheeks, well –' she paused mischievously to let Charlie's look grow more apprehensive '– then I'd be delighted!'

141

'Pig. But that's great! Can I fasten it on?' She squatted to unzip Cate's skirt and planted a kiss on the bare pubic mound thus revealed. With a little help the straps were buckled in place then Charlie kicked off her trainers, peeled down jeans and pants and shook her long brown hair down over her shoulders. She handed Cate the lightweight bundle of thongs, saying: 'I wonder . . .'

'Sure, kid, I'll colour you up a bit. This won't do much more than raise a blush.'

'No, it's not that. I mean, I want that, but . . . oh . . .' Charlie was positively squirming with embarrassment.

'Come on, girl, spit it out.'

'Well, there's something I'm going to have to do anyway before that thing's going to fit.' She nodded at the cylinder in Cate's hand that was about to be inserted into its base. 'But I don't suppose you'd want to . . . to . . .' At last the penny dropped: wow, this was going to be a first. Cate put on her best schoolma'am tone.

'Are you telling me, young lady, that you propose to empty your bowels in front of me?' But she couldn't keep it up and dissolved into squiffy giggling. 'That is pervy, girl, and I love it. Let's have one last little shot of the fire water and get on with the job.'

And they did. Charlie knelt on the floor, legs spread apart over an elongated silver tray. On instruction Cate took some scented oil and lubricated inside the mouth of the exposed sphincter muscle. She could feel what was in the colon and sniffed at the tip of her withdrawn finger with a grimace. What the fuck was she doing? But as if in answer she felt the liquid well up in her cunt and picked up the martinet to swish it vigorously back and fore across the split-wide buttocks. Once they were nicely pink she inserted the black phallus into its mounting and gasped as it poked her clit. Then she got down behind Charlie and said: 'OK, honey, it's over to you.'

142

The girl strained visibly and a dark head appeared. As it thrust further and further out the anal ring expanded to allow its passage then, incredibly, expanded still more. Cate watched, riveted, as the whole monstrous length pushed out and fell onto the bright metal surface. There it lay, smooth, brown and steaming, like a magnified version of the thing that hung from her body, and the stink of it seemed to fill the room as she pushed hard and deep into the slack empty hole.

'God, that is fucking big,' said Charlie in a small breathless voice that spoke even to Cate's befuddled consciousness. The rigid mass of plastic was a different proposition to the squishy turd and her insides needed time to adjust. So she pulled out and began to work gently in by degrees until Charlie's cries and pelvic quiverings showed an arousal to match her own. Only then did Cate give herself up to the sensations in her cunt and allow her body and her partner's to thrust their own way to the final and mind-obliterating spasms they were seeking.

When she came to, her head was muzzy and there was a bad taste in her mouth. Then she recalled the tears in the alleyway and winced for shame. How could she be so pathetic? And after that – oh, God – after that was the shit and the arse-fucking. In fact, that was better. Drunk and dirty was allowed, drunk and maudlin was not. But what had happened to her companion in debauchery? Cate had a vague memory of stumbling about in the shower, then surely they had both come to bed. She got up and rescued a T-shirt from under the drained vodka bottle on the floor, then stumbled blearily through the rest of the discarded clothes to the door. There she stopped and stood blinking at the sight that presented itself. In the brightness of the sunshine that streamed into the living room was Charlie, quite naked, slashing her best senior cane through the air.

'Wow. *She* must have done something real bad.'

'Cate, don't creep up on a girl like that. But, hey, this is something else.' She swished it again several times then gave a big sigh. 'I bet it hurts like fuck though, eh? I'm such a wimp.'

'Well, it sure can do. My friend – ex-friend – Gena discovered a way of toning it down.' She looked fiercely at Charlie to warn her off referring to the sob story of the evening before. 'Come into the kitchen. I'm going to die if I don't get some strong coffee and I'll tell you all about it. And cover up, young madam. Do you think I want to see your butt any more after what you did last night?'

Charlie stuck out her tongue. 'I don't recall you backing off in horror. Quite the reverse, in fact.' But the bravado was undermined somewhat by the pink flush on her cheeks and Cate chuckled in spite of her sore head. It was good to see a little shame in the morning light.

She ground beans while Charlie retrieved sweatshirt and knickers and as the machine bubbled and hissed she told how Gena had found a book by a professional dominatrix who had been a mistress in an English private school in the 1950s.

'She caned with a book held under her arm and the girls got to keep their underwear on.' Cate poured out the coffee and put the mugs on the table then continued. 'That way you can't get a full swing and the action's all in the wrist. She says it still hurts – no point in it, otherwise – but it limits its effect to something most girls can take.'

'You mean she wanted a way of being able to dish it out a lot without doing actual bodily harm?'

'Yeah. Apparently, though, there was one prefect who was really up for it and she got the full works every few weeks. But then they were found out when the head marched into her study without knocking and caught the two of them, literally with their pants down, having sex after a caning. Apparently the girl was so wealed there was the threat of an assault charge but when she swore it was her choice they were both kicked out and set up as a team in London, whacking guys who were nostalgic for their schooldays. Now, *there's* an occupation.'

'So did you get to try it out? Her method, I mean, with Gena.'

'No chance. I left to come here.' Seeing Charlie's look she went on briskly to forestall expressions of concern. 'But there's no time like the present. Are you game, girl?'

By way of an answer Charlie drained her coffee and fetched the cane. Placing it on the table, she produced the harness from behind her back and without asking lifted up Cate's top to strap it in place. When she was done Cate handed her a chair.

'The lady says to use one of these. If a girl's touching her toes she's gonna worry about keeping her balance, but if she's propped over this she'll have her whole mind on the sensations in her rear end.'

'Will I do like this?'

Cate took a handful of the offered buttock and squeezed it through the snug black cotton.

'Perfect.' She picked up the length of rattan and flexed it. 'Now she didn't actually use a book, because she practised with one till she got the action. But this thing tends to get a hold of me, so *I'd* better. Just to make sure.'

'Er, yes, please. I saw how Marjory wasn't sitting at all comfortably the other week. That was you, eh?'

'Yeah, it was. But she wanted it hard. Don't worry, the book's got to work. And if the worst comes to the worst you can always run; the door's not locked.' She grinned and Charlie nodded but she wasn't smiling as she went out to bring back the dildo.

145

'So it's six of the best and then I get old blackie here, right? Like before. He's oiled and ready when you are.' So saying, she took up position over the chairback holding on to the seat while Cate picked up a copy of *The Compleat Spanker* from the sideboard and clamped it under her arm. Not only was the subject matter appropriate, it was a slim paperback that would keep the arm to the side without weighing a ton.

She lined up her rod against the stretched material and thought of the mistress who had no doubt contrived this to be at least a daily task. There must have been other girls besides the prefect who found it all rather exciting, even if they didn't let on. Just like Charlie, who was by no means a born masochist. Cate raised her arm awkwardly from the elbow and brought the cane down as best she could. It was very feeble, if accurate, and there was no reaction. A second attempt was little better, but the third somehow found the wrist movement required. There was an 'ooh' and the bottom wiggled.

'If you want to put the first two down to practice . . .'

'You're on, girl. So that's number one.' Two more were better yet and the hips jerked at each. 'See if you can keep still for the last three, OK? Then stay put and I'll do the rest.'

Charlie did as told, though tremors ran up her thighs when the six were done and she moaned: 'God, that's incredible.' Cate clipped the cylinder in place and held her breath as the spur nudged her clit, then reached for the waistband of the black panties. The fucking was long and slow and she savoured every moment. Hands clasped tight round Charlie's hips, she looked down at the red-streaked buttocks rising out of the bunched cotton, the anus stretched wide around the embedded black shaft. Now that was something she could get used to, no doubt about it, and in time this girl would learn to take some real stripes . . .

* * *

Afterwards Charlie removed the device from its mounting and took it to the bathroom where there was the sound of running water. When she returned and handed the thing over her face was serious, even solemn.

'Cate. Maybe you won't phone Gena, I don't know, but you could write. Get in touch. At least *try*.'

'I told you earlier. Topic closed. Forget about that exhibition I made of myself last night.'

Charlie turned down her mouth. 'Look, Cate. I can't do this again. It was great but that's it, you know. I'm with Cassie, we sleep together, right? It's not a wild sex life, I mean we both get fucked by a lot of men, so we just pet a bit at night. It's what we want. Now I'm going back to make it up to her 'cos she's my best pal. I do crazy things now and then and she lets me off with them. Usually she does, anyway.'

After the speech she went out, leaving Cate sitting at the kitchen table, stunned. So that was all just a 'crazy thing', was it? The depression of the morning before rolled back in waves and when Charlie returned dressed and made to give her a hug she pulled back stiffly.

'Just go, yeah?' Now Charlie looked downright miserable but she said nothing and Cate took her to the door. With an effort she said: 'I'll see you around.'

'I'm sorry, Cate. I think I've really fucked this up. And I only wanted to help.'

It was all she could do not to slam the door shut on the retreating figure. Back at the kitchen table, she sat fuming at the idea it had all been misplaced sympathy. Then she railed at herself for mistaking good sex for the start of a good relationship. 'Get a fucking grip, woman.' She said it out loud, then said it again. But it did nothing to halt the flow of tears which, already begun, proceeded regardless to run their bitter course.

14

Ceremony

I'm going to start with the day I was marked with the claws, which was even more DREADFUL than I feared, although two good things came of it. One which certainly wasn't intended was that Annie – our maid who had the INTIMATE job of changing my bandages – became my SPECIAL friend, something which has to be kept totally SECRET. The other was that I was able to say goodbye to the horrid cane except for errors (which I've avoided apart from a SPECTACULAR one I'll tell about later). Of course the Cat (which I've never even seen, let alone FELT) will come out for the grand ceremony at the end of the year, but I don't believe it can hurt as much as those burning stripes! I've decided to make this little JOURNAL of what's been happening so that if there is a DISASTER Annie will smuggle it out and send it to our cousin in London. There is such an air of foreboding in the house as the time approaches.

I must stop here for the present. My brother John's training steps up a notch tonight (unlike me, the poor LAMB gets no respite from the rod!) and I am due to go to the chamber this evening to play my part. When I come back I'll try and begin writing it all down properly in order, and not RAMBLE ON like Annie says I do if I get half a chance.

148

For God's sake, what were these claws? While she had the stomach (or at least the loins) for tales of quite severe whipping, the idea of what sounded like ritual wounding made Judith rather queasy. Who was this girl? The hasty writing spilled out over the ruled lines of an A4 book inscribed inside the front cover with the initials 'J A at I' and dated 1980. Unlike the Edwardiana she had studied at the British Library this account brought her within striking distance of the present day, but she had no idea of its origin. Harry had shoved the envelope into her hand without explanation as she hared off to the station at the end of her extended sojourn in the big city. That had cost her dear, thanks to 'Miss' fucking upstart Carpenter, who had left marks plainly visible after nearly a week and still tender when she shifted in her seat. She didn't really blame her boss for sanctioning the beating; it must be some kind of mid-life crisis that had made her besotted, and it couldn't last. If the jumped-up bitch wasn't putting out cunt *or* arse there had to be some almighty crunch on the way. But how long would it take before it blew up?

In the meantime Judith intended to keep well out of the way at her desk in the stacks and provide no more opportunities to be given a summary dose of pure bloody hell. From her high window the often bustling quad of term time was almost deserted in the summer sun, and she had been sitting musing over Miss James's real interest in the recent history of their namesake cat. While the Archive had a principal concern with the testimony of devotees of corporal punishment, there was more to the Nemesis cult than the cataloguing and classifying of experiences of the whip. The director had a personal axe to grind here, Judith was sure, and she was determined to get to the root of it. And for now she would keep her findings to herself. She turned back to the handwritten pages to read on. Maybe this was the manuscript that was going to enlighten her.

John is coming on well, so much so I would say he's ready. But Grandma is a stickler and I expect she will put him through his paces right up to the end. What happens in these sessions is that she stands at the back of him in her long black dress and SWISHES his bum (ouch! ouch! ouch! I FEEL for him). He's leaning flat up to a ladder that's propped against the wall and I kneel in front of him so that if his cock goes down I have to pet it till it gets HARD again and then the caning carries on. But tonight he stays stiff without my help like he must be on the day of my birthday – I'll be eighteen whole years old! – when he has to PLANT it in my cunny.

That's the word Annie uses for my private part, and she likes to kiss me there. She says it tastes so sweet in among all the fair curls: what I know is it makes me nearly faint away. I didn't have any IDEA of all this before she showed me but now of course I find the magic button with my fingers when I'm alone in bed at night and then I sleep like a BABY afterwards. It started after I was ripped with the AWFUL claws right down both flanks (I know it has to be done for the CEREMONY so I'm not really complaining). When Annie changed the dressings I would go face down with a bolster under my hips and she stroked me till I went all wet and gooey inside. I've tried to kiss her in that place, too, but she won't have it; says she'll smell of HIM (that's her husband, the groom) because he's always at her. I suppose she means his cock goes in her cunny (like John's will be in mine) but I also saw once when I pulled up her skirt that her backside was all PURPLE like John's is after training. Is it something they do all by themselves? I can't really make sense of it because until the ceremony mine will only get like that if I've made a MISTAKE.

And that reminds me that I said I'd write about when I did. I should explain that what happens on my birthday is a FLAGELLATION ritual where the man is whipped right through the time he fills the woman (that's me!) with his sperm. So it wouldn't do AT ALL if he went limp because it hurt too much, and that's why there are these training sessions with the cane. The idea is that I stroke him or take him in my mouth – I can do either, it's up to me – when the pain makes him shrink but I have to be careful not to OVERDO it. We are not supposed to WASTE the fluid because come the big day there must be plenty to do the job. But of course, that's exactly what happened on this occasion two weeks ago, and the first I knew of it was when I felt his thing give a jerk between my lips. I pulled back AT ONCE but it was too late and I just sat there like a ninny while the stuff SPURTED all over my face and my hair.

So now I've torn it. Before I could wipe a blob out of my eye I was marched to the trestle in an iron grip and pushed down over it. Then Grandma lifted my skirt and gave my behind a real WHACKING with the beastly stick. I didn't dare move but just had to take it though I made a BIG noise. Now I think about it that wasn't such a good idea because it made her even crosser and when I went back to my task (oh, yes, we weren't finished yet) I could hardly concentrate with my whole rear end just throbbing like crazy. At least when at last I got back to my room there was the COMPENSATION of taking my lamp to the mirror to goggle at the MASS of stripes, then lying down on my bed with my legs spread and . . . (I shall draw a veil over this since there will be PLENTY of indiscreet things to come!)

Lamp? For a minute it had sounded more like 1880 than something from just over two decades ago. But the Woolworth's pad and the excitable script were clearly modern even if the house hadn't arrived in the age of electricity. It must be somewhere really isolated: the naivety and lack of prurience in the writing suggested there was no contact with the media culture that mostly reached down to girls of eight, let alone eighteen. Where was this place? There was as yet no answer. All she could do for the present was carry on in the hope of turning up a clue.

Then with only TWO WEEKS to go before D-Day there is a big change. I am over my bolster at the end of the bed and Annie is at her PRIVATE work between my legs when the door opens and her HUSBAND is there. Before I can move a muscle he has pushed her aside and grabbed my wrists in a BRAWNY hand which presses them into the middle of my back. So I'm pinned down helpless and he proceeds to smack my bottom while he tells me that this is what I get for LEADING his wife ON. This accusation hurts as much as the spanking – what does he think I am? – but there is no stopping him. He is big and strong with a wild ginger beard and my poor cheeks are soon HOT and SORE. When eventually he lets me free I look back to see him reach into his trousers and out pops a MASSIVE cock.

Annie yells: 'No! No! She's got to be a VIRGIN,' but he just brushes her away. I realise he isn't thinking CUNNY at all and I see Annie look at me anxiously but I stick my bum up in the air to show willing. I've had her fingers in THERE too and I like it. So while she OILS me I take hold of his thing. It is longer and thicker than brother John's with a PURPLE head and it dribbles in my hand. There's no need to stiffen up this one! Then he's at the back of me and pushing in – and in – and in. If there is any more I feel that it will come out of my THROAT. But this is NEW and exciting and when he pumps out inside me and his balls slap against my cunny I go off too!

Annie takes the two of us to the wash basin and cleans off what he has dredged up from DEEP in my bowels (it's not my fault if he's a FOOT long) and by the time we are sweet-smelling again he is as HUGE as before. This time SHE goes over the pillow but when he gets behind her he goes into her cunny. I have never seen this done and I stare, taking in every DETAIL of how her lips down there move round his shaft. But Annie wants me on the bed and I open my legs so she can put her head in there. We make a good threesome, I think, and when he shoots off again with a lot of grunting she makes me MELT right away with her mouth.

Judith pushed back her chair and made her way down the circular stair. It was time for a 'melt' break all of her own. Locked into the bathroom she brought herself to a quick efficient climax, in imagination straddling Harry's erection while her behind smarted from his paddle. Then she emptied her bladder slowly, in spurts, savouring the jets of hot piss through the sensitised flesh that were almost as good as coming all over again. This was no use: she would have to make some (non-punishable!) excuse to go back to the BL and get the real meat inside her. Judith made a wry face as she washed between her legs. If anyone had told her a month ago that she'd be pining for a guy's cock she'd have laughed in their face and declared that her bedside drawer contained something better than any man could offer her.

Back at her desk she skipped on impatiently through the manuscript. Page after page appeared to be devoted to descriptions of triangular sex between J A, Annie and the unnamed husband, in which spanked cheeks were parted to allow access to his rampant cock. The man was a prodigy and his seminal exploits were recounted in prose that broke increasingly into overheated italics.

It was all quite arousing, but ... Suddenly the penny dropped. 'Overheated' was exactly the word: this was the product of an overheated IMAGINATION. Not that it was all an invention; the bizarreness of the 'training', for instance, gave it the ring of truth. But the reason this was being set down was because it turned the WRITER on. She was filling her time by writing a kind of auto-pornography, complete with the cliché of a veritable stallion of a groom! Judith was prepared to believe that first, shitty bum-fuck and Annie's playing with the girl's cunt, but then it all became mechanical and repetitive, as if generated on the basis of infrequent and limited experience.

And there were reams of the stuff. Then, with a mere half dozen pages left, she came upon the heading

IT IS DONE!!!

Now, surely, she would learn something of what this crazy household was all about.

Annie has just bathed all the RAW places and I am lying face down on my bed to record the events. It starts in the afternoon when two PRIESTESSES that I have never seen before arrive to take me to the ceremony. In the ante-room they give me a silver cup to drink from. It tastes BITTER but I get it down while I am stripped and EXAMINED to make sure no man has been in my private part. When we go into the chamber itself the first thing I see is my NAKED brother tied hand and foot with his wrists pulled up above his head by a ceiling rope. Next to it another one hangs down waiting for ME. There are bindings over his mouth and eyes: his only function is to be a cock that will squirt the SPERM into me whereas my part will take another nine months (ALL GOING WELL). Now I am tied too and join him stretched up, half-hanging and half wobbling on my toes. The flagellation is under way and the women in their white ROBES circle us and strike out with their white leather CATS. While my backside catches it, as expected, so do breasts and belly and back and legs, over and over again. My head is reeling – it must be from the POTION – and each lash of the thongs is like a FLAME. Soon my whole body is on fire and just as I start to slip away – in my mind I am burning at the STAKE – the rope is released and arms catch me as I fall.

There is a marble slab between two pillars where they put me on my back and the COLD shock of it on my whipped body brings me wide AWAKE. Now it is the turn of my ANKLES to be hoisted up and hooked to the columns which spreads my legs wide and pulls me down so my BUM comes right off the edge. I'm going to FALL and I cry out, but one of the women holds me while the other fastens a strap under my shoulders to FIX me in place. Then they take up position each side of John who, in spite of being covered in deep red stripes, has the biggest HARD-ON I have ever seen him get. It almost makes me giggle to think that if anyone touches it by mistake it will GO OFF there and then and RUIN everything.

However I'm not smiling for long because a woman in a silver mask appears carrying a BLOOD-RED cat with knotted tails. I just have time to think it must be Grandma before she begins to whip the flesh inside my thighs right up to the cunny itself. I have NEVER EVER felt pain like this and I just yell and scream and howl until she stops. One priestess wipes away all my tears and snot though I can't stop sobbing straight away, especially when I see how she has cut my skin. I wonder how much of the COLOUR of that terrible instrument has come from other poor creatures like me and I SOB even more.

Now I'm feeling WOOZY again and it's all nearly over. They have taken my brother down, still tied, and are manoeuvring him into position. Then in one lunge his thing has torn right into me and he's GRINDING away. At first it just HURTS but as he starts to make noises behind his gag my body begins to RESPOND. But it's all TOO MUCH and it's like a black cloud comes down and swallows me up and I don't know a THING until I'm back here.

After this there was a whole blank sheet, then a single paragraph on the next.

It is a month since the ceremony and it has WORKED! There is no more need of John and he has been sent away. I have my books back and come and go as I please. So I head out riding in the hills most days, whatever the weather, but I keep well away from any PEOPLE. Often when I get back to the stables Annie's husband is there and he pulls down my breeches, then leans me over the workbench and spanks me with his BIG hand. He is no longer interested in my bottom except to smack it and when I am good and HOT he takes me in my cunny from behind.

Now there were several empty pages and on the last one of the pad just three sentences.

The time is close and I am getting very big with the twins. I can't do anything except read and there is nothing to write about. Now all that is left to me is to wait.

Judith pressed her legs together, imagining only too well the slapping of a bare bum amongst the smells of horses and leather. The ending, though, sounded an ominous note, and the fact that she was reading it at all meant surely that the 'disaster' feared from the start had occurred. But what could it be? Whatever else was going on this was clearly about breeding from a brother and sister and it had given rise to twins, who could easily be another brother and sister. Now if *they* were raised to breed again say eighteen years on, it would be happening right about *now*! Judith's mind reeled at the thought of these incestuous couplings stretching back in time and on into the future. Was this to do with the occult? It sounded a bit like the seventh child of a seventh child sort of thing: siblings producing siblings who produced siblings until – until what? Where was it supposed to lead?

She got up and stared down at the grass several floors below where a group of tourists aimed their cameras at the old clock tower opposite. Its hands were at ten to two and Miss James would be back at quarter past. An idea was beginning to form in Judith's mind and she sat down again in front of the manuscript. Now if she played her cards right she could get a few days in London on 'business' (to reprise the stable scene but among the books!) *and* pull off an investigative coup under the nose of the jumped-up American. But first she needed to know the whereabouts of the house named only as 'I'. Maybe, just maybe, that could be simply done and, praying that Harry was lunching in as usual, she turned to her computer keyboard.

15

Mis(s)fire

The director drew her chair up closer to the observation window as her secretary Grace ushered Marjory Rowleigh into the room. Centre stage was a newly constructed block of solid oak with a domed top flanked by ledges and hung with straps and buckles ready to secure its very first occupant. She had been acquainted with the deputy principal of the business college for some time but had become only recently aware of her propensity to undergo rigorous corporal punishment. There was something decidedly stimulating about the idea of an immaculately professional persona hiding a body, the severity of whose markings would keep their shocking existence in mind at all times.

She watched the demure Grace take the jacket and skirt of the dark suit and hang them in a corner cupboard. The blouse followed, revealing that there was no underwear of any kind to impede the process Samantha James always considered to be 'correction', whether or not there was an antecedent fault. There was none, of course, in this case, but she held the firm belief that a strict application of the rod had a purging effect that was not dependent on the existence of an identifiable misdemeanour. Now today's subject stood in her elasticated stocking tops, displaying the ripe flesh of a woman of nearly forty, as if gathering herself for

158

another painful demonstration of the thesis. Then her face cleared and she knelt in position, stretching over the wooden surface to rest her elbows on the far side. The young woman tightened the restraints around calves and forearms, then fastened a belt across the top that pulled the full-breasted torso hard down to the block and stepped back.

Marjory had become all and only *posterior*, imprinted yet with the results of her last disciplinary encounter and between whose spread hams bulged brown-fuzzed vaginal lips. It was a blatant, arresting sight and Samantha looked round to see the other spectators hunched forwards in their seats. Their presence behind the one-way screen was in no way surreptitious: the one with her bottom so prominently bared had invited Judith and her own young friends Charlotte and Cassandra to watch. But she preferred them to be out of sight, leaving her alone in the room with the assistant who would, after it was over, help bring her back from the edge and, of course, the chastiser herself who chose that very moment to make an entrance.

A stir ran through the audience at the appearance of the figure in a black bodysuit with clunky boots and fine leather gloves. Topped with the shining bob and scarlet lips, the effect was strikingly provocative. A total covering could be more arousing than any amount of the nakedness already on display, and the director's loins liquefied at the thought of laying visible cane tracks on the buttocks that rippled under the sheer material. If only . . . if only . . . But Cate Carpenter had been given her word, and so it must be. No doubt the purpose of the evening's entertainment – beginning with this soundest of sound thrashings – was to divert her lust for the American assistant into other channels and she was resolved to make the most of the two attractive girls when the opportunity arose later. She understood, though, that they were to be treated gently and so was quite happy for the present to observe, having seen that the instrument quivering in the young blonde's hand was a full-length penal cane whose application was sure to have a quite startling effect on the recipient's rump.

Indeed, the impact of the first strokes made all four watchers wince while the grunting body creaked its leather bonds against the wood. At six there was a cry and a hoarse 'Please, I can't ...' to which Grace responded by inserting a pear-shaped gag into the mouth and tying it firmly behind the head. At twelve the buttocks were welted in deep purple lines from flank to flank and after a pause for the muscular spasms to pass the rattan was measured carefully against the upper thighs. The director recalled with a small shudder an initiation of her own from the days – long past – when she was accustomed to submit to discipline herself. The memory of it was disconcertingly strong, but she drew compensation from the fact that having inside knowledge of such atrocious pain enhanced the thrill of seeing another made to suffer it. And what a trouper Marjory was!

However, after nine more, all laid on below the level of the genital fig, the figure slumped in its bonds and the head drooped. The director sighed: all good things must come to an end. It seemed clear that even this stalwart was at a limit of sorts and the chastising fury stood poised with signs of struggle written on her face. Plainly there was consideration for the victim that said stop and stop now: this is already extremity enough for anyone to bear. But it was in conflict with the powerful urge to inflict yet more pain on the helpless body on the block and the cane was raised again. When it swished across the crown of the backside Samantha James felt an electric shock through the centre of her being that left her breathless through the two strokes that followed. Then with a clatter the instrument of torture was discarded on the floor and the wielder of it stalked out of the room. For several moments no one moved then Grace leaned over to release the straps and revive the woman after her ordeal. It was her task to tend Marjory's injuries and it served as a cue for the viewers to get awkwardly to their feet to go upstairs for the next stage of the proceedings. There was no conversation as they went out to the lift and the director could think of only one thing: the throbbing in her clitoris that Cate Carpenter had caused with those last three strokes. To see a young beauty in the grip of a true sadistic passion was a rare thing, and far from serving to refocus her desire on other targets, the demonstration had redoubled its urgency. She had to have her, and have her that night.

The plan to distract her – if it were such – had badly misfired.

Cate sat in the dressing room with her head in her hands, oblivious to the remains at her feet of the flimsy garment she had ripped off in a fit of self-disgust. After a while there was the sound of water from the shower area adjoining and she got up and pulled on the pair of jeans and T-shirt that lay beside her on the bench. She tapped on the door but there was no response so she turned the handle and stuck her head into the room. There was a rectangular examination table alongside the cubicles and Marjory lay on this face down, with a large cold compress draped over the afflicted haunches. At the wash basins Grace was busying herself putting another set of icecubes into a bowl.

'I, er, I came to see if I could help.' Cate knew it was a mistake before she'd finished speaking. The girl looked up and her face darkened. With lips pursed in hostility she said: 'No thank you. I think – we both think – you've done enough damage for one day.'

It was quite out of order for a lowly secretary to address the director's favoured assistant in this way but

Cate backed out with a muttered 'Sorry, sorry,' and closed the door behind her. Then she fled down the corridor to the rear entrance and out into the warm summer dusk.

It was an hour before she returned and even then she couldn't face the critics. The outer office was deserted but voices came from within the director's office, so Cate slipped quietly into her own quarters. But no sooner had she sat down in the corner to collect herself than the connecting door opened and Charlie was there. She shut it gently and came over.

'I thought you might be here. Hey, cheer up, it isn't all bad. Grace is really pissed off but you sure impressed your boss. She's got Marjory spread-eagled for a really detailed inspection of her arse. You should see it, up like a fucking balloon.'

'Shit. Is Marjory OK?'

'Course she is. Tough as old boots. While Miss J is applying some dead special stuff to the injured bum, Mrs R is making a close study of Cassie's juicy bits. Having a whale of a time!' But the bright tone sounded false and Cate reckoned it was an attempt to disguise how much Marjory had been shocked by her treatment over the block. It wasn't like before when she held on to that stool; this time she'd been tied and gagged, for fuck's sake. And her trust had been abused.

'Look, Cate, I'm really sorry about the weekend. The last thing I wanted to do was upset you. I tried to explain . . .'

Oh, God, Charlie seemed to think she was responsible for the earlier excesses of the punishment room, at least in part. Cate felt like saying she was her own boss and would take any blame that was getting handed out. But while she stared crossly, the sexual magic worked again. Despite the unhappy frown, the girl was ravishingly pretty in a velour mini with her hair flowing about the shoulders. Then Cate noticed the hands cradling her seat and catching her eye the girl blushed.

'Miss James persuaded me to sample her new strap and it's got some sting to it. I was told to go away for five minutes to let the colour come right up.' She wriggled and rubbed and pouted, and it was all too much. Despite protests that she had to get back, the young student was marched to the desk and bent over with her dress up round the waist. Cate stood marvelling at the flesh that had been attended to by such an expert spanker: there were no individual discolorations at all, only a uniform cerise glow that suffused the whole rear end. Quite unable to resist, she stooped and buried her face between the hot downy cheeks.

When Marissa crouched splayed to get head after a whipping, in her spare frame the openings gaped wide. But there was depth in the furrow that separated these plump little buttocks and it was heaven. She wanted to lose herself there and forget everything. Against her lips the cunt lips were slippery with the girl's excitement and laced with the tang of sweat and urine. Mindful of what she had seen it doing Cate probed the anus with her tongue, savouring the acrid hint of what lay deeper inside. Before long the hips were squirming and taking a firm hold of them she worked her mouth hard into the clitoris. The action elicited three sharp cries, alarmingly loud, and in the next instant there was the sound of the door opening behind them. Cate sprang back and Charlie jerked up, pulling at her clothing but it was too late. Beside the director in the doorway was Cassie, and her eyes were filling with tears.

'How could you, Charlie, how could you?' she wailed. 'You've gone and done it again.'

Miss James was affected in a different way and her voice was icy. 'For one who doesn't *do* that, you seem actually to do it rather well. Or so our young friend's response would indicate.' For a long second there was silence, then she lunged forwards. With one hand she clamped Cate's arm while she slashed down with the cane that was in the other, hissing: 'Liar! Liar!'

Cate wrenched herself free and backed up to the wall, two lines burning into her lower back. She opened her mouth but no words would come out. When the director spoke again it was with a visible effort to maintain self-control.

'In my scheme of things, Miss Carpenter, a deliberate lie requires to be corrected. Given your own disciplinary proclivities, I do not see that you could disagree with that statement.' She held out the length of rattan and pointed to the floor in front of her. 'Therefore you will come here and touch your toes to receive the award you are due. And you will do so at once!'

Mute and rooted to the spot, Cate put up her palms in a gesture of refusal. The heart was banging in her chest and her mouth was dry.

'Very well.' The speaker drew herself up and stood formidable in her gleaming white shirt and black breeches. 'Miss Carpenter, I hereby terminate your contract. Take what legal action you care to take: that is my final word and will remain so. As you would put it in your country, you are *fired*. Now get out.'

There was a timid spattering of applause from the company that now crowded into the office with expressions that ranged from Grace's grim triumph to Judith's open delight. Crushed, Cate found her way to the door and made an exit. There was only one face that let her take away even a crumb of comfort and, strangely, it was Marjory's. Pale and drawn as she was, and with good reason to wish Cate out of her life, she had been shaking her head in disapproval of the outcome.

16

Post-Mortem

Cate made the taxi-driver wait with her luggage while she climbed the steps of the Georgian townhouse and pushed at the bell, still hardly able to trust the note that had been left on her mat late the night before. But the words had been unequivocal: *Please don't run. You can have my spare room while you decide what to do. Marjory.* When the door opened the older woman looked at the younger one and at the cab with its engine running.

'I meant what I said, Cate. So please fetch your things and come in.' When she returned with her two cases Marjory gestured at the stairs. 'On your left at the top. Why don't you go and install yourself? Don't say anything now –' she looked at Cate standing awkwardly, at a loss for words, then moved toward the downward flight at the back of the hall '– just join me on the ground floor when you are ready.'

It took only five minutes to stow her things in the elegant wardrobe and dressing table, then Cate had a good look at her surroundings. A single tall window looked across an expanse of green to a similar row of houses on the other side. In the early Saturday evening the street was quiet; although a stone's throw from the city centre, it formed an enclave blocked off to through traffic. Through a door to the back she found her own bathroom with a view of the small walled garden when she opened the frosted pane. On an impulse she stripped and got into the shower. Marjory had given the impression that she wanted a few minutes alone so, now Cate was there, she may as well try to wind down.

The house was warm so, once dried, she found a pair of grey cut-offs and a navy tank top and pulled them on. She had stayed underwear-free ever since the resolution in Seattle and there was no reason to go back on it just because things had taken a turn for the worse. Turn for the worse? That was a fucking joke! She had been thrown out on her ear, given the bum's rush, ejected on the spot without ceremony. But there was no way – absolutely no way ever – that she could have bent over for ... for ... Well, it would have been a real beating, that was for sure. A thrashing far worse than the one she'd handed out to Judith and it would have been in front of her and all the others. Cate shuddered and tried to put the thought out of her mind. There was no point in dwelling on it: she'd refused and that was that. The question was where to go from here. She sighed and stood up. One step at a time. The first thing was to try to square things with her unexpected and undeserved host.

At the foot of the lower set of stairs the door was ajar and Cate pushed it wide. The long room ran from the half-basement front with its iron railing right through to the French windows opening on to the lawn at the back. Just inside them stood a waist-high trestle with a leather-covered top that was raised at the front. It looked ideal for Marjory's 'bad girls' to bend over for spanking and petting when she was too sore to take them across her knee. As she would be right now. The street end was furnished with a heavy desk and two large bookcases between which the lady herself was drawing the curtains that hung down to the thickly carpeted floor. She had changed into a kimono-like gown that did little to disguise the curves of her body and Cate thought again how handsome was this woman some fifteen years older than herself. Under the cultivated urbanity of the deputy principal there was a strength that drew her while at the same time it added an edge of apprehensiveness to her guilt.

'Marjory, I – I –'

'I know, Cate. You believe that you went too far yesterday and you regret it. I imagine you regretted it almost at once. And you want to put things right, but you are afraid that an apology will fall short of what is required and may in fact be a little insulting. Am I correct?'

Cate nodded dumbly, disconcerted by the accuracy of the diagnosis.

'Can I therefore make a proposal? Thanks to your efforts, I am rather in need of a massage and I have here just the thing for it.' She went to a small cabinet and took a bottle from its drawer. 'Do you think you could oblige me, Cate?'

'Oh, yeah, sure. I'd be pleased to.' The opportunity to make recompense was exactly what she wanted, though it was hardly going to be a trial to put her hands on the woman's fine body.

'Very good.' Marjory draped herself over the trestle, legs spread and Cate lifted the silk hem and folded it up round her back. She had braced herself for what she would see but the reality still shocked her. After 24 hours there was still some swelling and the bruising was horrendous, with the lower buttock and upper thigh on the left one solid mass of purple and black. So she forced herself to begin there and with the gentlest touch she could manage smoothed a little of the herbal oil over the discoloured skin.

'Ah! Ah! Oh, dear, I'm afraid you're going to have to excuse me. I'll get used to it as you go on.' Racked with

167

guilt, Cate proceeded and thankfully the recipient of her attentions did quieten down. After a while she began to move in response to the action of the hands, becoming plainly aroused, and Cate touched her fingers to the slippery dark meat of the exposed genitals.

'In the drawer, dear. I don't want to impose, but it would finish things off rather well, you know.' There were half a dozen assorted dildoes from which Cate took a long one with a good grip and once she set to work the figure on the trestle was quiet no longer. Afterwards there was a silence while the deputy principal subsided, the air of the room heavy with the scent of her secretions. Cate wiped her fingers, uncomfortably aware that her own pantiless crotch was leaking arousal and she was glad when Marjory pushed herself upright and spoke.

'Thank you, Cate, that is much better. I feel quite *renewed*. Now, I do have one more suggestion, but I'm really not certain that you're ready for it.'

'Try me, Marjory. What is it?'

The older woman smoothed down her robe and went to the cupboard in the corner of the room. Then she looked at the younger one as if weighing something up. 'I think you were justified in refusing to take Samantha's cane. She had no right to demand retribution on the spot and in front of such a hostile audience. But it does still leave you with a gap, does it not?'

A gap? Cate was unclear where this was heading, but there was something ominous in Marjory's tone.

'Correct me if I'm wrong, but it's my understanding that you have never received any serious corporal discipline. So while you know – in the way anyone does – that it hurts, you have no specific idea of what you are doing when you inflict it.' She opened the tall narrow door and removed an instrument very like the one used the day before in the Archive. With one end resting on the floor it reached up to Marjory's chest and Cate gulped in the realisation of what was being proposed.

'Just a single stroke is all I have in mind. Believe me, I am not aiming to get my own back. Think of it not as punishment, but as a learning experience. Do I have your consent?'

Cate nodded, unsure what to say. After what she'd done to Marjory, she could not balk at one stroke.

'Very good. Over the trestle, I think. And it will not be necessary to take down your trousers.' Cate got into the position her host had adopted for the massage and took hold of the handles at the sides with sweaty palms. She felt Marjory grip her waistband and pull the cotton garment up into her cleft then smooth out any wrinkles in the cloth. There was a whirring sound and an instantaneous impact that drove her hips hard into the padded top. Then, with a screech forced from her throat, Cate was on her feet, clutching at the line of agony.

It seemed a long time before she could trust herself to speak. Staring at the floor she said: 'Thank you. You were so right, I had no idea.' Then she managed to look the older woman in the eye and it was as if a weight fell from her. The stroke may not have been intended as retribution, but it felt like she had made amends and Marjory smiled.

'Let's say no more about it. Is that agreed? Good. Now if you follow me up to the sitting room I can pour us both a well-earned drink.'

An hour passed and then another while the glasses were emptied, refilled and refilled again. Mostly it was Cate who talked, prompted by questions about her life in Seattle and her discovery of the world of s/m. Eventually Marjory got up, suppressing a yawn.

'Excuse me, Cate. It's no reflection at all on what you have been telling me which was quite fascinating. I simply had not realised that you are almost as much a novice as I am. Perhaps you weren't aware that the room downstairs was only finished a fortnight ago.

When I decided to indulge my inclinations I wanted a study and, for want of a better word, a workroom.' She yawned again. 'Oh, dear. I'm afraid I didn't do very well for sleep last night. Somehow it was difficult to get comfortable.'

'Oh, Marjory –' Cate stopped when she saw the stony face break into a sly grin. 'OK, OK. You got me going there. But, since you brought the subject up, just hold it right where you are a minute.' She ran down the stairs and was back at once carrying the four-foot length of rattan. 'One more? To make sure the lesson is learned, yeah?'

'If you insist, my dear. Then I think we should call it a night. There are things that need to be discussed in the morning. Now, if you'll be so good as to pull your trousers up tight and bend over the back of the couch, I'll do what you ask.'

In the bedroom, Cate stripped off her clothes and explored the fresh stripe that burned hard and hot an inch below the first. At least she had managed to take it with a tad more dignity, though she was uneasily aware that it had been far from a pure act of penance. There was a distinct itch in her groin that grew as she swivelled in front of the mirror to get a good view of the marks. She had never before thought of herself as being on the receiving end of a whipping, but as she studied her reflection she felt a frisson of pride at the nicely rounded buttocks she saw there. They would be a disciplinarian's delight, no doubt about it! But now her need had become urgent and Cate lay back on the bed with a half-pleasurable wince as the sore flesh pressed into the cool sheet. She eased a hand down between her legs and spread them wider. It had been weeks since the last time but tonight she was good and ready. Fuck, was she ready. Marjory's cunt had started her off and then the cane had set the seal on it. With the very tip of a forefinger she circled the stiff button then pulled back for a moment and did it again. And again. Each time the sensation climbed higher, and a touch higher still until in the end she trembled for an instant on the brink of an impossible precipice, then hurtled down and out into limitless space . . .

In the morning Cate woke early and let herself out into the back garden. Beyond the high brick wall the silence of an early Sunday morning was broken only by the sound of birdsong and she sat on the bench that had been placed amongst the flower beds filling one corner. She breathed in the air that was fresh and cool while the sun was still low in the sky and sank into a reverie. Time passed and Cate came to herself feeling the sunlight on the back of her neck, marvelling at the ease she felt inside. Yesterday's angst seemed a million miles away, though its direct cause – summary dismissal from the Archive – was just as real today. Somehow the bodily encounters of the evening had penetrated her mind: Marjory had worked a spell that had banished the demons. She shook her head at the fancy. Was that lame-brained or what? Then she looked up, saw her host at the kitchen window and made her way inside.

The small bright room was filled with the smell of coffee from the bubbling machine and there was a basket of hot rolls on the table. Cate went straight up to Marjory and kissed her on the cheek, squeezing the flesh at the top of her hip. 'Thanks so much. For everything. I don't deserve it.'

The deputy principal looked at her and looked away, plainly embarrassed. 'What nonsense. Of course you do. Now sit down and join me for some breakfast.' They ate in silence for a few minutes then she said: 'I hope you won't think I'm interfering, Cate, but what would you say to taking the investigation you started on in Seattle a little further?' She refilled their cups from the steaming jug then continued. 'I was given a piece of information yesterday on the telephone that I feel I should pass on. It's about your employer – ex-employer I should say, I suppose. Let me explain. When she attends to young Grace's bottom, she has a habit apparently of thinking aloud, seeming quite to forget that the cheeks she is reddening are attached to a body with a pair of ears.'

Cate smiled at the image but wished Marjory would come to the point.

'I've learned several interesting things that way from my trusty informant. Well, on this occasion she paced up and down in between whacks, quite distracted. It seemed she had discovered the whereabouts of a remote house and Miss Wilson – Judith – was to be sent north to find it. It is there, so Grace understood, that they still practise the ritual of the goddess that you were talking about.'

'Nemesis. It's a ceremony with the Cat, some kind of a special whip.'

'She said too that the house had a name. What was it now? Inglewhite, that was it. Inglewhite.'

For a moment Cate's mind was a blank; then she remembered. The old woman's story that she had been so impatient with. After the fire that had destroyed all traces of the cult she'd heard her aunt saying, 'Inglewhite will have a copy.' It wasn't a person, but a place. When she explained the connection to Marjory, the older woman got up and came back with a key.

'This will let you into the basement at the back. Now, far be it from me to encourage snooping, but you need to know what Miss Wilson knows before you head north as well. Samantha is up to something and I don't think she should have things all her own way. Besides, think of what a coup it would be to return to America with all the means to stage such an ancient rite.'

It was nearly dusk when Cate let herself out of the Archive into the deserted quad. Fired up by Marjory's scheme to attack Judith's desk, she soon found its contents engrossing. The Professor's papers were interesting in their own right, but when she came across the handwritten account by A J at I – Inglewhite, it had to be! – she read oblivious to her surroundings until the fading light brought her to a stop. Even then she sat on in the gloom pondering the strange ritual of flagellation and impregnation, breeding – but for what? There was a lot to mull over.

Back at the house, she noticed the drapes were closed across the half-basement windows and a light was on inside. Marjory had talked rather mysteriously of a plan to put things right between two of her young friends, saying it would be as well if they didn't see that Cate was staying there. So she let herself in quietly and crept down the stairs and along the passage to the back door. Outside she saw the French windows stood slightly open and a streak of light fell out across the patio. Then she heard the deputy principal's cut-glass tones, clear in the stillness of the night.

'No, Cassandra, I don't think that is anywhere near enough. Charlotte has been a very naughty girl and she needs a thorough whipping.' It was impossible to resist and Cate put her eye to the gap, holding her breath. Charlie was over the trestle, wrists and ankles fastened to its legs with silk bands while another gagged her mouth. The head was twisted back with the eyes standing out and big tears rolled down the face. As Cate watched, enthralled, Cassie swung the martinet with a will and the body jerked. The rear end on display was already well-streaked and was plainly going to become even more so.

Cate unzipped her jeans, worked two fingers into her moistening cunt then put them in her mouth. The tang of her own arousal made her wetter still, but it also brought to mind the disastrous first encounter with Marissa three months ago. But they'd had some fine

173

sexy times between that and the sorry end of it all when she'd just slunk off with her tail between her legs. Cate shook her head and concentrated on the scene in front of her. Eyes fixed on the thongs that lashed again and again across the ripe bouncing curves, she needed only a few deft strokes against her clit to bring herself off, teeth clenched to keep from making a sound. As the spasms subsided she saw a contented-looking Cassie hand over the whip, then lean forwards and put her lips to Charlie's glowing behind. Kiss-and-make-up time: it looked as though Marjory's plan was going to work. As she went softly upstairs Cate made a decision there and then that she would go back and reclaim Marissa. If a novice like Cassie could bring a wayward lover to heel with a whip, how much more could she hers? She was going to flog the nonsense out of her and Marissa would love it!

Cate pulled off her jeans in front of the mirror, remembering what it was like to have that head busy between her legs, but with an effort kept her hand away from the place. First things first. She sat down on the bed and smoothed out the photocopy she'd made in the stacks when the light had nearly gone. It was a note on an official memo sheet headed 'Harold Jameson, Rare Books Catalogue Department, British Library,' and with a little difficulty she made out the scrawled message.

Jude – The house is called Inglewhite and it's in Lancashire fell country, miles from any proper road (see attached map). If you're thinking of going *be careful*. The old woman is reputedly completely crazy so who knows what reception you'll get. Come down on *business* soon, eh? Love, H.

Attached map. Shit. Either the lady had it stashed somewhere or she'd missed it in the dark. Well, she wasn't going to find it now and she could hardly go back in the morning. Never mind, she would find a way. For the present her head was full of images of Charlie tied to the trestle and Cassie about to kiss it all better. Cate was jealous of the passionate love they would be making, no doubt right at that moment, but she could conjure up the memory of her own exploration of that secret furrow. It was the best she was going to get that night and she lay down resigned under the covers to let her hand delve where it was itching to go.

PART III

17

Send-off

The summary dismissal of the boss's favourite caused a ripple of conversation as the small group filtered back into the main office.

'Good fucking riddance!' Judith was scowling at the memory of her short but vicious beating at the blonde American's hands and Grace touched her arm.

'I did try to see a better side, but she's been way out of order from the start. I mean, pushing out your friend while you were away, and now see the state of Mrs Rowleigh.' The ill-treated Marjory referred to was in fact making her excuses and, when she had gone, Miss James settled herself on the sofa and started on the two young students. In no time she had the one caught *in flagrante* held fast over her lap while she made soothing noises to the still-tearful other and fondled her between the legs. It seemed the director might have her hands full for some time so Judith caught Grace's eye and made a gesture towards the door. The potent cocktails dispensed had made her bold enough to take a chance and she hoped the outwardly reserved young secretary was feeling the same. In response, she gave a little nod and a wink then cleared her throat ostentatiously.

'Er, excuse me, Miss James, but if you don't need me any more I'd like to get an early night.' Judith shrank a little, fearing the response to something she could easily construe as impertinence. But the recent dramatic confrontation seemed to have acted as a tonic for, after laying on another hearty slap and waiting for the squealing to die away, she looked round and beamed.

'Of course, my dear girl. You've played your part, as indeed has Judith. So why don't you both run along? I'm going to be fully occupied with these scamps.'

At the foot of the stairs the two young women let themselves out of the back door into the balmy air of the quad and slouched up against the wall in the shadow of the doorway.

'Loved your knickers, Jude.'

'Thanks. Whole point though with these string briefs is *not* to see them because the trousers are supposed to stay up for a whacking. Supposed to. With this stickler we've got here, it's odds-on they're going to come down anyway.' They both giggled, then Judith put her hands to Grace's hips and looked her up and down. 'Great outfit. The proper little schoolgirl but with a secret: there are no pants under her smart pleated skirt. So when it's lifted and she's found out she gets spanked twice as hard.'

The talk was making Judith even hotter than she had been earlier watching Miss James apply a leisurely but firm paddle to Grace's soft white cheeks while her own were still stinging from the cane. She knelt down and cupped the warm bottom in her hands, then stuck her head under the skirt and started on the wet labia. The girl began to moan almost at once and Judith felt hands run over the stubble of her haircut as she worked her to a rapid climax. Then she unzipped the skirt and pulled it right off.

'OK. Now spread wide. All the drinks you've had tonight, there should be plenty of liquid in there. Just let it out bit by bit.'

'Jude, are you sure? I never, er, I mean . . .'

'Hush, just let it come. I'll take care of things down here. Trust me, you'll love it.' She fixed her open mouth

180

onto the mouth of Grace's vagina and a dribble started which turned into a hot jet. Again and again the spurts came, each one with a gasp of pleasure from the girl whose fingers cradled Judith's head while she swallowed. Eventually the flow dried up and she got to her feet.

'Oh, wow. I had no idea, no idea at all . . .'

'Yeah. Well, I owed you one for the witch hazel, remember? But look, girl, I'd better go. I don't want to get you in trouble.' Missing Harry as she was, Judith would have liked nothing better than to take the secretary home and fuck all night and all the next day. But the thought of him reminded her of the resolution she had made to be faithful. Well, sort of. OK, what she'd just done was sex, but it wasn't as bad as being fucked herself. All she'd really done was make the girl happy and that was all right, wasn't it? However, it seemed Grace had other ideas that were going to upstage the slightly tipsy inner debate.

'No way do you take off right now. Not before you get to come, too. And I have here the perfect thing for the job – every schoolgirl's best friend.' She delved into the inside pocket of her jacket and with a flourish produced a luminous green vibrator that started at once to give out an angry buzz. 'Right, let's have those pants down and let's have you down on all fours.' Judith made a token protest but when Grace straddled her and spread her legs she gave in, glad to be taken in charge. 'Now unless you want a spanking on top of these marks you'll keep still while Miss Jenny here makes her entrance. But of course, once she's well inside you're allowed to wiggle as much as you like.'

That night Judith was disturbed by confused dreams about Harry and Grace. In the end they went off arm-in-arm and she woke up sweating. Out of a heavy grey sky rain was drumming on the sloping roof below her bedroom window and she turned over but sleep

181

would not come back. She got up and mooched about the flat until at last it reached the time she could join the Saturday lunchtime drinkers in the pub. When she came back in it was after three and there was an envelope inside the door. She recognised Grace's writing at once and her pulse quickened, but the note inside was from Miss James calling her to a special meeting on Monday at 10 a.m.

Judith sat down on the bottom stair with the paper in her hand. It must be important if she'd sent Grace round with it outside normal working hours. Damn it, if she'd been in she would have seen the girl again, and – and what? It had to stop. She was only lusting after the secretary so badly because her request the week before to go back to the BL (and Harry) had been turned down. She had messed up badly, letting slip that he'd already emailed her lots on the house which the boss promptly demanded she hand over. No doubt the summons was to do with it all, and she might just get another chance to argue the need to go south.

Come the day, Judith dressed in a white nylon thong and new white trousers. She had the feeling that she would be bending over at some point in the morning and looking good might get her the favour she was after. In the mirror she saw the dark crew-cut and eyes set off by the white long-sleeved roll neck that covered her small braless breasts. As with all her tops it was short enough not to hide the full curves of the close-sheathed buttocks that she was going to flaunt once more quite shamelessly. OK, that would do. Now she had better go and find out what she was wanted for.

'Ah, Judith. Come in, come in. You are very prompt.' The director got up and came round from behind her desk. There was an excitement quite at odds with her usual air of laconic authority. 'What do you say to being dispatched on a mission? I would have sent Miss Carpenter, but since she has left us the task falls to you.

And I am sure you will do very well, even though it will be quite different from your usual manuscript work. I'm afraid there will be no time for more research at the British Library before you go; instead your information will have to come from the field. Though let me say I am aware that you have a more than professional interest in returning there, and on reflection I feel it's no bad thing to have a personal contact in such a place. Therefore I shall make an effort to accommodate your visits there in future.' She smiled and Judith tried to assimilate what she'd heard. Somehow the lady knew about Harry and was giving the liaison her blessing. Well, in the longer term she supposed that was good news, but before she could register a response the rather worryingly manic Miss James had swept on.

'But for now, Judith, I am sending you north to Inglewhite and I want to mark the occasion with a little ritual of our own. So would you please indulge me by taking off your trousers?' Judith stared. There was only one ritual she knew of in this office to do with the removal of trousers and that involved a cane from the rack in the cupboard. However, there were worse things in life than submission to her boss – at least now the American was gone – so she obeyed with only the smallest of sighs.

'Good. Now put your boots back on, my dear, and let me have a look at you. Turn round, would you? Oh, yes, very fine –' Judith knew the words meant eyes fixed on the cheeks divided by a thin white strip of material and blushed '– I'm sure I have told you before that you have a bottom simply made for chastising.'

But she hadn't. Told her, that is. While the director had never concealed the pleasure she took in Judith's corporal discipline, neither had she declared it. This was a new and embarrassing departure. But there was no time to consider the matter for she was handed a thick piece of leather with a cloth and a small bottle.

'Now, sit down here at the desk, Judith. I'll explain to you exactly what I want you to do and while you listen you can give my new instrument a good dose of oil. I do hope you understand that when I apply it to you later it will not be as a punishment – after all you have done nothing to merit such – but as a kind of send-off on your journey.'

What was required of her was to 'infiltrate' the house and send a report of the ritual practices Miss James was convinced were to take place in the next couple of weeks. It was simple to describe – if scarcely simple of accomplishment – but the director's excited mood made her unusually verbose and the blade of the leather paddle was well slick before it was taken from her. Then the tall desk was brought centre-stage and Judith bent over it in the customary way.

'Excellent, my dear. Now just try to relax.' The paddle began to smack down on each buttock in turn, gently at first then with gradually increasing force. It was astonishing: quite unlike the effect of the angry cane, this sting, although it grew steadily more fierce, was building up a heat that fed straight to her lubricating loins. Then the unthinkable happened. Miss James's discipline was always a meticulously formal affair where there was no contact except with the device used to inflict it. But now there were fingers in the waistband of her thong and a voice was asking: 'May I?'

In disbelief Judith croaked, 'Yes,' and felt the thong peeled down and away from between the buttocks and then, incredibly, fingers pressed into her brimming cunt. It sent a jolt right through her body when they found the clitoris and began to work it between them. In only seconds she was about to explode.

'Miss James, if you do that – uh – any more – I'm going to – uh – going to –'

But she was cut short when the paddle cracked again hard across her behind four times. The pain brought her back from the edge, gasping, and then the fingers returned to their manipulation. And so it proceeded until Judith was a sweating seething mass of sensation. When she cried out at last: 'No more. Please, no more!' the touch stayed firm and took her to the very top. And, coming down in a welter of hot meltings, she thought getting a send-off like that could make her want to go on more journeys.

Afterwards there was only one possible thing to do and she squatted to unbutton the director's breeches, in her buzzing brain the awkward thought that she had been in the same position just the other night with this woman's secretary. What a *slag*. But when the silk knickers were lowered past the wet curls what she saw wiped any such notions from her mind. There, between the engorged oozing lips, was a spur of inflamed flesh the thickness of a child's finger. Jesus fuck. If that was a clit, then . . . Bewildered, she looked up.

'I'll tell you some day, my dear. But for now please be gentle. It is very sensitive.'

Judith pushed her head forwards and lapped with her tongue. Then she took the dark meat of the protuberance between her lips and gave it a tentative nip with her teeth. There was a cry from somewhere beyond pleasure and pain and hands wrenched her shoulders while pungent juices flooded into her mouth.

18

Trade

Cate woke early and made a snap decision. If she wanted the location of the mysterious house then she had to go to the source of the information she'd lifted from the Archive, and go in person. That way she could pass herself off as still working for Miss James. So she got up before Marjory was astir, wrote her a note and left for the station. With a degree of luck she would be in London well before noon, track down her man at the British Library and be back before the end of the day.

On the train she rehearsed the story she would tell of a last-minute decision that Judith needed back-up but had gone off with the only copy of the directions. Could she make it plausible? Cate was far from sure but she would have to run with it now. Her destination turned out to be directly opposite the terminus and she asked at the main desk if she could get to see Harold Jameson in Rare Books. He wouldn't know her name, but she was from the Nemesis Archive and he'd done some work with them. The librarian went to an intercom on the wall and pressed a button several times. Then she spoke into it, cast a glance back at Cate and spoke again. When she came forwards it was to summon a flunkey who looked down his nose at her before leading the way in silence to the opposite end of the building. At the exit he pointed to a house on the end of a ree-lined crescent, shook his head with a look that said, ff you *must*, and left her to negotiate the traffic.

'Ms Carpenter, I'm Harry. Come into my lair.' He was a large man filling the doorway with a resonant voice unconstrained by the proximity of any reading room.

'Cate, please. With a C.' She shook the sizeable paw on offer and followed him through into the office.

'Now, what can I do for you? Archive business, I gather.' In response she blurted out her request whose justification seemed suddenly painfully thin.

'Well, I don't know, now. You see I've been working with your colleague on this one and I'm not sure that I should give out the information to anyone else. Tell you what, why don't I just give your boss a ring –?'

'No, don't do that, Mr Jameson –' Cate broke off but it was too late. She'd blown it. The cataloguer was looking at her with a kind of wry amusement.

'You must call me Harry. If you want this to be, er, unofficial, then perhaps we can cut a deal. Do a trade: I give you what you want, then you return the favour.'

Favour? The eyes were not unfriendly and Cate was more curious than apprehensive. 'But what kind of favour can I –?'

'Well, Cate, there's a couple of things. Without being more specific at this point, let's just say you have a certain reputation that makes me think you'd be willing to help with the first.' He went over to a stand inside the door and from amongst its assortment of umbrellas and walking sticks he drew out a cane which he handed to her, saying: 'I gather you're a dab hand with one of these.' Harry's matter-of-fact expression tempered her embarrassment and she took the yard of medium-weight rattan by the handle and swished it.

'Arnold! In here now!' The inner door opened at once and a lad in maybe his late teens came through it. 'I've decided to bring forward the punishment you were due to receive this afternoon. Remind me what it was for.'

'Trying to remove a book, Mr Jameson.'

'And what kind of a book, Arnold?'

'A triple-X classified, Mr Jameson.'

'And what is the penalty for that, Arnold?'

'Six, Mr Jameson. With the cane.'

'For a first offence, Arnold, yes. But this was the second time you have been caught. So the tally should be –'

'– twelve, Mr Jameson.'

'Correct. Now, we're going to take advantage of Ms Carpenter's presence to have her administer the strokes. Not only is she an expert with the cane, but she is also a very attractive young woman. I have to say, Arnold, you do not deserve this special treatment, and you are to make sure you thank her properly afterwards. Understood?'

'Yes, Mr Jameson.'

It was plain that the interchange was a ritual into which she had been incorporated, no doubt to add a frisson for one or even both parties. But Cate was not complaining: the boy was undeniably cute and, while perhaps not exactly willing, certainly compliant. Harry ordered him to drop his trousers and bend over, saying that the underpants could be retained seeing they were in the presence of a lady, and besides their outline perfectly defined the part of the body to be dealt with. Then his head was pushed down between the tree-trunks of Harry's thighs while his hands clamped the wrists and pulled them up into the small of his back. Cate looked with a smile at the snug triangle of navy briefs that enclosed the neat out-thrust buttocks. He was going to feel a dozen concentrated in that one area. If this was doing Harry a favour, he could call on her any time.

She took aim and lammed into the centre of the target, leaving a line of impact printed across the cotton. There was a muffled noise and the boy writhed, but in the older man's grip he wasn't going anywhere. Five more strokes created clearly-marked horizontals from the band at the waist to the elasticated legs. Halfway. Cate paused to let the twitching in the hips and thighs subside, then laid the second instalment of six, one by one, into the spaces left between the first. After the last she had to master an urge to yank down the skimpy garment and feast her eyes on what was underneath. To judge from the way the red-faced youth shot upright and clutched at his behind when he was released, it would be quite a sight. Then as he rocked she saw that what had been a modest bulge at the front was now long and thick in its thin sheathing. She had seen this effect before but it still surprised her that such obvious pain could make a cock stand rigid. Harry moved between them, blocking her view, but Cate was almost certain he put his hand to the boy's erection.

'Pull up your trousers, lad, and thank our guest,' he said briskly, adding in an undertone, 'I'll see to you at the usual time.'

Arnold obediently tucked in his shirt and fastened his belt. 'Thank you, Miss, oh, sorry –' He put his hand to his mouth in confusion.

'I should think so, Arnold. She is not your primary school teacher, though one like her might have knocked some sense into you. *Ms* is the correct form of address.'

'Thank you, Ms Carpenter.' He had recovered some composure and the flushed good looks were very alluring as he made his exit. Cate thought if she could fancy both ways why shouldn't Harry, and she wondered exactly who did what to whom when they had sex together. But then the cataloguer said something that brought her firmly down to earth.

'Thanks, Cate, though I don't suppose it was too much of a burden. Now, as for the second thing . . .'

Shit. She'd forgotten there were two. And the way he was eyeing her this one wasn't going to be nearly as appealing.

'I'll come straight to the point. No doubt about your skill with one of these –' he picked up the cane and flicked it through the air '– but what about your judgement of who gets it and how hard? I hear you were out of order with my Judith, once. In fact, way out of line.' Cate looked at the instrument in his hands. Oh, God, he wanted to get revenge by using it on *her*. She backed towards the door holding her hands up in front of her.

'No way. No fucking way.'

'Oh, dear, language. You young women these days.' But then he laughed and returned the rod to its place. 'What I had in mind was a good old-fashioned spanking with this here hand.' He waggled its broad fingers and grinned at her. 'Though it does get sore very easily and by the time we've included an extra dose for swearing, I may have to get out my paddle.'

Cate scowled at him but she was secretly relieved. A hand-spanking – even a paddling – couldn't be that bad, could it? And if it was part of the deal, if it was her trade for what she needed, then she could grit her teeth and take it. Cate took a deep breath and forced herself to speak evenly. 'OK, I'll do it. But I want the information I need first. Just so you don't spank me and then tell me to fuck off.'

'I meant what I said about language, Cate.' He went to the drawer and took out a segment of the large scale Ordnance Survey chart. 'It's all marked there, exactly the same as Judith has. Though I'm locking the door before you put it in your bag and not unlocking it until you've removed your skirt, bent over my desk and taken your medicine. Do we have a deal?'

Remove her skirt? Well, she could hardly be hand-spanked over it. Perhaps it was past time to revise the no-underwear policy, a thought confirmed when Harry shook his head, tut-tutting, as it came off.

'Oh, dear. The full professional suit, stockings and smart shoes and underneath it all no knickers. I might

190

have said keep them on for modesty's sake but now you've done it, young lady. I suppose it goes with the f-word, really.'

In spite of her predicament Cate almost chuckled. It was difficult not to warm to this big man with his pantomime of fogeyish disapproval. Then he placed two thick cushions on the desk and over she went, heart thumping. This was it.

The first blows were more like cuffs coming from underneath and she felt how they made the cheeks lift and bounce. After a while he said, 'You're too tense; just relax and go with it.' She'd been keeping her legs tight together for fear of displaying how the boy's caning had aroused her, but now his hands slid between the stocking tops and she let him ease them apart. Now the slaps started in earnest and at each one she gave a little grunt. Gradually the hurt and the shame of her position was subsumed into a new state of being in which she was nothing but a pair of hot stinging buttocks and the sopping vulva in between. Something shifted deep inside her and a shocked Cate found herself arching her back and thrusting the spanked area right out.

'This is for the swearing.'

She felt the pressure of cool leather and then a volley of smacks that set her behind on fire. Something had to give. Digging her nails into the wood, she strained back at him with a hoarse gasp and his hand was on her wet lips.

'No. Not the cunt. In there. Please, in *there.*' Suddenly she was desperate for this man to do what Mark had done that night back in the spring.

'Oh, the c-word now, is it? I'm afraid that's going to cost.' After a moment's pause, a finger pushed a blob of something cold into the anus she was offering. The paddle came down six times with an energy that took her breath away and she felt his hardness force open the ring of muscle. Only when his hand clamped over her mouth did she realise she was yelling and then his fingers were where she'd said not, exploring. But Cate was past caring as the jerkings of her body broke into the full seizure of orgasm.

On the journey home she sat with her prize of the map open on her knee in a kind of trance. As the carriage clattered over points and junctions she was aware only of the violated rear end that glowed under her skirt. The caning had thrilled her as always, but this was something fresh. The domina paddled and buggered – oh, God, what would Gena say about it all? The thought brought her back to earth with a bump. She would write to the girl, apologise humbly for the crude grope that had driven her away, and say she would see her (if she could be forgiven) after the trip north. Marissa could only be dealt with in the flesh – suitably *bared* flesh – but it had to be a good idea to get in touch with Gena before she turned up back at the club in Seattle. In fact, she could reach her there without delay by email. Pleased with the decision, Cate tried yet again to study the route she would have to take to Inglewhite, but just then the train rounded a bend in the track. The motion drew her attention once more to the newly sensitive part of her anatomy and she fell back into a sexual reverie that lasted until her own station came into view.

Marjory had the Tuesday afternoon off and once lunch was done they sat down to talk over the venture. The map showed that the house holding the secrets of the ancient ritual lay in the depths of fell country to the north of Preston, separated from the trunk routes to the west by a maze of narrow lanes that connected small hamlets and farms. Isolated as these were, the place they were interested in was one stage further removed at the end of a long winding track through the hills. As they examined its location it transpired that Marjory had been a keen hiker in her youth and she took charge of the planning.

'I think there's only one thing for it, Cate. You won't be able to drive the last part except in something like a Land Rover and that would be far too conspicuous. The only way you'll get there without announcing your arrival is on foot.'

'Sure, Marjory. Two city blocks and I'm wiped out. Can you see me in the middle of nowhere, climbing hills?'

'No, I'm serious. Just take a look here. From the contours you can see that the track goes all the way up one valley, crosses a ridge and then zigzags down into another. If you went cross-country you could cut straight through and come out at the edge of this patch of wood above Inglewhite. It'll be ideal for a recce of the house: you'll see any people going to and fro without any danger of running into them while you make up your mind what to do.'

That was it: what the fuck was she going to do when she got there? But there was another, more practical problem. 'OK, Marjory. Let's suppose I hoof it. What do I do for gear?'

'My dear girl, it's been the driest weather we've had for years and it's set fair for at least another week. All you'll need to wear in these hills is sweatshirt, jeans and trainers on your feet. I can give you a rucksack with an anorak and a bedroll and if you add a few provisions you will be fully equipped. Oh, this brings back the old days. How I wish I could join you.'

In the evening they batted back and forth ideas on how Cate was to extract the crucial details of the rite, but came to the conclusion that without prior knowledge of the members of the household it was impossible to fix on a strategy. She was just going to have to play it by ear; if the worst came to the worst she could possibly intercept the report that Judith would be sending out (if

193

Grace's intelligence were to be believed). The topic exhausted, at least for the present, Marjory suggested a drink.

'I don't suppose with your background that you drink gin, Cate. But I've got all the ingredients for a proper martini if you'd like to try one.' It sounded like a good proposal and when she emerged from the kitchen with a large cocktail shaker and glasses they settled down in the sitting room. While they drank Marjory asked whether the visit to the BL had gone smoothly and Cate told her tale of the cataloguer with a penchant for spanking young women's bottoms.

'You *are* coming on, my dear. You'll soon be well-rounded in more senses than one, if you'll forgive the pun.' Cate giggled, then stopped. There had been a notion in her head since the morning and under the heady influence of the alcohol she had to get it out.

'What I didn't say was that I also caned a young guy – a very handsome young guy – in his underwear while his boss held him down. And these days I think – well, I *think* I think – that I shouldn't hand out what I can't or won't take myself. Yeah?' Marjory nodded but before she could speak Cate ran on. 'It was a dozen – hard – with a kinda standard instrument like maybe a yard long. If you got one, do you think you could use it? On me, I mean, of course. Like I did to him. Only trouble is, I don't have a pair of underpants to my name.' The finish sounded lame and she looked into her glass and emptied it.

'Cate, dear girl, if that's what you want, certainly I'll oblige. I'm very glad you asked, especially when it was difficult. My only concern is that you might be trying to go too fast.'

'I want to square up for yesterday before I go off tomorrow. If that makes any sense.'

'Yes, I believe it does. I think I can supply both of your needs and when I have perhaps we should do the thing sooner rather than later.'

'Right. As soon as you're ready.' She managed a firm tone but fear gripped the pit of her stomach.

'I hope you won't think me inhospitable when I suggest we postpone further drinks until recovery time afterwards. So, if you want to go downstairs, Cate, I'll be with you directly.'

Ten minutes later Cate was hugging the trestle in a pair of bottle-green school knickers that Marjory must have been wearing around the time she was born. By request her wrists and ankles were secured with the same silk bands she had seen used on Charlie two days before. She feared will-power on its own might not keep her body in place and if the worst came to the worst she would be able to stop the beating with a single word. In the moments before the ordeal began she was trying to hold on to the phrase Marjory had used: 'recovery time'. There was time *beyond* punishment, if she could just get through to it. Then the rattan whacked into the fleshiest part of her seat and speculation was at an end: there was only pain and the need to survive it.

The deputy principal did not stint her task and stroke followed burning stroke in a measured sequence until the count was reached. Each one made Cate give out sharp cries and wrench at her bonds while its effect reached a peak, after which there was a brief respite before the next cut repeated the process. When the final crisis had passed Marjory untied her and she sagged weakly along the length of the padded top.

'I'll leave you alone now. When you feel able to come upstairs, I'll have another martini waiting.'

In the corner of the couch was a large soft cushion and Cate perched on it swigging gratefully from the tall glass. Yesterday's spanking had left her a bit sore, but the present indescribable tenderness of the butt belonged in a different league. From the armchair her erstwhile chastiser was looking concerned.

'You managed very well, dear. I was worried I might have overdone it.'

'I asked for hard, Marjory. But, beside the young guy in the catalogue room, I'm no stoic.' She thought of all her vocalising with a touch of shame.

'Ah, but by the sound of it he gets plenty of practice, Cate. Though I do have to say that's likely to be the best hiding those knickers have ever had. Why don't you keep them as a souvenir.'

'Well, thanks. They'll go down a bomb as a piece of fetish wear back home.'

Marjory laughed. 'I dare say they will. The genuine English article, once to be found clothing many a private schoolgirl's bottom. And I can tell you, it was just as well they were regulation wear. When a culprit was bent over at the front of the class for the strap, at least there were no surprises when her skirt was folded up.'

'Ouch.' In her present state Cate winced at the thought even of leather connecting with her rear end. 'Did it happen often?'

'I'm afraid it did. Our senior mistress was a dragon who believed we were all guilty of some punishable crime. But it wasn't so terrible, and I know I wasn't the only one who found the spectacle quite stimulating. Especially when a well-developed girl was on the receiving end. It was a broad tawse most of the time that didn't really hurt too much, but it certainly made the cheeks bounce! Now I think of it, it seems obvious that the dragon herself took more than a punitive interest in what she was doing, but such an idea would have never entered our heads at the time. But here I am wittering on while you're sitting there with an empty glass. Do let me give you a refill.'

'Only if I get a proper briefing on these schooldays of yours. It's like they're from another planet than my own.' Marjory was quite happy to recount some of the formative experiences provided by her rather exclusive education while Cate drank and plied her with questions. Eventually the older woman looked at the clock.

'You mustn't encourage me any more, Cate. I've enjoyed reminiscing, but wouldn't you say you could do with an early night? And I'm not just thinking about the journey you'll be taking tomorrow. I find myself that certain after-effects of a good thrashing can take quite a while to emerge, but when they do, well, one needs to be alone.'

Cate blushed at the pertinence of the remark. For some minutes she had been aware of an increasing state of lubrication – as yet absorbed by the well-lined gusset between her legs – that couldn't really be explained by her host's stories, sexy though they were. No, the lady was spot on: now she was out of shock the throbbing ache of the bruises had set off another throbbing that demanded to be satisfied.

After they had said their goodnights Cate went up to her bedroom and found a large hand-mirror in the cupboard. Standing in front of the dressing table she peeled down the green pants with their sodden crotch and explored what she found with her fingertips. The whole area was hot and ridged and the slightest touch made her flinch. Then she held the mirror to give her a rear view and saw the mass of reds and purples. Oh, God. That's what the guy would have looked like after she'd finished with him. And now it was what *she* looked like. Her cunt dripped and she cupped her hand to it and when she pressed into the labia she came at once in spasms more violent than any she had known before. Then, exhausted, she crawled into her bed and slept.

19

Tanning

As soon as she was in the car Judith knew the ultra-tight 501s were a mistake. She had gone for stout boots and a unisex zip-top affair but couldn't resist showcasing her best feature. So it should have been no surprise really that when a flashy Jag came to a halt it wasn't her thumb that was on the driver's mind. As they sped north he delivered a flow of suggestive talk about the 'freedom' of young women these days while his hand kept sliding from the gearstick on to her thigh. She cracked short of her intended destination and demanded out but instead of stopping on the main road he shot down a narrow lane for several hundred yards. Then he pulled over into a grassy clearing, switched off the engine and lunged at her. Somehow she released her seat belt and half-tumbled out of the car. He was not pleased but he made no move to come after her. Instead he leaned over and said with venomous scorn: 'Nothing but a tease. I ought to have known. What girls like you need is a bloody good spanking.' Then he pulled the door shut, reversed back on to the side-road and roared off leaving her staring at a cloud of exhaust fumes.

Judith smiled grimly and sat down on a fallen tree. He was quite a hunk and if he'd only hauled her over his knee and carried out the prescription, then he'd very likely have got what he was wanting in the first place.

More fool him. But now she had to work out where she was and how far she had to go to reach the beginning of the Inglewhite track. The map seemed to put her at the southern edge of a network of tiny roads with little option but to leg it vaguely northwards until she found a place she could identify. Well, there was no point in hanging about so she stood up, hoisted the bag on to her back and set off in a positive frame of mind.

An hour later she was rather less cheerful. At first the bright sunshine had raised her spirits but the relentless tramping, mostly uphill, was taking its toll. The jacket had come off but she was still sweating profusely, the unsuitable jeans were chafing the inside of her thighs and the unaccustomed boots were making her feet sore. And, to cap it all, there was still no real clue to her location. Not a single vehicle had passed and the few farmhouses she had seen were set back from the road, unnamed, with a forbidding air about them. They were not places that invited a passer-by to knock and ask directions and in any case she didn't want to alert anyone in the locality of where she was going. It hadn't helped that the lanes ran mostly between high banks, so there was no wider view from which to take her bearings. Then, all of a sudden, after puffing her way up a sharp gradient Judith found herself at a junction on the edge of open country.

And there it was. Surely, it had to be. The metalled road ran to left and right but in front of her was a track that meandered up a gently sloping valley and disappeared over a ridge. She leaned on the gate and checked the map. Yes, she was right: there was only one house any distance at all from a road in the whole area. She took a long drink from the bottle of water in her bag then splashed some of it over her face. There was a good breeze coming off the hill and at last she knew where she was. Using the stile stones built into the dyke to climb over it, Judith set off at a jauntier pace despite her aches and pains. Things were looking up.

When she came to the second gate there was the sound of an engine in the distance. Behind her the road was out of sight and with luck it could be just a passing car. But the note was steady for a few seconds and then it changed. Whatever it was had moved off and was heading in her direction: they must be going to the house. There was a low wall that ran for a few yards at right angles to the gate and she crouched quickly behind it, holding her breath while the engine noise got louder and louder. The vehicle stopped right beside her and she risked a peep: it was an ancient pick-up. Now *that* was too good a chance to miss. When she heard the scraping of rusty hinges Judith leaped out of cover and pulled herself up into the back of it. The door banged and she burrowed under a pile of sacks while they travelled through the gate, then lay, heart in mouth, while it was closed behind them. Then the door banged a second time and they were off.

It wasn't the most comfortable of rides bumping and rattling over ruts and potholes and it didn't help that she had to keep her head under dust-filled hessian while two more gates were negotiated. Then they drew up once more, the engine died and she heard the driver get out. After a pause she stuck out her head and breathed the air with relief, though there was a sickly-sweet smell to it that she couldn't place. It looked all clear, so she jumped down but before she could move there was an iron grip on her arm. He towered over her, making resistance pointless, and Judith allowed herself to be led into one of the outbuildings that flanked the yard. OK, then. She had wondered how she was going to approach the household and now it had been done for her.

The place was a stable for two horses with a sizeable workbench in the middle of the floor at one end. From this he took a length of rope and tied her wrists tightly behind her back, then he buckled her ankles together with a strap and pushed her down on to a straw-covered pallet in the corner. 'Stay there,' he ordered and picked up her bag.

She wanted to ask what the fuck else he thought she could do, but on balance decided that the sassy comeback was not good policy. And before she could change her mind he had disappeared out of the door. By now it had dawned on her that this must the the groom of the diary she had read, though nearly two decades on. The ginger hair and beard were not the wild things the girl had described but neatly cropped, tending to confirm Judith's suspicions she had embellished the tale. But what about the other proclivities she had given him? Well, the way she was trussed up, she was going to be around to find out.

It seemed an age before he returned and the first thing he did was to light a large paraffin lamp that hung from the ceiling. It was still bright outside in the late afternoon but not much of it filtered through the one grimy window. He stooped down close to her and unfastened the ankle-strap then stared her in the face. 'Behave,' he said firmly and set about unlacing her boots. It was bliss when she could waggle her sore toes, but then he pushed her back and reached for the buttons on her jeans. When they were off he pulled her to her feet and she stood in front of him in socks, white T-shirt and black thong while he looked her up and down. Her heart was nervously a-flutter, but there were too the tell-tale stirrings in her groin.

Now he took off the leather apron he was wearing and spread it over the middle of the rough bench between a pair of vices. From the back he lifted her by the upper arms and laid her face down across it in one movement. Her feet didn't touch the ground and with her hands still tied behind her she was stranded, wriggling on her belly. She could hear the horses moving the other side of the partition and her nostrils were full of the reek of leather. It was of course a tannery smell she'd caught in the yard and she choked back an hysterical giggle as she felt the huge hand on her bum. Tanning – of a somewhat different kind – was exactly what she was in for.

He spanked with only moderate force but steady persistence and after several minutes had passed Judith was squirming with the glowing smart of her rump. Then the thin band of material was peeled away from between the buttocks and a finger probed underneath. The 'hot-wired' cunt she shared with Grace had been lubricating from the start of the proceedings and he showed his appreciation of its state.

'Good *girl*,' he said and made her squeal with three hard slaps across the bottom. He was evidently a man of few words and all of them would have done for a dog. But then what was she at that moment but a bitch in heat for whom words were neither here nor there. She felt his cock nose into the wet opening and his hands position her hips so she would take its rigid length in up to the hilt. Unlike Harry's fucking, this was brutally simple, but it was exactly what she needed, and with his coarse-haired thighs ramming into her stinging cheeks she climaxed in the seconds it took him to do the same.

'All right, G, you've had your fun. Both of you, by the looks of it. You can bring the girl in and for God's sake untie her wrists, she's not going to run.'

He was still erect when he pulled slowly out of her and Judith felt petulant at being deprived of a second instalment. In the doorway was a woman of about fifty – *his* age, she supposed, was more than that; though the weatherbeaten complexion made it hard to tell – who was looking at them as if they were a pair of unruly children. He zipped up his trousers but Judith couldn't face pouring herself back into the 501s and settled for retrieving the thong. When they went in the back of the house she steered the two of them through a door to the left while the groom went straight on. They were in a room with a single bed and a table on which had been spread out the contents of her bag.

'I'm Judith and, er, you must be Annie.'

'I am indeed. And did you get an introduction to that husband of mine you were being so free with?' Judith felt her colour rising but Annie burst into laughter. 'It don't worry me, girl, I'm only setting you on. I can't be doing with him any more and the poor man has to take his pleasure where he can. Not that he often goes without, but we did just lose a maid who was soft on the old bugger. You help yourself if you like what he's offering.' She lowered her voice and leaned closer. 'We got more important things to talk about than him. I been looking at what you wrote and I'm not going to apologise for my nosiness because I reckon we might be able to help each other out. So you just sit yourself there while I go and make us a cup of tea and then we'll see if we can do a deal.'

Given that Judith knew about the central insemination ritual, it didn't take Annie long to bring her up to date. J A's twins had been trained up and last year they were ready. But then the whole thing came unstuck: after they'd done the ceremony the girl didn't fall pregnant. Twice more they tried with no better luck before they found out she was infertile. So now the old lady sat all day brooding in the attic while the maid had been sent to take the girl to the other branch of the family in the south and bring back her cousin Joan. And they were going do the thing with her in ten days' time.

Annie shook her head disapprovingly. 'I don't reckon it's any surprise they're having trouble the way they're inbred.'

'So what's the point of it all? What happens if they get it to work this time?'

'No good asking me, girl. It's way above my head. But there's books and a pile of papers I can let you have a look at. Maybe you can make some sense of them.'

203

'Great. That's just what I need if I'm going to send off a report. But what is it that you want *me* for?'

'Well, I'll tell you. That maid I said we had leave, she was part of it. There have to be two on the day, as you know, and there's a few things to do first. The new girl will have to be whipped when she arrives and there'll be a couple more sessions with young James.'

'That sounds OK.' Judith remembered the bits about keeping the boy's erection up under punishment: she could manage that fine.

'There is one thing, though. You can't start without getting a taste of the cat yourself from the old lady. It might not be too bad and then again she might really lay into you. I can't say, it all depends on her mood. I can set that up for the day after tomorrow if you want.'

Judith made a gesture of submission. Spanking was one thing, but she *never* wanted the more severe treatments. However, when needs must . . .

'All right, I'll see to it. Now, we'd better get you organised. For a girl going on a big journey you weren't carrying much.' Judith looked sheepishly at what was on the table. Apart from the manuscripts and her own notes, there was a bottle of water, a sandwich, a pair of socks and a multi-coloured pack of five satin thongs. Talk about the bare minimum. The problem had been that, lacking an idea of what she was going to do when she got to the house, she hadn't been able to pack clothes to do it in.

'Don't worry about it. I think we can fix you up with Jeanie's old stuff. I didn't tell you that she took ill soon a month after the birth and there was nothing they could do. When they got her to hospital she only lasted a week.'

'Oh, God.' Judith had warmed to the girl who got carried away with her tales, and it turned out she had hardly outlasted her writing.

'She was about your size, give or take. Look, I'm sure she'd have wanted you to use anything, you being so interested in her story and such. Come on up with me now and we'll have a sort through.'

The wardrobe was crammed with rather girlish clothes but there were several frocks in plain muted colours and some flat-heeled shoes that Annie said would do fine around the house. She also dug out a blonde wig to hide the dark crew-cut and then showed Judith back down to the bathroom next door to her own. After she had wallowed in the tub for a while she emerged in the new disguise to find soup and a plate of salad ready in the kitchen. It was just the two of them – for G liked to eat early and then kept his own company in the stable or the small tannery – so Judith plied her with questions about the history of the house while they ate. Only when the evening light began to fade and the lamps were brought out did it dawn on her that Inglewhite was still without electricity.

'All except the leather business out back, and it's just a clanking old diesel thing he's got that would never do for in here. We got the stove for cooking and the water; there's plenty of wood and he fetches coal when we need it. So we're cosy enough. I don't really think about it.' She opened up a foot-high hurricane lamp and trimmed the wick before setting a match to it. 'Here, take this one. You can read by it if you turn it up and just carry it with you when you go anywhere.'

Judith took the bright lamp gratefully and said she'd call it a night. In her bedroom she stood looking at the apparition in the mirror with its blonde curls and dress that flared over the hips. Taking off the wig, she sat for a while, trying to make some notes about what she had learned that day, but was overcome with yawning. Then she heard footsteps leaving the kitchen and climbing the stairs: Annie must have gone to bed. Out of her window she could see a light burning in the stable and decided she was going to pay it another visit. There was no moon and she needed the lamplight to pick her way across the cobbled yard and through the half-open door at the other side. G was bent over a saddle harness with the tilley lamp picking out every line in his face. He made no sign but she was sure she had been noticed and sat quietly on a stool in the corner watching him work. Then without looking up he spoke.

'She take you on, then?'

'Yeah. She said I have to be whipped first. On Thursday. I thought . . . I thought you could show me what they'll use.'

He put a buckle-end on top of the vice and tapped it carefully with a hammer, then picked up the whole mass of straps and put it over by the wall.

'Nervous about it?' He looked full at her and Judith nodded. He went over to a wall-cabinet and took out a roll of oiled paper. It unwrapped to reveal a bunch of cream-coloured tails bound into a cord handle and he pulled her up from her seat and placed her hand on it.

'Ever had the cane?'

'Well, yes –'

'I mean proper, like. Bare bum and hard as he could lay it on.'

Or she. 'Yes. Yes, in fact, I have.'

'Well, it won't be no worse. Different, but no worse. If that's any comfort.'

It wasn't, when Judith thought of what the American bitch had done in just six strokes, and she no longer wanted to examine the whip. When she felt G reach under her skirt she turned him round to undo the ties on his apron. Taking the hint, he spread it as before over the bench and she went up on tiptoe to lie across the greasy leather. The big hands massaged her bum and thighs and he said: 'I better take it easy till after.' He spread her legs and felt deep into the wetness between them, but she stuck her arse out in reply to the words and got the half-dozen crisp smacks she was hoping for

206

to make her cunt brim over. Then he fucked her with long slow squelching thrusts and she heard the horses through the partition stir and whicker until their noise was drowned out by her own orgasmic cries.

Early in the morning she went back across the yard and he was with the horses. 'You ride?'

'I used to, but that was way back.' She stood close to the big animal while he inspected a shoe then he took her through to the workshop. Face down, ready, she wriggled her buttocks at him.

'Don't fret, girl. I'll give you a right royal tanning next week.' The flat of his hand stung her twice then he was inside and she came at once. When he pulled out she knelt down and licked their mingled juices off him while he stiffened under her tongue. She fondled the thing with its oozing purple head then took it full into her mouth and sucked until he spurted another shot of salty fluid. Then he pulled her up, turned her towards the door and slapped her behind. 'Go get your breakfast. Then I'll take you out.'

20

Proper Cat

In retrospect a well-caned bottom was not an asset on a long train journey, requiring as it did that she spend a lot of time standing in the buffet car. Nor did it improve the ride in the cab that threw her from side to side hurtling round narrow bends to reach the start of the track. But once she began to step out across open country the aches and pains were forgotten and now Cate lay at ease on her bedroll examining the buildings a few hundred yards away from her down the valley. Inglewhite consisted of four ramshackle but quite sizeable constructions that clustered at the back of the main farmhouse which was a substantial dwelling of three storeys under a slate roof. She caught a glimpse of figures in the yard but the light was beginning to fade and the binoculars could supply little more detail. Tired by the unaccustomed hill-walking, she turned over and yawned. Where she was – in a small clearing at the edge of a tree plantation – would do fine for the night and she was going to stretch out and sleep.

Awake at first light in the unfamiliar surroundings, Cate washed her face in a stream that was keeping its flow despite the dry weather, and breakfasted on biscuits and what was left of the orange juice. She would have to make a move before long, and the house was the only direction it made any sense to take. But now he morning was growing warm and she was feeling drowsy when a movement caught her eye and she reached for the glasses. A bearded man came out leading a horse, mounted it and rode out of the yard. Prepared to dive into thicker cover, Cate relaxed again when he travelled only a short distance down the track then branched from it and cantered away. After a while he vanished over a distant ridge and she allowed herself to nod off. When she came to it was midday and there was no sound except a skylark high above her. In the heat she stripped off and lay with the sun on her back. It must be all the fresh air or something but again she was fighting a losing battle against the urge to doze.

Then out of nowhere there was a whinny right at her side and she rolled over, clutching at her jeans. He was an enormous figure in the saddle, blotting out the sun until he swung down off the horse and pushed it away to graze. Cate got to her feet and he took her arm and turned her round, his gaze on her marked rear end.

'Been naughty, is it, or do that get you going?' It was the groom from the house and if she co-operated he might help her, but words would not come. She wanted to explain that normally she wielded the instrument and the stripes he could see came from a special experiment-cum-penance, so the answer was really both. But it was far too complicated so she settled for the feeble 'Now and then.'

'So would "now" be now, like? Or would that be a bit soon after "then"?' He looked hard at her and Cate swallowed. She had to get a grip on the proceedings. Assuming this was the man in Judith's old diary, she knew his predilections, and if she was going to be spanked on a still-sore butt she'd better arrange something good in return.

'Depends. I need to get into the house to find out about the ceremony.'

'American, eh?'

'Yeah. I'm going back as soon as I finish my research.'

'I can land you in the thick of it. You'll get to know the lot from there.' There was an amused glint in his eye that Cate did not like one bit. But if she turned away this chance it was unlikely she would get another. She dropped the jeans she'd been holding to her crotch and stood naked in front of him.

'OK, you're on. So it's you to play.'

He went without a word to a capacious saddle bag and took out some things. First there was a small bundle of thongs, then a bottle of liniment and finally a heavy waxed coat which he folded up and placed on a tree stump in the middle of the patch of grass. Cate got the picture and went over it, legs wide. She guessed an inspection was coming and saw no point in pretending to a modesty she did not feel. All that interested him was arse and cunt and that was exactly what she was presenting him with. With the palms of her hands on the ground taking her forwards weight Cate was quite comfortable and lay passive as his fingers explored the residual bruises from Marjory's efforts with the cane and began to massage in some of the soothing oil. When he had satisfied himself that she was producing her own flow of fluids, he picked up the miniature cat and swished it backwards and forwards across her bottom and thighs. It was not much more than a fly-whisk that at first barely tingled but as he persisted it began to sting like a horde of tiny insects biting. After more liniment there was more light whipping and he alternated the two until her whole posterior was a prickling, melting mass of sensation that had to be released.

At last there was his cock nosing between her hot cheeks and she heard the hoarse demand of her own voice. 'Arse. Fuck me in the arse.' Just like she'd done with Harry; it was as if the uniquely female part of her was being kept for women only. Was it Marissa she had n mind? Cate couldn't tell and further self-analysis was put on hold as the thick length penetrated deeper and deeper into her colon. Oh, God, was he big. Light-headed with all the stimulation, Cate moved with him as he thrust in and out, gathering momentum, and when she felt him jerking in her tight muscle her own spasms swept her away. He moved inside her still as she came slowly down and then he pulled out and she cleaned them both off at the stream. Three anal fucks with three different men and two of them in this one week. And the last was the biggest yet. Whatever anyone else might think, she was going to mark it down as progress.

Later in the afternoon he took her down to the house crouched at his back, the saddle sticking to the sensi-tised flesh below her raised dress. When they arrived there was no sign of anyone stirring and he took her into the stables.

'You stay here till I fix you up inside.' He lit a lamp hanging over the workbench and Cate put her things on the bunk bed he indicated in the corner. She smoothed down the short grey outfit he had said would do (not that there was a big choice in her rucksack) and watched him unroll a length of oiled paper. Inside was a whip of the same design as the one he had used on her but it was a good two feet long and the creamy-white tongues were as thick as her little finger.

'Go on. Pick it up.' The handle was greasy to the touch and her nostrils wrinkled with the whiff of newly tanned leather. He must do it himself out the back. She counted ten tails, one more than the expected nine, then swished it through the air. The supple weight betokened a serious instrument and when she slapped it lightly across her palm the tails curled and wrapped round it in a way that made her shiver.

'That there is a *proper* cat. It's my estimate you'd be happy to watch one being used.'

His eyes were fixed on hers in the harsh light of the tilley and Cate felt abashed that she was so easy to read. Shit. It had to be totally lame to balk at acknowledging an interest the man plainly shared. With an effort she managed to say: 'Sure I would.' The words at least amounted to a yes even if they still concealed her real excitement at the prospect.

'Then we'll go in and see the show.'

She followed him across the yard and into a dark passage that turned to the right. At its end he opened a door and pushed her in, putting a finger to his lips and pointing to a bench just inside. They were in a space not unlike a small chapel, except that where the altar should be there was a marble slab end-on between two white columns on which torches burned with an eerily bright, smokeless light. Two nearer columns, also bearing torches, were joined by a cross-member a few feet from the ceiling into which were fixed three stout iron rings. To the centre one were roped the wrists of a young blonde in a short brown cloak at a height that obliged her to stretch up on to the balls of her feet. She faced towards the massive slab and in front of her was a white-robed woman with a shock of snow-white hair and a nose like a crow's beak, who was holding out a duplicate of the whip Cate had just examined.

'You know that no one can serve Her until they have been served by this instrument that is dedicated to Her.' The old voice quavered but there was a keening note that commanded attention. 'Do you therefore submit your body to the Cat that you may so submit others?'

'I do.' The reply was scarcely audible from the back but it was obviously acceptable.

'Gag her and bare her.' When she stood back another woman, middle-aged, came forwards to do as bid and Cate saw there were three other figures on seats near the front. Two looked like maids while the third seemed to be a young man. It was difficult to see much detail in the strange light but none of them was identifiably Judith. If she hadn't made it then the field would be wide open for an exclusive investigation, one that Cate could claim as hers alone.

The cloak was removed to reveal a long back and a slender waist that flared out into broad hips with a jutting behind. When the chastiser came out into full view and swung her weapon it was plain that age had not diminished her vigour. The helpless, suspended body twitched and jerked with each *hiss-crack!* of the descending thongs that curled now over the shoulder blade and now into the armpit until the whole back was a network of red streaks. Then the initiate was turned to face front and the woman assisting took a glass of water and dashed it into her face. The head jerked back, eyes wide, and then contorted in agonised disbelief as the lash attacked the small high breasts. But while Cate stared she saw only one thing and that was in her mind's eye: a dark cropped head that in sudden recognition she knew to be hidden under the fair curls. It was the missing Judith who was strung up from the cross-beam getting a taste of the 'proper' cat.

Now it was the turn of the belly and thighs to be marked by the relentless tails after which the drooping head was once more doused into life. Drawn in again by the corporal spectacle Cate saw the body turned back away and the whip begin its work on the final posterior quarter. She had thought Judith's a beauty of an arse when it was tight over a desk at the Archive, but here the full meat of it was on display as the force of the lash made one cheek then the other lift and bounce and ripple. Herself lubricating freely, Cate thought what bliss it would be to get her head between those molten mounds. Once her tongue got working she'd soon soon take the girl's mind off her smarting welts. She put her hand on the trousered lap beside her and felt the erection that stiffened further at her touch. As the cat was cast aside and the final splash of reviving water dripped off the victim's face, Cate took hold of the man's hand to pull him to the door and out to the stable. Judith's cunt might be on her mind but her own cunt was impatient for the instant action of that thick cock on her clit. So much for females only. It was still a good principle but there were times when a girl just had to do what a girl had to do.

21

Pain and Pleasure

It was the arms that all but undid her. Bad though the whip was on the soft flesh beneath her breasts, it came in discrete slices of anguish that were eventually at an end. But the torment of her strained sockets was a constant as each cut of the lash defeated the attempt to take more of her weight on to her feet. So it was almost a relief when the old lady started in on her behind for it signalled a conclusion. And she could make a better effort under the familiar pain to plant her legs and push up.

At last unroped, Judith sagged against Annie on the blessedly short walk to her room. No doubt it was true that the marks would fade much sooner than cane weals but for the present she could not bear to be touched and rejected the offer of any aftercare except a cup of hot sweet tea. Alone she stood in front of the mirror and winced at the sight of the cross-hatchings scored from neck to knees; had she known about the first-hand experience of the Nemesis Cat that was in store she would have told Miss James exactly where to stuff her inquiry. The rump she stuck out at the glass was crimson and the welts were hot and hard under her fingers. For the first time she became aware that she was wet between the legs and then it hit her. What she needed was not a bathe or a massage but a good fuck. And she needed it right now.

Draping the cloak over her sore shoulders she stole quietly out across the yard, but a breathless voice coming from inside stopped her dead, hand on latch.

'Oh, God. Oh, yes. Jee-sus, that's good. Yes, oh, yes!' There was no mistaking that sound: it was the American who had been the bane of her life at the Archive until she was sacked. What the hell was she doing here? Judith pushed the door and there they were, in the act. She was in *her* place face-down on the apron; he looked faintly ridiculous with trousers down and a hairy arse poking out under the shirt. But what mattered – what she'd come for – was the hard shaft on the other side of him and that was occupied. Occupied fucking Cate bloody Carpenter. The bitch. The bastard. The dim figures at the back of the chamber must have been them. They had watched her whipped and then gone off to have sex. Too demoralised to attack, Judith crept back to her room, guts churning in rage and self-pity, and curled up painfully on the bed. And when the tears started she let them take their course until she fell into an exhausted sleep.

When she woke it was eight in the evening and her shoulder joints were so stiff she cried out. But a little gentle exercise was enough to make them bearable and already the traces of the cat had started to fade. If it weren't for *that* woman she would be OK. Then again, what did she expect G to do? She used him simply to attend to her nether regions and faithful didn't – shouldn't – come into it. Though the fact that he had been up to the hilt in the interloper when she needed him still made her boil and she decided to take her mind off it by going through to the kitchen. She pulled the maid's costume over her head with some care and stepped into the flat shoes then she heard the sound of an argument and tiptoed out into the passage to listen.

'I tell you, woman, the old bat won't know no difference.'

'He's right, Annie. It's the only way to get this thing done with before she goes completely round the bend.' The first voice was G, pleading and exasperated, but the second was unknown to her. It must be the other maid, her counterpart, who had been away to fetch cousin Joan from down south.

'We can keep her under lock and key out back –'

'But she's going to want to *see* her.' That was Annie, unconvinced.

'We put a gag on the tart. Just stick to the story that she had second thoughts when she got here, but she'll come round in time. The old lady'll have no problem with that and just so long as she believes it's Joan we're home and dry.'

There was more, but the voices fell too quiet to follow so Judith ducked back into her room until she heard him go out the back door and footsteps go upstairs. Annie was shifting pots around on the stove and looked sharply at her but she put on a yawn and said she had just woken.

'Annie, can I take you up on the oil, if you've got time? And I'm starving.' As she hoped, the older woman seemed pleased to see her recovered and willingly attended to what was left of the marks. Then when Judith was sat at the table she said: 'Did I see the other maid back? And is Joan with her?'

'Yes, Martha came back today. But there's a bit of a problem because the girl's taken against what she got to do. And we're going to have to work on that. Now that's enough questions. You get on with your soup.'

Judith did as she was told – the hunger had been no invention – and turned over what she'd heard in her mind. Annie had avoided a straight answer to the question about Joan, tending to confirm that she had failed to come as planned. That meant there was only one likely conclusion. Since the time she had seen the American in the act, she had become a captive and they

217

were going to pass her off as the absent cousin. So if the plot was carried through, Cate Carpenter would get the ritual dose of sperm in place of Joan at the end of the next week. It was certainly something to think about.

In the morning Judith went into the stable where G was slicing through a new piece of leather. 'I saw you here with her. After I was whipped.'

He carried on working with no sign that he was aware of her presence until he had finished the cutting. Then he laid the knife down and faced her. 'Will you let me look?'

She held her arms up for him to pull the dress off over her head, then he took down the lamp and moved round her with it. 'You'll live. Arse caught it bad, though.' He found a brown corked bottle and returned the tilley to its place. But when he took off his apron and spread it as before, Judith shook her head. No way was she going over where the American had been just hours before. So he sat down on a heavy upright chair and she draped herself across his lap. The embrocation smelt sweet and spicy and as her juices began to flow she felt his hardness pressing into her belly. After a while she unbuttoned his heavy trousers and straddled him, lowering herself carefully on to the rigid pole of his cock. Then she rocked, her face in his rough shirt, until the sensations in her groin sharpened into full-blown climax.

Afterwards, he said: 'I had to keep her sweet then. Not any more, I don't.' It wasn't exactly an apology, but it was getting on for one, and when he asked if she wanted to see how the leather was made out of skins she put her maid's frock back on and went with him in good spirits. With interest she followed him through the huddle of small buildings that contained a drying shed, a tanning room where alongside more modern chemicals an ancient process was used involving the pounding in

218

of animal grease, and finally an area where the product was dyed and rolled into a thickness needed for the special whips. She could not suppress a small shudder at the sight of a freshly made ceremonial Cat so soon after her traumatic encounter but she forced herself to handle it while G explained how it was put together. Then he opened a cabinet in which hung a variety of such instruments and produced a braided black quirt that tapered from the thickness of her thumb to a narrow flat tip. There was a hide spread over the back of an old couch and he used it to demonstrate how a straight swing drew a line right across its surface while a sharp flick of the wrist brought the last inch or two cracking down on one spot. When she'd got the hang of it he led her outside to a door secured with stout bolts top and bottom.

'You'll find her the other side of that, tied up. Go and enjoy yourself. Just keep in mind we don't want marks showing a week on.' Judith stared open-mouthed, feeling the leather sticky in her hands as he walked away. At the corner he looked back with the nearest thing she'd seen yet to a smile. 'Then again, you know yourself the light in there's not that bright.'

After he'd gone she stood and rehearsed the reasons her old enemy deserved a good thrashing until she felt herself psychologically equipped to mete it out. Inside, however, she was met by a pathetic sight as the figure on the bed struggled to its knees and held out the roped hands imploringly while incomprehensible noises came from the gagged mouth. But Judith hardened her heart and shook her head.

'If you co-operate with me and take your punishment –' she flicked the whip and watched the eyes grow wide with alarm '– then I might consider letting you speak. If only so you can tell me what the fuck you think you're doing here.' She walked to the head of the bed and saw that the American's legs were hobbled in leather ankle cuffs connected by a short length of chain. 'OK, *Miss* Carpenter, get yourself on all fours. It's payback time.' For a moment it seemed there was going to be rebellion for the neck stiffened and the brow furrowed, but then obedience won out and the shoulders went down. Crouched as she was, the long T-shirt that had covered her rode up her back, leaving the prominent posterior completely bare. It was a delectable sight and Judith indulged herself by making the whip end dance over the twitching buttocks and into the dark furrow between them, while announcing what was to come.

'The first thing is you got Helen sacked. That would have to be worth a minimum of two dozen lashes –' she paused wickedly to savour the head shaking and sounds of protest her proposal evoked '– but there are mitigating factors. Miss James *was* looking for an excuse to do it which reduces your responsibility, and when we consider how sweet and sexy Grace is, the outcome is actually not a bad one. So suppose we halve the twenty-four and then halve it again that would just leave six. OK? I hope you're grateful. Get ready for them.' Judith eyed up the length of braided leather: if she stood back and forward a little it ought to be possible to lay on long strokes to curl from one flank right round to the other. She had to be careful to keep the pain within bounds for, while the lady was tied, she wasn't tied down.

Nevertheless, they were six beauties that made her victim jump and mew into her gag and brought back to mind the time a year before in France when she had been taught to use a cane. As with that instrument, her new toy raised on the white flesh an instant welt that darkened as she watched, and though not primarily of a sadistic bent Judith thrilled to see the visible correlates of sharp punishment. And why not? Many of the past writers she had studied at the Archive would have taken the pleasure in administering merited corporal correction for granted.

'So that's the first lesson. Now we come to the occasion when not only did you get me caned, you got my trousers taken down and then laid on a half dozen that have to be described as *hard*. So if that doesn't rate double that number, I don't know what does.' Again she let herself enjoy the anguished reaction before continuing. 'To be fair, though, it is possible that the boss would have punished me anyway, so what do you say to another smart six? Good, I'm glad you're going to be sensible; I wouldn't want to have to call in help to hold you down. He's much stricter than I am and you really don't want to find that out for yourself, do you? Head right down, now. That's it.'

Judith felt a little ashamed of milking the situation, for though she had said nothing that wasn't true she had no intention of fetching G. This was between the two of them and the upshot was a repetition of the first six except that the effort it took the young woman to maintain her position was palpably greater this time round. Afterwards Judith put a hand on the bent back and examined the crimson ridges that now covered the whole area of the buttocks, noting that the exposed genitals showed no signs of arousal. With the roles exchanged her own cunt would have been brimming; merely to have been placed in that position, arse up, would have been enough to start her off. Well, maybe that was as it should be: Cate Carpenter was not supposed to be enjoying herself. But still Judith decided to finish with something a little lighter.

'I don't suppose you realise that I saw you over G's workbench. You got juiced up watching me suffer and then you got him to fuck you. I ought to have you strung up by the ankles and then flog the backside off you. Can you give me one good reason why I shouldn't? Eh?' She snapped the flat end of the whip repeatedly across the livid flesh as she spoke and the American reared up and shook her head beseechingly. Tough as she undoubtedly was she looked close to weeping and it was too much. Judith had lost heart for any more games and reached over and untied the rope that held her wrists. At once the hands flew to her behind and rubbed frantically while the gag was removed.

'I'm too fucking soft, that's my trouble. But I still want an explanation of why you're here, or else . . .'

'I just thought I could find something out, to take back with me. To the States, that is. It's just when I got sacked I had to do something and when I was trying to make things up to Marjory, she suggested –'

'You saw Marjory? After what you did?'

'She, er, took me in. Gave me a place to stay. And I really tried to, to . . .'

Judith saw her blinking back tears that might be the start of a serious flow and put up a hand. 'OK, OK. I didn't know any of that. Look, let's leave it there for the talk. I want one more bit of contrition and then I'm done. Lamming into your bum has made me horny, so you can get on to your knees on the floor and bring me off. And don't say you don't, because we now know that you do, remember?'

It was perhaps an unkind cut to refer to the occasion that had got the lady the boot and for a second time it looked like there was going to be resistance. But then she hunkered down and Judith lifted her short frock up round her waist and put her legs apart. At first all she could feel was a gentle nuzzling, then the American's tongue came out and her hands crept round the back and squeezed. 'I always did love your butt,' she mumbled, lapping like a cat the length of the labia again and again until Judith's sensations reached – and passed – their shivering peak. Still the hands and tongue worked on and it was too tempting by far. This young lady was enjoying herself and that wasn't the idea. Well,

222

not the whole idea, and Judith allowed herself to indulge one last unworthy pleasure. Digging her fingers into the expensively cut blonde bob she pulled the face tight up to her vulva and released a stream of urine straight into her mouth.

22

Laying Plans

When she woke Cate swung her legs off the bed and shuffled over to the sink, the chain between her leather anklets clinking on the concrete floor. After squinting into the dirty cracked glass on the wall she stripped off the crumpled T-shirt and washed herself down from the single cold tap with a face-cloth. At least the lumps on her behind had gone away but it was still tender and she was without any means of climbing up to assess the damage in the mirror. It had been quite a day that she had started roaming free on the hillside yet ended quite literally pissed-upon in captivity. Despite the affront, though, she had to admit to a certain erotic frisson at the idea of it, especially after she'd really got into giving Judith head. Now it would be something else again if she could subject those full cheeks to a good thrashing – a repeat of the one in the Archive would do just fine – and then get her face in between them . . .

The sound of footsteps on gravel brought the dreamer out of her reverie with a start. She reached for the grey dress and pulled it quickly over her head as the bolts scraped back to reveal Judith herself. Flustered at the materialisation of her fantasy object, Cate took the offered mug of coffee and drank from it before she looked up to see her visitor as embarrassed as she was.

'I, er, I think I owe you an apology. Not for the whip; my mate Helen would say you got off bloody lightly.

224

But, er, at the end . . .' Plainly she thought she had gone too far.

'I'm not in good position to fall out with you, Judith, am I?' Cate waved her arm at the fetters and the bleak surroundings. 'So let's say what's done is done, yeah? But there is one thing: the name is *Cate* so will you use it? Please.'

'OK. Deal. Er, Cate.' Judith dropped on to the bed beside her then stiffened with a pained face and a muttered, 'Ouch!'

Cate looked at her and smiled knowingly.

'Hey now, young lady. Don't tell me. You've not gotten yourself –'

'Caned? On top of yesterday's dose of the Cat? Oh, yes, I have. And it's fucking sore.'

It was almost too good to be true and it put all thoughts of her own predicament out of Cate's mind. She just had to take advantage of the girl's apologetic mood to make an inspection. 'Come on, lift up your skirt and let me see while you tell me the story.'

Judith did as she was told, bending forwards to display a pair of finely marked buttocks. 'Oh, wow,' said Cate softly, tracing with a fingertip the dozen or so double-edged tracks that crossed the background bruising of the day before. Apparently the punishment had been earned because she had taken pity on 'the boy' and sucked him off, though the significance of this crime passed her by. Cate's attention was concentrated on the one thing in front of her eyes and she was just bending forwards to apply her tongue to the hot swellings when the door opened again and she jerked away.

'What *are* you two doing?' It was the maid Cate had seen at the whipping and she wasn't pleased. 'Judith, you know this one's supposed to be kept on her own. Now come on, I'll tie her arms and you tape up her mouth. And make it quick! The old lady'll be here in no time and if she finds out we're sunk.'

Finds out what? Still bemused by the turn of events that had transformed her from groom's playmate into cuffed prisoner, Cate allowed herself to be bound and gagged without a fight. No sooner had they done with her than the feared figure herself was in the room. How old was 'old'? It was hard to say for a hood concealed much of the face, though what was visible was deeply lined. She carried a cane in her hand – in all likelihood the one lately used on Judith – and with it jabbed at Cate's bruised hip, making her shrink back.

'What's this? Martha, I told you she was not to be touched. Did you think you could beat her into submission? Stupid girl!' The voice had lost its ceremonial quaver and was now sharp with anger. 'Get over at once!'

There was no glimmer of protest or even of hesitation as the maid pulled down her knickers, lifted her dress and reached down to grasp her ankles. Cate glanced at the real culprit but she was looking firmly at the floor, no doubt driven by the urge to save her striped rear from further mistreatment. By contrast, the surface now in view was quite unmarked and the broad swell of the cheeks pressed together in a line that kept the private parts out of view. Despite the anxiety of her situation Cate watched with interest to see how the rod would make the pale flesh quiver. Six strokes were each absorbed with little more than a grunt though the lines that sprang up at once testified to the force of them. Then the girl was ordered to 'go right over' and she obeyed by parting her legs and placing her hands flat on the floor ahead in what was plainly a well-practised move. Now the body was tilted forwards and above the underwear stretched across the thighs was visible the thickly-fuzzed vulva. And it was at that level, right into the crease, that the cane cut six more times to much greater effect. But while she squealed and yelped and wobbled precariously, Martha stuck it out until she was allowed to stand, red-faced and breathing hard.

'Pull your pants up, girl, and stop all that silly wriggling. I may be 83 but my arm is quite capable of repeating the dose. Now, you two, spread our cousin's legs for me to have a look.' Cate gasped and squirmed as the long bony fingers went into her vagina. While her state of arousal made the inspection mercifully easy, it did not, alas, go unnoticed. 'Well, well,' the old lady cackled, 'this one liked what she just saw. Juicy Joan, we shall have to call you. Only take to the lick of our Cat in the same way and we'll all be happy.' She finished with a wink and a crude leer that made Cate blush while her mind was rebelling against the seemingly inescapable conclusion. While she was struggling, the woman turned and spoke to the maid, who was still holding her punished bottom.

'She's no virgin, Martha, but I suppose we'll have to make the best of it.'

'They swore she ain't been near a man for six month, ma'am. So she can't already be expecting.'

'In that case, we follow the plan. Try to talk sense into the girl. I warn you that if I find out that anyone has laid a finger on her again, neither of you will sit down for a week.' The eyes flashed round the room once more and she was gone. In her wake Cate saw Martha round on Judith, spluttering with rage.

'I had to take that hiding because of you, bitch. Why did you wallop her? Don't answer that, I don't want to know. What I do want is to leather your arse, right now, in the kitchen before I throw you out on the moor.'

'Martha, I'm sorry you got it. Look, you need me for this to come off. If you kick me out it's not going to happen.' She held up her hands. 'OK, OK. I'll go over the table for you, if that'll make you happy. As long as Annie's there, yes? Just give me five minutes.'

The girl frowned at Judith, plainly exasperated, then stomped off. In the silence Cate sat quite still while the full realisation crystallised of her role in the unfolding

227

drama. In her mind's eye she saw the ritual penetration that she now recalled from her hasty reading in fading light of the material on Judith's desk. That she could wear, maybe, after several beers, which of course she wouldn't get. But it was the intended consequence of it that took her breath away: nine months of pregnant incarceration and then giving birth to – to what? Judith had been fumbling with the rope and now her hands were free Cate gingerly peeled off the tape and faced her.

'Juicy Joan. Juicy fucking Joan! You knew, didn't you? You knew all along what they were going to do.' After the initial shock her anger was rising fast.

'Er, I didn't want to worry you unnecessarily.'

'Unnecessarily? *Unnecessarily?* Oh, so you were gonna leave it till I was tied down with my legs open? And then it would be "Sorry, Cate, I didn't like to say before, but . . ." Jesus fuck, woman, I gotta get out of here!'

'Calm down, calm down. What we need is a plan of action.'

'Too fucking right, sister.'

'Look, I've got to go and offer my bum up for yet another roasting. After that's over I'll be able to think straight. I'll get back to you, promise. Just keep cheerful.'

If there had been anything to hand to throw at the retreating figure, Cate would have thrown it. As it was, she sat glowering on the bed, willing Martha to make the punishment in the kitchen long and painful. But then, as she thought of that tasty butt bouncing and reddening even more under the hard smacks, her fury ebbed and her groin ached. Damn the woman! It was difficult to hate someone who evoked such lust. There was no point getting agitated; Judith would be back later and they could maybe come up with some scheme. In the interim it would calm her down if she could get some physical release. So Cate lay back with her knees

228

drawn up and closed her eyes, slipping a hand into the wetness between her legs. In amongst the trauma there had been plenty of stimulation, and with an effort it was possible to imagine she could hear the sound of leather on flesh carrying across the yard . . .

Meanwhile, in an annexe of the British Library several hundred miles to the south of Inglewhite, the cataloguer of restricted materials was occupied with a fantasy of his own. In front of him stood the second American woman in the space of a week to be asking questions about the remote house of the Cat. This one was even younger than the first and the mannish suit, the short back and sides and a distinctly pugnacious tilt to the snub nose all said to him: men keep your distance. It made him itch to put her over his knee and smack her bare bottom. Not out of anger or spite – he was comfortably bisexual himself and she seemed a perfectly decent (or indecent) girl – but simply in order to lay the first male hand on what he was sure would be a delectable behind. Given her connection with the Carpenter woman, it was a fair bet she had an interest in the subject, so if he played his cards right . . .

Harry Jameson coughed and pulled himself up; there were practicalities to tackle first. 'So you came all the way over here just on a hunch, really, Ms –'

'Everybody calls me Gena. But yeah, you're right. I'm worried about Cate.' She hesitated a moment and he felt the cool blue eyes weighing him up. 'It's maybe easiest to give you the whole picture. If that's OK.'

'Carry on, Gena. The name's Harry and my time's yours. There isn't much on this Saturday morning.' She lowered herself on to the edge of his desk displaying the promising curve of a hip. The move could easily have been pushy, even arrogant, but with her it seemed to signal only that she was going to talk straight and Harry sat back to listen.

'You see we were friends, best friends, back in Seattle – but then we fell out and she left for England the next day. That's a couple of months since and there was no contact till I found an email waiting for me at the club I run on Tuesday morning. It was real nice and apologetic about what had happened and said she was going on a trip so on Thursday I phoned her workplace to find out when she'd be back. Well the secretary told me she didn't work there any more and when I told her to get a grip she came right out with it. Cate had been sacked.'

'Uh, oh. No wonder she didn't want me to contact the Archive.'

'Yeah. The thing sounded fine when I thought it was official, like just more of the work on this Cat she'd done back home. But now I wasn't sure. In the end I got through to a woman she'd been staying with who wasn't happy about it either. Said Cate had taken off early in the morning to find this place way out in the wilds without any proper plan of what she was going to do. But she said you could show me exactly where she'd gone and so I got on a plane. I want to go after her, Harry.'

'I like that. You don't sit around worrying, but get up and do something about it. Can I ask you something? This, er, falling out you had, was it anything to do with the lady being too handy with a cane?'

'No.' The freckled face had reddened a little and Harry thought he might have been too nosy. But after the eyes had found his again she went on. 'We weren't lovers. I do the rounds of a whole bunch of fluffy femme-types and I didn't want the thing with Cate mixed up in that. But then she tried to grab me one time and I stormed out. So why did you ask?'

'I have a friend Judith who works at the Archive and your Cate contrived to lay into her something shocking.'

'Yeah. Can't say I'm surprised. She did have a problem knowing when to stop but she *was* working on it. I used to carry the gear to her s/m gigs, so I know. But I guess that she's been pretty down over here, so she won't have been behaving well.'

Harry was having trouble keeping his feet on the ground. Here was this young woman from the USA, at most half his age, talking in a quite matter-of-fact way about subjects he never mentioned unless sure of his audience. For him to be devious – never in any case his strong point – was not only unlikely to work but as a response to Gena's openness was positively distasteful. He would make an effort to match frankness with frankness.

'First of all, I think you're right to have a bad feeling about this place up north. The Judith I mentioned went there too just before Cate, so I have an interest in helping you. Maybe we could come up with a plan to check on them both.'

'Sounds good.'

'Before we do, though, you've levelled with me so I'm going to level with you. I have a trainee assistant with a taste for discipline and when Cate was here she obliged me by giving him rather a sound thrashing.'

'I bet she did. But I don't, well –'

'You don't hand out the big stick, is that it?'

'No way, no. Nor take it either: spanking's about my limit.'

'Fair enough. I thought as much. I expect he's still marked from Monday, but I had it in mind to give him a good going-over with a strap and I'd like to do that in your presence. It would add a sense of occasion.'

'OK. I don't see why not.' She seemed unperturbed so Harry took a deep breath and plunged on.

'There is something else, if you'll just hear me out. Cate noticed the erection my boy gets when he's punished and it's my guess you've never handled a man's member before. Now –'

'Are you asking me to get a hold of his cock while you beat him and then –?'

'You've every right to walk out now. But for one thing it would give him such a thrill and for another you could think of it as broadening your own experience while in a foreign country.' There was a silence in which all Harry could hear was the beating of his heart and all he could think was that this time he'd definitely gone too far. But then Gena looked up with a rare grin breaking through the habitual solemnity of her expression.

'Fuck it, why not? I haven't seen a whipping since Cate left and the first I get to be at I also get to make a guy squirt all over me. OK, but I guess an essential piece of equipment is gonna be a king-sized handkerchief.'

The event passed off well. Gena was interested in inspecting the blue lines that remained from her friend's efforts earlier in the week and Arnold was over the moon that he was to be masturbated by one of the Sapphic sisters while the tawse stung his backside. Then, when the boy had been dispatched to await his boss's later pleasure, Harry took a chance he would never have dared before, detecting the arousal in Gena's quick breathing and bright eyes.

'Tell me to eff off, please, if that's how you feel. But I want to ask you if you've ever been properly spanked?'

'What do you mean: properly?'

'I mean so that you come like he did, but without the helping hand.' He went to the desk and took out the paddle that had been used on both Cate and Judith. 'Just with the aid of this.' This time the silence was longer and at the end of it there was no grin: Gena's face was set tense.

'I must be fucking crazy. Where do you want me?'

He made a quick calculation that over the knee would be too much contact at this stage and put a big cushion on one end of a long table. 'Over here. Uncover your bottom and get comfortable. Then I'll do the rest.'

It was quite a boyish behind but with fuller cheeks than the one he had just attended to and they rippled delightfully even under the first light smacks. For a while the olive skin showed little trace of its treatment but when he upped the force of the slaps it soon acquired a pink glow that deepened with each gasp evoked from the recipient. When her movements showed him they were nearing the end he laid the paddle aside and brought the flat of his hand down into the juiced-up base of the buttock cleft until the climax took her. The smell of her was sharp on his palm and his erection strained in his trousers, but he knew, alas, that this one was not for the taking.

When she had pulled up the black briefs and tucked the shirt back into her trousers she nodded down at the painfully obvious bulge in his. 'If you wanted, I dare say I could –'

But Harry cut her off, shaking his head.

'The boy will deal with that. I heard him listening at the door and no doubt the handkerchief got its second dose of the morning. So while he's still bending over after I've tanned his arse some more for impertinence . . .' He offered the rest to Gena's imagination and saw her colour rise just a little. God, she was pretty; it was no surprise that her friend Cate had grabbed her. 'I'll make enquiries about Inglewhite but it could take a few days. Will you be OK?'

'Yeah. The woman I'm staying with knows a couple of students who are showing me around. I thought the English were supposed to be strait-laced, but these two . . .'

Harry laughed. 'That sounds fine. Leave me your number so I can reach you. And have fun.'

233

23

Escape

Minutes later that same Saturday morning, while a British Library assistant in London found himself impaled on a rampant erection, Judith too was bent over, but the cause of her squirming across the kitchen table of the house on the moor was somewhat different.

'Ah! Ah! Oh, Annie, please. Take it easy. Oh – oh – oh. I'm so-o-o sore!'

'Good grief, girl, I'm being as gentle as I can. Though I can't remember ever seeing Martha so riled. She was going to walk right out of the house if she didn't get a crack at you. So what could I do? You should be thankful I managed to stop her when I did. Now just keep still while I get some lotion on these places down here and we're done. And, for God's sake, try and keep this bum of yours out of any more trouble. Whatever you do, don't go anywhere near that one out back until the rite next week. Got it?'

In her room Judith tried to get to grips with some of the material Annie had given her which had lain untouched since her painful induction as ceremonial maid. Among the items was a record of the preparations made fifty years ago for an event similar to the one in which the American was to be pressed into service in a week's time. A cursory perusal of the text seemed to show that the lead role had not only been difficult to fill but when it was the girl had not been fully persuaded until the last minute. That was no surprise: the girl in the memoir from twenty years back had on reflection sounded a little naive if not actually simple-minded and then she'd pegged it for her pains shortly after giving birth.

The problem was what to do about her old enemy, currently fettered as securely as any member of a chain-gang. As far as Judith could see their first – and last – opportunity to break out was going to be when the cuffs came off just before she was speared with the boy's cock. And it was an understatement to call that cutting it fine.

The foolscap file was making her arms ache and she put it down. Being forced to stand, thanks to Martha's enthusiastic strapping, was not conducive to the study of manuscripts. Besides, in its wake she was feeling randy as hell and found it difficult to keep her mind off what G's stiff shaft could do for her. Pulling back on her wig – Annie had stressed it was not a good idea to let anyone see her dark crew-cut – Judith slipped out but was disappointed to see that the pick-up was missing from its usual place. He must be away for supplies and could well be gone for hours. Well, what about the Carpenter woman? Cate, she had to make an effort to call her that. Cate had been dead keen earlier to get her face in where it counted but they had been interrupted. OK then. She would have her chance right now.

Judith crept round the side of the workshop heart in mouth until she was out of sight but when she reached the outhouse that held the captive there was a padlock clamped through the top bolt. Again she looked round but there was no sign of life so Judith bent down and put her ear to the wood and hissed: 'Cate. Can you hear me?' Then she saw that a vertical plank had warped, pulling its nails out from the lower cross-piece of the door, and when she tugged the bottom foot of it came away in her hand. 'Cate, it's me Judith,' she said softly into the hole and there was at once a face on the other side of the narrow opening.

'What are you doing? I thought you'd never come.'

'I can't get in. Someone's fixed the bolt. I got a real hiding over there, that's what took me so long. But I may have an idea.'

'I hoped you would. Get well leathered, I mean. Shit, I don't mean that, I didn't *hope* . . .'

Judith couldn't resist a chuckle at the transparency of the sexual interest. 'Don't worry, I know what you meant. Here, do you want a feel?' So saying she crouched down in front of the gap within reach of the exploring hand that lost no time ranging over the bare backside under her frock.

'Oh, wow. This is so lumpy and hot, even more than I imagined.'

'And what were you doing, my dear, during this imagining of yours?' The hand drew back and there was a short silence in which Judith could almost feel the embarrassed flush of the confined blonde. 'Sorry, Cate. When this bum's recovered you can give it a good slapping. But now I'm as horny as you were sounding, and you've got two hands: one for you and one for me . . .'

Then there were no more words for a while as Judith gave herself up to the fingers in her cleft that teased the clitoris until she was maddened with desire. While she came she could hear the hoarse panting behind her that echoed her own, but when she opened her screwed-up eyes there was a shock waiting. Firmly planted on the ground in front of her were a pair of old-fashioned boots sticking out from a long skirt and Judith rocked back on her heels to see Annie glowering down.

'What did I tell you, not half an hour ago? Just what is it between you two, eh?'

'Nothing. I just took pity on her and let her, er . . .'

'And that's why you whipped her the other day? Out of pity? Look, girl, you get back inside or I'll have you taken up to the old lady for a dose of what Martha got. Now, in your present condition, *that* would give you something to think about.' Judith cringed back but saw there was the hint of a smile underneath the frown. 'I left some more papers I found on your table. If you would only just stick to your studies for the rest of the day you might stay out of hot water.'

On the other side of the door Cate let out her breath when she heard the footsteps die away across the yard. Of course, no one knew of her connection to Judith, although the housekeeper was becoming suspicious. They would have to play it careful, and it didn't help they'd been separated before she'd heard what the idea was for getting her out of the place. As it turned out, however, the need for caution was obviated by the fact that Judith did not return. Not that day nor the next, nor the one after. Meals were delivered by a tight-lipped Martha and in between times Cate shuffled to and fro in a restless anxiety about her future. But as the hours dragged by with no word of escape she fell bit by bit into a kind of erotic languor in which she began to visualise, in elaborate detail, the progressive disciplining of Judith at her own hands. So wrapped up did she become in the prolonged waking dream that she forgot altogether having repented of the caning in Miss James's office, and now clung to the memory of those long curving weals while slippery fingers played between her legs and time stood still . . .

Meanwhile, Judith was not under lock and key but the kitchen door opposite hers was kept open so that any movement was likely to be noticed and stopped. The atmosphere in the house was fraught and it made concentration difficult; nevertheless she struggled on to produce a précis of the relevant documents she had been given. But when it came to making an interpretation of their significance she was reduced to chewing her pencil or doodling in the margins of her pad. On the Tuesday afternoon Annie was summoned upstairs and Judith sneaked out to the workshop, hopeful that she could procure the services of G's cock. But he shooed her out, saying it was more than his job was worth, so she crept back and sulked for the rest of the day. Come Thursday, however, the supervision had become lax enough for her to chance a visit to the captive's door and lift up the broken board.

'Cate, it's me. Cate, are you there?'

'Judith. Where the fuck else would I be?' Not without reason, the voice sounded far from happy.

'Look, this has got to be quick. I've racked my brains and we've only got one chance I can see. We have to make a break for it when the chain comes off.'

'Correct me if I'm wrong, but isn't that *after* I get whipped?' The tone was icy and Judith quailed.

'Well, er, yes. But I'll be as easy on you as I can. That's a promise.'

'Gee, thanks a bunch. I can't wait. Before you go, Ms Scholar-of-the-Archive, perhaps you can tell me what it's all *for*? Since I'm going to be flogged with this special Cat anyway and then, *if* we botch the escape, ritually fucked, it would be nice to know what it's designed to achieve. Is it kind of magic? Or is there something real?'

'Beats me. Some of the outfits were just whipping clubs, like yours for Christ's sake. I'm not sure anyone really knows if there's more to it. But look on the bright side. Day after tomorrow we'll be out of it all in the hills, safe. Trust me.'

While Judith was imparting assurances to her less than convinced listener, Harry was at his desk in London unusually at a loss for words. In front of him stood a snub-nosed and freckle-faced schoolboy in the kind of uniform that was already on the way out when he himself was of an age to wear it. Although he had recognised that the 'boy' was in fact the young Gena of last Saturday's acquaintance, that in itself did not prepare him for the removal of her jacket. Under cover of its respectability lurked a skimpy nylon shirt moulded to breasts and nipples that left exposed a band of flesh above the grey flannel stretched tight over thighs and crotch. With the addition of knee socks, heavy boots and a rakish cap, the impression made was almost shockingly lascivious.

There was only one thing for it, and it seemed to be what Gena (or should that be Geno?) expected. The two upright chairs that had done service for Judith were placed in position and the provocative boy-girl went across Harry's lap. After the drum-tight seat had been well paddled she lifted herself for the shorts to be peeled down and allow the bare-handed bare-bottomed climax to be brought about. When she stood up he saw the pubic hair shaved into the shape of a heart atop the glistening labia, then his handkerchief was plucked from his top pocket with the words: 'I insist.' Once the distended organ was unzipped and in her hand the contractions began and through half-closed eyes he saw her arrange the cloth in order to watch until the discharge was over.

Afterwards he bought her coffee. 'As I told you on the phone, Gena, I've had a hell of a job trying to find out what's going on at Inglewhite. All I got was gossip that a cousin who was supposed to arrive didn't, but we don't really know what that means. What we do know is that there's been no message from your Cate or my Judith for more than a week. What I suggest is we give them another couple of days then head north. I'll get a Land Rover so we can drive to the door if we have to and I'll book us into a hotel for the night somewhere near. How does that sound?'

'Great. But see if you can get us a room with good thick walls.' He stared for a moment at her expressionless face before it cracked into a grin, then he grinned too.

'Right. But you, young lady, be careful what you wear. I don't want the management thinking I'm into under-age boys.'

Cate came to with the sound of bolts being drawn and there were two figures in the room. Her head was muzzy and as her eyes focused she saw the light was fading. She tried to speak but her tongue wouldn't work. Shit, there must have been something in that cocoa last night. There was another cup being held out and she turned her head away but a voice said: 'Come on, girl. That was a sleeping tablet you got to take you through this last day and you'll soon come out of it. But this now is to steady your nerves while we get you ready.' It was the housekeeper and she drank. Anything that was going to take the edge off her rising panic was welcome.

'Now, the first thing is we're going shave you. It'll be simple if you just go along with it but if you don't I'll get help to hold you down and it'll be done anyway. So what's it to be?'

The head was clearing and the lemon-flavoured draught seemed already to have had a calming effect, so Cate let herself be laid on her back, knees apart while Martha got to work with a bowl of hot water, soap and a safety razor. When the operation was complete the sight of her bare pubis made her chuckle and she wanted to point out that it was a waste. After all she would be gone, wouldn't she, before her legs were spread to display their efforts. But she caught herself just in time. Jee-sus, she was fucking light-headed with what they'd given her.

So Cate bit her lip and allowed the rest of the preparations to be made. First the anklets were un-

240

locked and removed, then more water was brought and she was washed from head to toe. While she sat in a fluffy towel trying to suppress the urge to giggle, her hair was blow-dried and she was fitted with a pair of soft white leather boots. The finishing touch was a white cape which fastened at the neck with a brooch that made an impression even on the cotton wool that had replaced her brain. On it was engraved the emblem of the Cat she had first seen in the tourbus, and the space that separated there from where she was now was a chasm that made her drop, giddy, on to the edge of the bed.

'Take a deep breath, girl, while we put these on. Once we get you in there it will soon be over.' The woman produced a metal bar a foot or so in length with a hook in the middle and strapped Cate's wrists to each end then she wrapped a new chain round her ankles and snapped the ends of it shut. 'Come on, up on your feet and let's be heading in.' Outside the yard was completely dark and she swayed between the two women as they led her across it. Judith's promises of escape seemed far away from the enactment that had caught her up and Cate moved forward without any sense of resistance to her fate.

In the chamber the torches flamed just as on the day the groom had sat her down at the back. This time, however, she was to be the star of the piece and yet she was eerily detached, watching as if from a distance as her wrist bar was secured to the overhead beam between the two pillars. Beside her hung the boy, similarly cloaked, and they faced the marble slab while the masked and white-robed figure of the old lady delivered herself of an incantation. In no language Cate could recognise it grew wilder and more outlandish until its abrupt end left the last syllable echoing into the silence. At once the handmaids, also masked, threw a powder over the brands which blazed with a brilliant white light. Silk bands were fastened over both captives' mouths

241

before their capes were removed and they were turned back to back. Then the white Cat was raised in front of her and she saw with sudden fear the eyes that were fixed on her face: they were not Judith's and she was going to receive no mercy.

As the flagellation proceeded, the burning cuts jerked the two pairs of buttocks into repeated collision and air was filled with the hiss and crack of the two ten-tailed whips. On a second command each body was rotated to bring them face to face and through a red mist Cate looked down on the distended staff that stood out between the scored thighs. In the moment of respite she thought of the first man she ever flogged on her test in Seattle. That one's seed had splashed over the floor, whereas this one's was intended for her. Except that Judith was meant to have a plan. As she was pushed closer to him she felt the wet stiffness rub her belly and saw with a shiver that the eyes opposite were completely vacant. Whatever may have been there had long since departed. Then the leather tongues bit into the flesh below the shoulder blade and focused her attention on the survival of the next several minutes.

At last, when the cheeks of her behind had been turned into one raw throbbing mass of heat, the cats were laid aside and she was supported while the wrists were released. In her ear a voice whispered: 'Get ready,' and she almost laughed. How could she get ready when she could hardly stand? But somehow, she did. When the chain was unlocked from round her legs Judith yelled 'Now!' and gave Martha such a push that her head cracked hard against the column. Adrenaline pumping, Cate sprinted for the door right at her back. First Judith knocked the housekeeper aside but in the process left her robe in the strong hand; then the old lady barred the way with her hand up but suddenly crumpled clutching at her chest and they were out into the moonlit night.

'This way. If we run for two minutes we get some cover. Can you do it?'

'Fucking have to. Off you go, I'll follow.'

Later Cate found it difficult to understand how a half-doped, thoroughly whipped body was capable of such a burst of energy for it was in fact rather more than five minutes before the two naked and gasping figures dropped down in a clearing on the edge of a small plantation of trees.

24

Moor and Beyond

It was a balmy night with a light breeze that came and
went, and small clouds drifted across the face of the full
moon. They lay side by side as the harsh ragged
breathing returned gradually to normal and Cate became aware that apart from the gurgling of a nearby
stream and the occasional rustle of leaves it was all
stillness. Why was there no one in pursuit? Then from
the direction of the house came the sound of voices,
urgent in the silence, and an engine started up. Doors
banged and headlights came on, and gathering speed the
vehicle moved off away from them down the rough
track.

'It must be the pick-up. Where's it going?' Judith's
voice hissed sharply in her ear and made Cate jump. But
then she remembered.

'When you pushed the old lady away, maybe you
didn't see. But I reckon something happened to her.
Something serious.'

'What, you mean like a heart attack?'

'Yeah. They'll be taking her to the hospital. Why else
go at this time of night? And that means we're safe for
now at least.' Cate got to her feet wincing at the
soreness of her body. In the middle of the grassy area
was a dark object that looked familiar. 'Shit, that's *his*
coat. It's still there. This is where he found me.'

Judith jumped up and examined the heavy waxed jacket. 'G was here with you. Cate, he fucked you here, didn't he?'

'In the arse.' Oh, God, what was she saying? 'Judith, I'm sorry. But how could I have known he was fucking you?' Or cared, then. It was in her mind but she kept her lip buttoned.

'Don't worry about it. That's all past now.' The tone was brisk, but not openly hostile. 'You'd better get across the thing – again – and I'll have a go at your marks.' There looked like the hint of a smile on her face and Cate obeyed, relieved, while Judith went over to the shadows. 'I stashed a bag here with some witch-hazel I nicked from Annie. Yeah, here we are. Now you just lie still while I get at the worst bits.'

She took her time and Cate slowly relaxed. Already the time in the chamber was taking on the character of hallucination rather than reality. But when she stood her knees wobbled and Judith supported her until she was steady.

'Cate, you hold on there, because I've got a good idea of exactly what you need to sort you out. Now if I know G . . .' She felt in the pocket of the abandoned coat and came up with a knife that she snapped open. Then she disappeared into the trees and returned in a couple of minutes holding a trimmed switch that she handed over with a flourish. It was about a yard long and the thickness of her finger and Cate gaped at it stupidly.

'Right. You've been at the rough end of things for a while and we're going to redress the balance. I promised you I'd take a spanking but I don't think you're up to that just now. But *that* is an ash-plant, and it will deliver a good hiding without too much effort.'

The instrument had a lively quiver in Cate's hand and she stared into her companion's eyes then kissed her on the mouth. 'Jude, this is going to *hurt*.' Judith kissed her back and lay down across the stump.

'OK, Miss Carpenter. I'm in your hands.'

Cate swished the flexible rod several times then brought it down. After three Judith said: 'Fuck, that is severe. But go on.' When she could see six dark lines in the silvery light her cunt oozed and a small tight voice said: 'I think . . . I can take . . . the same again.' Now her own whipping was totally forgotten and Cate felt supremely alive as she rose on to her toes and lashed the switch into the fold at the base of the cheeks. Each of the second six produced the same strangled noise somewhere between a grunt and a whine and when she threw the weapon down she saw its tip was shredded. She leapt on top of her victim and held her tight until the writhings lessened then sat back on her knees and ran her tongue along the hot black swellings. Then her face was hard in the cleft and she sucked and licked and nibbled and bit until Judith came, then came again. When she lay back on the grass, exhausted, the dark-stubble of the head went between her legs and she came too, almost at once, before oblivion took her.

In the morning they were wrapped together on top of G's spread coat and Judith gently distentangled herself and gazed enviously at the body beside her. The blonde hair shone in the morning sun and the ripe curve of the breasts was in marked contrast to the flatness she saw squinting down and fingering her own. When she looked up the eyes were open watching her.

'Jude, when you've got a butt like yours you don't deserve boobs too. That would be plain greedy.' She rolled over and stretched. 'Wow, I'm stiff as fuck, but I feel *good*. How about you, lady?'

Judith grinned at her lover of one night's standing and pulled her up by the hand. 'I'm just fine, *if* a touch sore. What do you say to a wash in the stream and you can inspect the damage you did.'

'Remember who cut the switch and positively demanded I use it. How could I say no?'

246

They ran giggling across to the small pool and splashed about, then Cate put a hand between Judith's legs and they were making love all over again. Afterwards Judith took out sandwiches and a bottle of lemonade and, suddenly starving, they ate and drank with a single-minded concentration. Still there was no sound from the house below them, so they sat back in the warm sun to decide on the next step.

'Well, Jude, we can't go marching back to civilisation wearing only our nice white boots. You can bet we'd have hordes of admirers, but we might also get locked up. So what have you got in the magic bag?'

As the words sank in Judith felt the colour rising in her face. 'Oh, no. Fuck. You see, Cate, I couldn't get hold of any of your things, they wouldn't let me near you. And I *meant* to put in more of my own stuff but, well, I, er . . .'

'OK, sister. Come clean. Empty the fucking thing so we can see what you actually brought.' Shamefacedly Judith picked up the rucksack and removed its contents. First she pulled out a thick file containing all her documents and notes and next there was a leather paddle she had pinched from G's workshop. Last came the clothes which consisted of exactly three items: a satin thong, a pair of jeans and a T-shirt, all hers.

Cate was silent for a moment then she exploded. 'You packed your manuscripts and your clothes: what the fuck did you think I was going to be wearing on the run from a naked whipping?' But then she began to chuckle and they both collapsed into helpless laughter. 'OK, sister,' she said wiping away the tears, 'I'm comandeering the top clothes; you can make do with the lingerie.'

While Judith protested Cate put on the jeans which hung loosely on her hips until G's jacket pocket gave up a piece of string to serve as a belt. Then Cate picked up the paddle and smacked it against her hand. 'It's good you put this in, girl. Just the thing to reward such rank carelessness, yeah?' The mere sight of it made Judith's loins stir and she dropped at once over the stump and pushed up her behind into the smarting onslaught that continued until she cried for mercy and begged for the throbbing in her clitoris to be given release. But Cate's tongue had no sooner made contact with the sopping vulva than there was the unmistakable sound of a familiar engine.

'Fuck it! What timing.' Judith was on her feet snapping the tiny briefs in place while Cate pulled the shirt over her head. Together they stuffed the papers and the paddle back in the bag. 'I worked out a route, but we've got to get moving before he comes after us on horseback.

'Right, Jude. You know where you're going so I'll follow on with the load. And that way I get to view the blushing cheeks in their snazzy black thong.'

In little more than an hour they had completed a loop that brought them to a derelict farmhouse a mere fifty yards from the track and only three times that distance from the road itself. As they paused in the hot noon air Judith heard the sound of hoof beats and the two young women scurried into the cover of a ruined byre. He was coming from the Inglewhite direction at a gallop and drew up suddenly below them. Through a chink in the stone wall Judith saw the horse rear and neigh while its rider stared ahead, then as quickly as they had arrived he had turned the animal and was gone again. And when the commotion died away she heard what he must have heard to send him back: there was a vehicle coming the other way down the track.

Peering round the doorpost she saw a Land Rover bump slowly into view over the ruts and potholes of the rough surface. She couldn't see who was behind the wheel but in the passenger seat was a figure wearing what looked strangely like an old-fashioned school cap complete with badge. Then with a whoop Cate was gone from beside her, bounding down the slope shouting and waving: 'Gena! Gena!' The driver pulled up and got out and Judith who had hung back now leapt forward too and found herself swept up in Harry's arms while the other pair hugged beside them.

The country hotel they were booked into was a rambling affair and Harry had secured for them a single-storey wing that contained three double rooms. Judith shrank back at reception all-but-naked under Harry's huge coat, watching Cate in her loose string-tied jeans with her friend in the tight grey shorts and cap over one eye. They made an odd crew but the desk clerk gave no sign he saw anything untoward and from the way he 'sirred' Harry she guessed extra money had already changed hands. When they were escorted through the long corridor to the back she noticed Harry speaking into Cate's ear and just caught the words: '– a proper spanking, you know, low down. There'll be no more talk of just best friends after that. You try it.' Then he glanced back and she saw his broad features for a moment take on the appearance of a small boy detected in a piece of naughtiness.

When the luggage had been deposited, the two Americans disappeared behind a firmly closed door and Judith was left alone with the classifier of Rare Books.

'I can't believe you came after us. How did you know we were in trouble?'

'We didn't. But Gena had a hunch and I'd heard things about that house. So we thought it better to check up on you both.'

'We: you and Gena. And then it was you who told Cate how to get there, wasn't it? I wonder how she rewarded you for the information. And just now you were telling her how to turn her friend on.'

'Hold it right there, Jude. I know all about a certain groom at Inglewhite: half the girls in the neighbourhood have had his children. And he has a reputation for a special interest in that part of the anatomy you're so well endowed with. And you were on the moor last night with Cate and those marks on your backside look very fresh. Do you want me to go on?'

'OK, OK. What on earth made me think I could get the better of you?' Laughing, Judith shucked off the coat and stood in front of him in her thong and boots. 'A cheeky young girl criticising a wise old librarian, well, she has to be asking for it, doesn't she?'

'Less of the old. But I agree that a firm hand could be required. Especially since I believe she knows it will be to their mutual benefit.'

'Oh, she does indeed.'

It was sometime later when the door opened without a knock as Harry was measuring a short cane against Judith's very rosy behind. The chambermaid in her confusion tried to retreat but he grabbed her arm and pulled her into the room.

'Oh, I'm sorry, sir. I thought the room was empty. I won't say anything, honest.' Seeing her expression gave him a sudden idea and he whisked up her skirt. Underneath was a red-streaked quite knickerless bottom and he chuckled while Judith stared.

'I do it myself, sir. I don't know anyone to . . . to . . . That's why I had to look when I heard –'

'All right, girl. Save your blushes. Would you like to join in – if that's OK with you, Jude?'

'No problem. I remember when I was all shy about these things. What's your name?'

'Penny. I've always wanted to be spanked, far back as I can remember.'

'Well, Penny. You'll get your wish, but there is one thing. Judith here could use a little servicing between her legs, if you get my meaning.'

'Oh, yes, sir. Begging your pardon, sir, but I do like

the ladies best in any case. Though of course if you want to . . . when you've finished . . .'

Harry took her at her word and after he had slapped her bottom to a crimson hue he unzipped and eased his erection into the well-lubricated vagina while Judith squealed and writhed on her back on the bed. Then while he poured out the drinks from the cabinet for the three of them he had another idea.

'Jude, didn't you tell me that this whole Cat business started because you wanted to fix your boss up with a young lover? Well, maybe we have just the candidate for the job right here.' He jerked his head in the direction of the maid and when Judith gave a broad grin and a thumbs-up sign he turned to the girl directly. 'Now you don't have to give me an answer until the morning, Penny, but what would you say to starting a new life where your bottom would be well attended to and you would look after a dark handsome woman in the way you've just been doing?'

Later still, once Gena was breathing in a steady rhythm, Cate slipped out of bed and stole quietly into Judith's bedchamber. She woke immediately and followed the visitor into the empty room adjoining, leaving Harry fast asleep. Inside, Cate put on the bedside light.

'I'm with Gena now and in ten days we go back to Seattle. But I wanted one last time if you did.'

Without a word Judith put a pillow on the edge of the bed and went over it. Under Cate's hands the buttocks glowed with the deep heat of prolonged spanking and she spread them wide to probe the sharp taste of the anus with her tongue. She thought of how she had twice laced those full globes with welts: the first time in a kind of twisted resentment and the second with a pure thrill in the aftermath of her own whipping. One day, who knows, she might get to do that again. But for now it was time for the lips and teeth to do their work and she bent her head to the dark meat of the splayed cunt.

251

Epilogue

'Be so good as to put the box down here, Penelope, and then you may go. I shall be home in an hour and I intend to take a long lunch break. Do you understand?'

'Oh, yes, Miss James. I'll have everything ready.' The young maid Penny, who had jumped at the chance to travel down with them only ten days before, had clearly scored a hit with the raven-haired director. And vice versa, to go by the happy grin she was trying to cover as she bobbed in her short black skirt before leaving in blushing confusion.

'A most obliging girl, though of course she is in need of a firm hand.' She's in the right place for that, thought Cate, exchanging glances with Judith. It was her last day before the flight home and word had come to Marjory of a parcel to be collected from the Archive. While Cate was curious about what it could be, returning to the place of her dismissal would serve another purpose. It might bring her to do something she had so far avoided even while knowing she would feel better in the end for facing it. But first things first. Her package contained the bag and its contents left behind when they had made their dash for freedom, though there was with it no word of explanation. Judith's, however, came with a letter that raised her colour a little when she scanned it, though on the director's insistence she read an extract aloud after explaining that it came from the housekeeper.

Since you ran off together, I'm guessing that the American is to do with you, so I am putting her things in this box. Well, I don't expect you heard that the old lady collapsed that night, which means it's all over. It was a shock but maybe it's for the best because everything was left to the boy. You know the way he is, Judith, so he just expects Martha to carry on his training even though there's no point to it. But it's all he knows. And now she's going to have his baby so there'll be a wedding and we might start to be like a more normal house.

G says to tell you there's a proper cat here for the taking and you'll know what he's on about.

Judith coughed. 'I think, Miss James, he means you can have an authentic Nemesis Cat if I go for it myself. And then she says that the groom wanted me sent this that he made himself.'

The thing was a black braided whip that Cate recognised at once with a frisson of distaste. Miss James examined it with interest and commended its craftsmanship, but when Judith held it out to her Cate demurred.

'I think you're forgetting that I have met this one before.'

'Oh, God. So you have. In the worst possible way. What am I thinking of?' She looked stricken.

'Water under the bridge, girl. Don't worry about it, though I will still pass on a second encounter.' Cate tried to smile reassuringly; she had no further quarrel with Judith. Far from it. But the whip had brought again to the centre of her attention what she had really come there to do and she made an effort to screw up her courage. Then Miss James cleared her throat in a way that indicated an official pronouncement.

'Well, I want to thank you young ladies for what you have done: Judith for your excellent research – in leather, it seems, as well as on paper – and both of you for stopping the rite in the way you did. It means that I shall be able to work towards mounting a ceremony myself at some future date. But I believe that Miss Carpenter deserves special thanks since she was – how shall I put this? – no longer actually an employee of ours at the time.' The director looked a little uncomfortable and Cate guessed the cause of it was also the source of her own unease. Right. It was now or never.

'Miss James, we have unfinished business between us and the main reason I'm here is to ask you to complete it.' Steeling herself, Cate looked at the floor while she unzipped her skirt and stepped carefully out of it. Having laid the folded garment on the arm of her chair she faced her one-time boss in her garter belt and stockings. Miss James was staring intently at her, eyebrows slightly raised, waiting. 'But, the way I remember it, you did not specify a number of strokes at the time.'

'A round dozen would satisfy me, Miss Carpenter. If that is acceptable to you.'

'Please, Cate. And it is.'

'Excellent. It shall be twelve of my very best.' The director was on her feet, looking positively cheerful. 'Judith, fetch the cane you presented me with and bring out the punishment desk. Good. I should like you to watch. Now – ah – Cate, if you would care to lift up your blouse and place yourself, we shall begin.'

With a deep breath the blonde American stretched over in the approved manner to grasp the legs low down on the other side. There was ice in the pit of her stomach and she was all too aware of the posterior vulnerability of her position. The instrument's touch was cool against her bare flesh as the disciplinarian measured her target and Cate tightened her grip, vowing that this would be the last foray into the masochistic position she was going to make for a very long time . . .

Nexus

NEXUS NEW BOOKS

To be published in July

CHERRI CHASTISED
Yolanda Celbridge

Yolanda Celbridge takes her brand of robust pornotopia to the USA once again as nineteen-year-old Cherri discovers her ability to submit to even the most arduous punishments, and to suffer the most extreme indignities until, try as she might, the girl can't live without them. And in the wide-open spaces of America, she doesn't have to worry about what the neighbours will think. A novel of craven submission and lustful hijinx from the author of *The Taming of Trudi*.

ISBN 0 352 33707 9

SILKEN SLAVERY
Christina Shelley

Chris is a thirty-year-old transvestite. He is firmly 'in the closet' and spends his evenings alone in his exclusive London apartment, yearning for understanding female company. His shyness with women is a problem, particularly at work where he supervises a lot of them! When his inner life is accidentally discovered, however, he finds his staff more accommodating than he might have thought, and embarks on an odyssey into willing she-male submission and enforced feminisation that will change his life – and those of his colleagues – forever. A tale of kinky cross-dressing and sexual fulfilment from the author of *The Last Straw*.

ISBN 0 352 33708 7

DISCIPLINE OF THE PRIVATE HOUSE
Esme Ombreux

Jem Darke, Mistress of the Private House, is bored. So bored that she rashly accepts a challenge to submit to the harsh disciplinary regime of the Chateau, where the Chatelaine and her depraved minions will delight in administering torments and humiliations designed to make Jem abandon the wager and relinquish her supreme authority. Only the Sapphic bond formed between Jem and the other captives will give them the strength to surprise their tormentors – only their acceptance of the strict rules of pleasure and pain will win them freedom. A Nexus Classic.

ISBN 0 352 33709 5

To be published in August

SATAN'S SLUT
Aishling Morgan

Aishling Morgan returns to the sleepy, mysterious environment of seaside Devon, explored in *Deep Blue*. Someone has been performing the Black Mass in an old, abandoned chapel at Stanton Rocks. The local priest, Tom Pridough, is convinced it was Nich Mordaunt, local high-profile pagan, and his friend, the stunning brunette Juliana. Tired of the churchman's confusion of diabolism with his own nature-worship, Nich too sets out to find out who is responsible, and all three become embroiled in a weird and perverse world of sex-magick beyond their darkest imagination.

ISBN 0 352 33720 6

BARE BEHIND
Penny Birch

Penny Birch is currently the filthiest little minx on the Nexus list, with thirteen titles already published by Nexus. All are equally full of messy, kinky fun and, frankly, no other erotic writer has ever captured the internal thrills afforded by the perverse and shameful humiliations her characters undergo! In *Bare Behind*, Penny discovers that a friend of her family, also on the fetish scene, may know more about her private passions than is good! In the search for him, she encounters the pop band Madman Klien, and she must submit to their most perverse desires if she is to find her quarry!

ISBN 0 352 33721 4

MEMOIRS OF A CORNISH GOVERNESS
Yolanda Celbridge

Accepting a position as Governess in the household of the eccentric, port-loving Lord and Lady Whimble, the young and ripely formed Miss Constance soon finds her niche giving special lessons to the local gentlemen, including the vicar! Administering unique attention to their unusual requests, she performs her duties with glee. Employing all manner of Victorian instruments of correction, not least Mr Izzard's box of hygienic but curious bathroom accessories, Constance is destined to have a very rewarding career. A Nexus Classic.

ISBN 0 352 33722 2

If you would like more information about Nexus titles, please visit our website at www.nexus-books.co.uk, or send a stamped addressed envelope to:

Nexus, Thames Wharf Studios,
Rainville Road, London W6 9HA

NEXUS BACKLIST

This information is correct at time of printing. For up-to-date information, please visit our website at www.nexus-books.co.uk

All books are priced at £5.99 unless another price is given.

Nexus books with a contemporary setting

ACCIDENTS WILL HAPPEN	Lucy Golden	☐
	ISBN 0 352 33596 3	
ANGEL	Lindsay Gordon	☐
	ISBN 0 352 33590 4	
BEAST	Wendy Swanscombe	☐
	ISBN 0 352 33649 8	
THE BLACK FLAME	Lisette Ashton	☐
	ISBN 0 352 33668 4	
THE BLACK MASQUE	Lisette Ashton	☐
	ISBN 0 352 33372 3	
BROUGHT TO HEEL	Arabella Knight	☐
	ISBN 0 352 33508 4	
CAGED!	Yolanda Celbridge	☐
	ISBN 0 352 33650 1	
CANDY IN CAPTIVITY	Arabella Knight	☐
	ISBN 0 352 33495 9	
CAPTIVES OF THE PRIVATE HOUSE	Esme Ombreux	☐
	ISBN 0 352 33619 6	
DANCE OF SUBMISSION	Lisette Ashton	☐
	ISBN 0 352 33450 9	
DARK DELIGHTS	Maria del Rey	☐
	ISBN 0 352 33276 X	
DIRTY LAUNDRY £6.99	Penny Birch	☐
	ISBN 0 352 33680 3	
DISCIPLES OF SHAME	Stephanie Calvin	☐
	ISBN 0 352 33343 X	

Nexus books with Ancient and Fantasy settings

Period

CONFESSION OF AN ENGLISH SLAVE	Yolanda Celbridge ISBN 0 352 33433 9	☐
THE MASTER OF CASTLELEIGH	Jacqueline Bellevois ISBN 0 352 32644 7	☐
PURITY	Aishling Morgan ISBN 0 352 33510 6	☐

Samplers and collections

NEW EROTICA 3	Various ISBN 0 352 33142 9	☐
NEW EROTICA 5	Various ISBN 0 352 33540 8	☐
EROTICON 1	Various ISBN 0 352 33593 9	☐
EROTICON 2	Various ISBN 0 352 33594 7	☐
EROTICON 3	Various ISBN 0 352 33597 1	☐
EROTICON 4	Various ISBN 0 352 33602 1	☐
THE NEXUS LETTERS	Various ISBN 0 352 33621 8	☐

Nexus Classics

A new imprint dedicated to putting the finest works of erotic fiction back in print.

AGONY AUNT	G. C. Scott ISBN 0 352 33353 7	☐
BAD PENNY	Penny Birch ISBN 0 352 33661 7	☐
BRAT £6.99	Penny Birch ISBN 0 352 33674 9	☐
DARK DELIGHTS £6.99	Maria del Rey ISBN 0 352 33667 6	☐
DARK DESIRES	Maria del Rey ISBN 0 352 33648 X	☐
DIFFERENT STROKES	Sarah Veitch ISBN 0 352 33531 9	☐

---------- ✂ ------------------------------

Please send me the books I have ticked above.

Name ....

Address ....

....

....

.... Post code...................

Send to: Cash Sales, Nexus Books, Thames Wharf Studios, Rainville Road, London W6 9HA

US customers: for prices and details of how to order books for delivery by mail, call 1-800-343-4499.

Please enclose a cheque or postal order, made payable to **Nexus Books Ltd**, to the value of the books you have ordered plus postage and packing costs as follows:
  UK and BFPO – £1.00 for the first book, 50p for each subsequent book.
  Overseas (including Republic of Ireland) – £2.00 for the first book, £1.00 for each subsequent book.

If you would prefer to pay by VISA, ACCESS/MASTERCARD, AMEX, DINERS CLUB or SWITCH, please write your card number and expiry date here:

....

Please allow up to 28 days for delivery.

Signature ....

Our privacy policy.

We will not disclose information you supply us to any other parties. We will not disclose any information which identifies you personally to any person without your express consent.

From time to time we may send out information about Nexus books and special offers. Please tick here if you do *not* wish to receive Nexus information. ☐

---------- ✂ ------------------------------